Best wi[shes]

Jae x

x.

Sleeping People Lie

JAE DE WYLDE

www.jaedewylde.com

Praise for The Thinking Tank

'A beautiful story; splendidly paced, poignant and compelling. It will have you riveted. With twists and turns, family secrets and romance, it is un-put-down-able!' Waterstones

'A superbly crafted debut novel, expressing deep compassion – insightful and thought-provoking,' Richard Demarco CBE OBE, European Art Foundation

'Sensitively written and delicately observed, an enthralling and suspenseful book that is literary but never difficult,' Leslie Ann Bosher, author, To The Manor Drawn

'I loved this book; loved, loved, loved it,' Deborah Fletcher, author, Bitten by Spain

'De Wylde has a flair for description of environment as well as of personal emotion'

'It's no surprise that The Thinking Tank is a Bestseller'

'I felt as though I was being let into a huge secret, almost like reading someone's diary'

'An honest, challenging, beautifully written story with a healing quality,' Ingrid Schippers, author Bloodlines, Touch Not the Cat

'Difficult themes — beautifully handled'

'I loved reading The Thinking Tank and found it eloquent, insightful, and thought provoking'

'It is always wonderful to discover great new writers. We have had such lovely feedback from our customers,'
Walkers Bookshops

First Published Great Britain 2012
by Summertime Publishing

ISBN: 978-1-909193-10-9

Design by Creationbooth: www.creationbooth.com

DISCLAIMER
All characters in this publication are fictitious and any resemblance to real persons, living or dead is purely coincidental.

I am near-paralysed as the snow falls

No longer do I recognise the person that I am

The faces I have worn

Do not protect me from the cruelty and the comfort

Of the world beyond

Each morning

The reality and the unreality

Of death's peaceful shadow on her beautiful face

Splinters into me afresh

I cannot see the light

My separateness is reborn

The snowdrops keep growing

And I cannot hush the silence

Jane Minshall
8th February 1999

Jae De Wylde

Chapter 1

Dear Em,

You can tell a lot about a person from their bottom. And it was looking at a person's bottom that began your story or *our* story, I suppose it should be. I'm not sure why I haven't told it before. It's not like I haven't had the chance. Somewhere in between the leaves of my scribblings I could have squeezed your story, our story, but I never have and it seemed unlikely that I ever would. It's you though, Em. You have finally made me sit down, take up my pen and tell your story, which began with a bottom and has never yet found an end. You, Em, you deserve to know what happened, why it happened and who was finally to blame.

Let's start with that bottom. It was just there, right before me, placed directly in my line of vision whilst its owner leaned over the chrome balustrade aboard the 54-seater coach. All 54 seats were taken and I had landed next to bottom man. Yes, it was a man, as it always is, that directed my future from that bottom moment, and with it yours.

Em, I was young and I was miserable. You truly cannot blame me for being distracted by that bottom for it was so enticing, framed as it were, by the stitching on the Levi jeans. There was an exciting roundness to it. A youthful promise dangled in the air as it moved back and forth in perfect rhythm with the hand that gesticulated at the driver and the hand that waved a map. It reminded me of one of those loop games, where you have to hold your hand steady and get the loop from one end of the metal rope to the other without making the buzzer sound. Bottom, hand and map were all moving in lazy harmony, in choreographed perfection as if sudden movement would be the end of the game and we would find ourselves *out,* so to speak. That bottom said *hey, I know what I am doing and I am master of my destiny.* So attractive to one starved of romance and ripe for passion.

The leather jacket that shimmied up and down with the waving of the hand had its attraction too. It whispered sophistication, its studiously crumpled butter-soft hide in perfect tan, not too deep and not too pale; an arrogant garment, in control yet with a frisson of recklessness adding to the whole enigmatic mix.

Now, it will sound to you as if I had never before seen the person attached to the bottom, leather jacket and waving hand but this was not the case. It was just that I had never seen him with my eyes wide open and yielding a passage to my heart. No, that's too precise, too corny. I wasn't thinking with my heart and I wasn't thinking with my head; it was rather a kind of recognition of something moving inside of me, nudging reason out of the way and allowing myself a space to feel what I wanted to feel, not what I was supposed to feel, and to sense instinctively that this was a significant moment. It was a moment that augured change.

This was the sort of person I had always imagined myself with; always regarded as way beyond my league. How much safer it would have been, Em, to forget the whole idea. Yet there it was, drumming in my head. Gosh, why had I never noticed that bottom before?

As he sat back in the seat, tucking the object of my curiosity and delight beneath him, I caught a waft of maleness as his scent tickled my nostrils. Citrus yes, but with a muskiness that seemed new and altogether inviting. Oh Em, that bottom, that scent, you cannot imagine how heady a moment, how dangerous the closeness and how fragile my resolve to muster immunity to this sensual feast.

He smelt delicious. Glorious. Sexy. Like someone I wanted to fuck. Fuck. Did I just use that word? That was bad of me. I am sorry. But you are making me honest, Em, in a way I have never been honest before, and so our story must begin.

'Oh, pardon me. I am so sorry.'

Not at all, entirely my pleasure.

'No, it's fine. You're busy. No problem. Anything I can do to help?'

'All done now, I hope. That's if this guy here has understood my directions. I think they're pretty clear, but we don't seem to be speaking the same language,' he purses his lips and shakes his head, drawing his hand back through muddy blond hair. I wrinkle my brow and make the first twitch towards a shrug and he breaks into a grin, 'but then there are those who would claim that we don't,' he says.

'Nicolas Bride, Nicky. American. Bad joke I guess,' he adds. He's holding out his hand and I am supposed to take it but my brain is rooted to the spot.

He drops his hand back into his lap. The nails are neat. Not over-groomed in a girly way but nicely ovalled with what my mother would have called 'healthy half-moons'. He covers his left hand with his right and picks with his forefinger at a raggedy hangnail clinging by a thread to his thumb.

'The language thing, you know, American and English,' he prompts, 'seems the same but doesn't – that kinda thing?'

'Oh that. Right. Sorry. I didn't...' So far this is not going well.

The bus stutters to life and the driver yanks a grey, frayed handkerchief from his pocket. He blows his nose noisily and adjusts the rear view mirror with little, frenetic taps, a Morse code of tiny movements until, satisfied, he punches his right foot onto the accelerator and clears his throat as the coach gruffly responds. He shifts about in his seat until he has us in his sight.

'Are we off then? Or might you 'ave more instructions fer me before we go?'

Nicholas Bride, Nicky, does not have more instructions. The myth of the language barrier serves, it seems, to shield him from the driver's sarcasm and half attempt at posh speak — or serves to allow him his rejoinder, sarcastic or not, I cannot tell.

'All set, my man. Tallyho!' He stands and taps the driver on the shoulder with the map, further straining Anglo-American entente. A crunch of the gears and the coach lurches into motion. I lurch towards my bottom man and find myself apologising all over again.

'Don't bother me none,' the accent thickly emphasized this time, 'Ain't too often a purdy gal falls for me these here days.'

God, Em, that was so corny and so utterly ridiculous that it should have put me right off. Buffoon or what? But something about him. Can't put my finger on it. Just something about him seemed sort of sad.

You know how, when you sit next to someone, there can be this kind of current zizzing back and forth? You can call it electricity or chemistry, but there's no one good expression, no *mot juste*, for that whole sexual tension when you are almost skin-to-skin, utterly aware of every tiny move that person makes. Every in-breath, out-breath, when your entire nervous system is on red alert, like the signals of your body are set to explosion mode and you are suspended in the calm before the storm. Well, that's how it was for me.

And yet, there was something more beneath the physical blueprint for attraction, that chaotic exchange of pheromones. God, I didn't even know if I liked this person but beneath that attraction, I felt something else. He somehow smelt sad, sad like the long, lingering death of a tulip as it bends its gentle head and lets its silky petals fall. I had no idea why I felt this and had no intention of letting him know. You're right, Em. It was nuts.

I click open the clasp of my bright red bag and ferret for lip salve, swirl it across my lips, grab a magazine and settle myself to read. Only then am I aware that my knickers have shifted into that most uncomfortable groove. Wiggling surreptitiously, pretend-groping in my bag, I manoeuvre them into a better place and finally flip open the pages of *Cosmo*.

A title, bold and brash strides across the page and I realise just too late that it reads *The G-spot Orgasm, Myth or Magic?* I can't help myself. I look up to see what I know to be true. He has seen it too and we blush in unison. Me, a global kind of blush that gets the chest as well as the face and leaves your nose all ruddy; he, a more gentle blush that colours up his cheeks and hides for a moment the paleness of his skin and the dusting of all but invisible freckles. I close the magazine and stuff it quickly back into my bag, cough politely and tuck my hair behind my ears. Its nutty brown lengths are tangled from early morning neglect and I dig in my bag again to hoik out a scrunchy, which I slip over my wrist, unwilling to fidget my way further into focus.

Tiny hairs on my arms are standing to attention, guarding me by a millimetre more from the presence of Nicky Bride, who begins scrutinising papers anxiously, feverishly even, flicking back and forth with pen in hand, fussing and tutting.

For several minutes I watch from the corner of my eye, tuning in to the conversation behind me:

'Did you know that Rose fancies Chris?'

'No – since when?'

'Valentine's disco. She saw him snogging Gilly and got mad jealous.'

'Well I heard that Chris was only doing that for a bet.'

'Bloody hell – does Gilly know?'

'No idea. But I bet Rose doesn't. Can't wait to tell her when we get back…'

Let them enjoy it all while they can; before the complications start. Before the pain gets real.

I can't stand the flapping anymore.

'You sure you're okay? I can help if you like?'

'How're your face – name skills?'

'My what?'

'You know, putting names to faces. There are just so many kids on this trip. It's not really my skill area.'

'So what are you doing on the trip then? If it isn't your *skill area*?' My turn to emphasize the vagaries of transatlantic-speak. Cheap, stupid, but curiously satisfying.

'A favour. I owed a favour and this is payback. Marcia's not well. She asked me to step in.'

'You mean Marcia isn't here at all? She should have said something. I could easily have sorted this.'

'Just seemed a solution all round,' he says. 'Plus I get to do some research. And once they're gone, they're gone, right?'

I glance around at the students, faces blank with morning sleep or still gossiping in clutches of conspiracy.

'No, Nicholas, wrong. They're never gone, just momentarily somewhere else. You are now, officially, the end of the line buck-wise.'

'Huh?'

'I mean the buck stops here – with us. I mean with you, although Marcia should definitely have asked me. I just thought she was on the boys' coach but I suppose that's just Pete and Cathy now. Do you know Pete and Cathy? Do you even speak French?'

'No, not really. Met them once over at the Arts Centre but only before some play. *Et oui, bien-sûr, je parle français, ayant etudié les langues comme premier diplôme aux Etats-Unis.*'

I ignore the French and launch in.

'Anyway, if Marcia's put you in charge, that means you deal with the families and any stupid niggles that crop up; homesickness, illness, running out of money, losing passports. It all happens, you know. It's not just a jolly. We have to be responsible all day, every day, and if Marcia's put you in charge, that means you. Maybe I'll go off and do my own research.'

I'm not happy. She should have called me. Marcia should have put me in charge. I don't deserve to be overlooked for some Yank who's only just arrived and who isn't even in the same department, even if he did study French as a 'first degree'.

What do we think he did for his 27th degree? Even if he does have a great bum.

Marcia, Cambridge graduate, MA and a God knows what else from Harvard, plum in mouth and hair, sometimes dark brown, sometimes with streaks like a badger on a bad day. Never turns up for anything extra-curricular, and too high and mighty to socialise with the likes of me. She should never have been made Head of Languages and only got the post because the Head went to the same college or something like that – a definite case of jobs for the boys. Bugger.

'Whoa, there; there's no need for all that. I guess she just thought that it was kinda mean to spring it on you at the last minute. And like I say, I owed her one.'

'Miss?'

A tousled-haired, smiley girl pokes me on the shoulder and tilts her head to one side. In her hand is a bag of sweets, grey and crumpled, warm-looking, like it's been rescued from deep in her satchel, treasure from the ocean bed.

'Yes, Franny. What is it?'

'Caro feels sick, Miss. I've given her a bag but she looks really pale and she keeps burping. Would you like a Fruit Salad?'

I take a sweet, thank her and pass it to the man by my side, 'Your reward,' I say.

'Don't worry, Franny. Mr Bride here will come and sort her out, won't you, Mr Bride? He's an expert on burps. And it'll be good for his face – name skills.'

Nicholas Bride shoots me a puzzled glance before he swings himself out of his seat to deal with the likelihood of vomit in the coach. I don't rate his chances with the driver if he doesn't get there in time and the thought turns into a giggle, which I hastily suppress.

'If it's so damn hilarious, maybe you'd like to go see 'Caro' yourself?'

There's a thing we do when we fancy someone, isn't there? Is it about putting up barriers that the other person has to knock down, just to see if they do? I know I'm not being fair and I know I want him to like me but this irritating thing that we all do, this challenge we throw up or gauntlet we throw down turns everything on its head. I want him to like me but I am being unlikable. How does that work?

I fiddle with the scrunchy, turning its faded brown velvet over and over in my hand, picking at a stray thread that runs along the seam and finally gather up my locks and tuck them into a messy tail on my head.

I can't resist the urge to check on the happenings behind me and lean across, perching on my elbow and crane my neck to see up the aisle just as Nicholas pushes his way back to his seat. Face to fly, I have absolutely no idea what to do next. I splutter into confusion, hurling myself backwards into my seat. Graceful, Sloane. Real class.

Grace is something Nicholas does, however, possess and I find myself gratefully accepting the truce when he speaks.

'This hasn't been going very well, has it?' he says with a sigh, 'What d'you say we start again? Nicky Bride, Boston, Massachusetts. And you are?'

'Felicity Granger, but my friends call me Sloane. From London, originally. How do you do?'

'Well, how do you do back.'

We both try a smile and it works. His eyes are somewhere between baby and a truer, deeper blue. The little crinkles at the corners suggest he is older than I am; maybe thirty-three, thirty-four?

I feel myself blushing again as he smiles back at me, as I wonder what he sees. Hair a bit of a mess, that's for certain, but the rest is not too bad. Reasonable figure, although not as much on top as I'd like. The French have a saying, *Elle a du monde au balcon*. Well, personally, I don't have a lot of folk populating my balcony – just enough to fill a generous 'A' cup or a skimpy 'B'. My legs are long though. Oh no, I could be taller than him. Oh sod it – that would be just my luck.

I feel obliged to break the few seconds of silence between us, more silence than it takes to smile, though not enough silence to class the moment as a love-at-first-sight experience.

'I'm sorry about all that. I was just upset. Not to be asked to take charge. It's what should have happened. And it's not as if I haven't done this sort of thing before. Well, I've done day trips, that kind of thing. It would've been good for my CV – for promotion and I *am* capable. It's just my snooty Head of Department doesn't think I am – either that or she feels threatened by the fact that I see through her, and I know she only got the job because of who she knows. You hear that sort of thing on the grapevine, don't you? Education is such a small world; small and smug and incestuous beyond belief. Not sure it's really what I should be doing but I *am* good at it. Good with the kids, good with the parents and I do love my subject but it's so claustrophobic sometimes and... Oh heck. I'm sorry, I have absolutely no idea why I am telling you all this. I don't really...'

'Relax. No harm done. I guess it's early and we're both a bit cranky. Caro's fine by the way. Just in case you were concerned...'

'Oh yes, of course I am. I don't want you to think...'

'Just teasing, Ms Sloane Granger. Where'd the Sloane come from? That's kind of curious.'

'Oh, that's easy. Maybe not for you, because you're American, but everyone gets it here. It's from the Granger. Felicity Granger, Lone Ranger, Sloane Ranger – you know, like Princess Diana. Twinset, pearls, bicycles down the Kings Road, that sort of thing.'

'Don't really see you as the twinset and pearls type.'

He has an opinion. He sees me.

'Oh, you should see me on parents' evenings. You have to look the part, you know, with these posh kids. Otherwise the parents don't take you seriously. Not at my age anyway. They have this vision of what a languages teacher should be like. Like their teachers I expect, all tweed and moustaches. Bet it's not like that in the States.'

'That depends on where you are in the States. We have some pretty traditional institutions, you know. I'm kind of familiar with one or two of them myself. Even as an artist, there are dos and don'ts. You still have to work to fit in.'

'I wondered what you did. Art. How come you're hardly ever in school?'

'Well, History of Art mainly while I'm here in the UK, and yeah, I guess there are some who'd put me down as an artist – sculptor, mixed media. I'm one of the Harper guys. You know. Here for a year then gone.'

'Oh, the Harper lecture. I didn't make it to that last year. Sounded boring.'

'Well, let's hope I can spice it up a little this time around.'

I can't believe I am being so shallow. I am just not being me. His next question takes me completely by surprise.

'So tell me, Ms Granger. I wanna know if you live up to your name. Are you, Ms Sloane, a lone ranger or is there a special someone to share the ride?'

Chapter 2

Sloane

The creak of a spring wakes me up. I reach for my watch and my little finger catches the wire of the gangly bedside lamp. The faux-Louis something rocks from side to side, forcing me from doziness to wide awake in five seconds flat. It steadies at my grasp and I take a deep breath as my heart regains its own steady rhythm. It is five o'clock and I groan.

It feels like seconds ago, but it was midnight I think, when I was standing at my bedroom window here in the hotel. The Paris sky was orange black with purple clouds, pregnant and ready to pop. From the restaurant across the way, the clatter of impatient clearing was still echoing its way between the elegant eighteenth century buildings, weaving in and out of the wrought iron balconies.

I breathed in the feel of Paris, recharging the Francophile in me, sucking in what I miss in the months when *La Belle France* and I have no rendezvous lined up; months, when I have to conjure her presence and her passion for kids who think anything closer than Martinique is a waste of space, and kids who'd rather be in Butlins than Boulogne.

I saw him then, Em and drew back so I, unobserved, could take in more of the man who fascinated me despite myself – despite a raw feeling that all was not well, a gut instinct that in some inner part of me, I knew this man. Knew what he was and that what he was would hurt.

He stood, motionless, staring up as if waiting to pull some message from the weight of the sky, his face part in shadow, part alight with the amber red of the neon sign, grim, laden and bearing no resemblance to the carefree guy seated opposite me earlier. I never did answer his question on the coach, Em. I merely blushed and looked away. He never did ask it again. Nicholas had no need.

La Joconde, that was the restaurant sign, although what the place had to do with the *Mona Lisa*, I had no idea. And that's where we all went to eat.

His suggestion, actually, 'It's where all the locals go,' he said. And he was right. 'Where else could you get this kind of menu with *escargots* included for this kind of price?' He was right, right, right. So how come he feels so wrong?

'Now you just have to try this,' Nicholas said, offering his fork, *rillettes de porc* dangling in fatty little strands. 'These are just awesome.'

Who says awesome?

I gave in. The offered fork was an intimate gesture and I captured the shreds of pork with my tongue in reply. Sometimes you take notice of what's dangling in front of you. Sometimes you don't.

'*Merde*, I can't believe it's raining like this. I thought the forecast was supposed to be good.' Pete is shaking out his brolly and sparkles of water fly at the rest of us like tiny diamond missiles. 'God, I've only been as far as the Odéon and my jacket's already soaked.'

The jacket is the inevitable. Brown corduroy, patches on the elbows, wear and tear visible and ignored. Pete, thirty-nine going on sixty and with the ambition of a depressed flea. His specs are always at half mast, clinging like *pince-nez* to the tip of his nose, a large, ruddy and over-aging protuberance, which lends him the look of some Shakespearian tragi-comedian.

'Since when can you rely on a forecast, let alone a forecast for Paris? *I love Paris in the springtime...*' Cathy breaks into song and springs aside like an enthusiastic cow as Pete bounds, dripping and swearing into the lobby of the *Hôtel Splendide*, 'and saying *shit* in French doesn't make it posher, you know, or any less rude. Why couldn't you just have waited anyway? Pete, the intrepid explorer, is that it?' Good old Cathy.

'Ta dah!' Pete produces a pyramid of scrunched paper from under the sog of corduroy with the flourish of a rabbit-bearing magician. 'Your favourite. I braved the storm just for you, my lover.'

Cathy pounces on the package, rips across the name *'Boulangerie Fargin'* and thrusts the torn paper back at Pete.

'Oh my goodness... *Religieuses*. Okay. You're forgiven.'

Cathy scoots over to the mahogany coffee table and pushes aside well-thumbed copies of *Marie-Claire* and today's *Le Monde*. She plonks the little cardboard tray down on the shiny glass top and licks *crème anglaise* from her thumb. With a little squeal, she swoops and peels the head from the body of a pastry 'nun' and bites horsily into the squidgy choux bun, sending a squirt of chocolate custard up her nose. She sighs magnificently, *'Ah, mais c'est parfait. Extraordinaire!* Utter perfection. I do love you, Pete.'

If only everyone were so easy to please.

'Come on then. Dive in.'

'No, you go ahead, Cathy. I'm fine.' The smell of crumbling hot croissants is still fresh in my nose from breakfast, a buttery, warm smell with a hint of vanilla; a smell that has France stamped on its spine and never fails to thrill. And I love the runny jam – the sort of jam that thinks it's a drink, refuses to stay on the knife and trickles stickily down your hand.

I pick up the newspaper and unfold its sheets, while Pete and Cathy guzzle. Looking at the two of them, I think that if you chopped them laterally and read what's inside, they would have *teacher* printed in concentric circles throughout. I envy that really; that knowing who you are, what you are, not questioning or stressing. It's just not who I saw myself to be and somewhere, secretly, I hope that Pete and Cathy are not a version of me, older and resigned, stuck, wedged in a vat of verbs, nouns, subjects, objects, active, passive.

Passive. Allowing time and terms to march on, each school year mirroring the last, each grateful student flying off, French unfurling into some exciting slice of life that I'll only ever see through the eyes of the odd student who returns to find us still festering in the staffroom.

I shake my head and rustle the paper, reading the date under my breath; *Le 22 mars 1991*. Okay, Sloane. If you are going to change something, change it before it's too late and you are gone, vanished, forever 'Cathified' with no return.

'Where's what's his face?' Pete has crumbs hanging from his mouth, like moist clusters of cold sores.

'His name is Nicholas, Pete. And you know it. Being grumpy is not going to help.' Cathy pulls a pink spotty handkerchief from up her sleeve and expertly wipes Pete's mouth and brushes flakes of pastry from his tie.

'Sorry, Sloane. Pete's just annoyed that he's not in charge, though God knows why he'd want to be.' *Good God, does Pete have aspirations after all?*

'I keep explaining that it was just quicker and easier for Marcia to sort it this way,' Cathy continues, 'She thought right up to the last moment that she'd be coming but she just felt too ill in the end. Knowing Marcia, she'll be here by the weekend anyway. Heavens, Pete, you've got custard on your trousers. Watch out.'

Oh my God, she really is going to wipe her hanky up and down his trousers in public. I try to look away but am drawn to how Cathy just keeps on looking after Pete. I think she must find it tedious somehow, this bumbling child of a husband but check my thoughts as I see that it's not like that at all. Finishing her task, she brushes her lips over his and he raises his hand and strokes her frizzy, caramel hair as she stoops.

'Now you've put custard in my hair! What are we going to do with you, Peter Bayes?'

'He said he was here for the Harper lecture. What's that all about anyway? I missed it last year. Something all about nuclear power, wasn't it?' I am pleased to have the chance to discover what's going on without revealing to Nicholas that I have no idea what he's doing or where he's come from. Or that I am remotely interested.

'No idea, but it was that bloke, Bleakley, the scientist with the mole on his face who ran the debate about energy. We didn't ever really get to know him, did we, Petey?'

Petey. She just called him Petey. That's what I love about school trips. You think you know a colleague but when school's out, there's no telling who they are.

'That's the trouble with the Harper thing. People come and go and unless they're in the same department you never make contact. They're in and out before you can say 'Yank,' although it's a bit different this year, of course.'

'Are they always American then?'

'Of course they are. It's the Harper scholarship – as in Abel Harper, the old boy who donated the lecture theatre and the bursary to go with it, same family as the Harper building. That Harper, *our* Harper,' Pete nods at Cathy, then towards me. 'These guys come for a year, as resident whatevers – scientists, artists, you name it, give some major lecture and then off they go again. All paid. A great big freebie courtesy of old man Harper; not a bad deal is it?'

'How long's that been going on for?'

'Search me. Donkeys' years. Abel Harper Senior's been dead a while now, hasn't he, Cath? There's a plaque on the wall somewhere I think. Doesn't mean that when they're all dead these Yanks will stop coming though… not that there's anything wrong with them, of course…' Pete coughs.

'Well, *bonjour*, all. How are we today?'

Cathy is the first to recover.

'Oh, good morning, Nicholas. Fine, thank you. Now that we're all here we can get on with the day.'

His eyes flicker around the room and settle on me, unsettling me. 'Thought it all went pretty well last night,' Nicholas says.

'Considering it's your first time...' It comes out of my mouth before it's been run through my brain.

Nicholas Bride ignores me. I feel uncomfortable and shift in my chair.

Pete nods and finger-nails up a crumb from the table. He eases it from nail to mouth with his tongue. 'Actually, it's the earliest we've ever had everyone partnered up and away,' he says, generously, 'and the kids seemed happy enough.'

Unattractively, I snort.

'What's up with you anyway? Not feeling so good?' Cathy asks.

'I'm fine. No, really I am. Just didn't get too much sleep,' I say.

Pete is right. It did go smoothly, although I wonder if the kids are quite as excited with the prospect in the cold light of day. I did that whole exchange thing as a kid myself and ended up with a real tomboy who wanted to climb trees and hang out with *les gars*. All I wanted was to bury myself in a book, ignore the boisterous boys and forget that I had landed in some strange family and wouldn't be let out of jail for three whole weeks. The babble of the language gave me headaches – straining to understand a word here and there – and I hated the battle with unfamiliar food. One nightmare weekend, we stayed with Elodie's grandma in Normandy. She had these live crabs in a basket and she plonked them straight into boiling water. I swear they cried. Pitiful little mewing sounds leapt from the saucepan and it was all I could do not to plunge my hand in, to rescue the unfortunate creatures from their fate.

I hated the crab, along with the mussels, the snails, the rabbit, the tripe, the Camembert and definitely the *rillettes*, which I still absolutely detest. Which begs the question, why on earth did I open my mouth to accept the nasty, meaty mess that Nicholas offered me on his fork? Why indeed?

'Well then, maybe you need a spot of fresh air. Perk you up, eh, Sloane. Do you two mind going to fetch the tickets while we sort out the rest of the paperwork?'

'Bloody hell, Pete, you're already wet. I don't think … and anyway, that means that you and Cathy will be stuck here. Someone's got to be near the phone. The kids have only just arrived and there's bound to be something...' Nicholas interrupts me in full flow.

'That's just fine, Pete. Sloane and I will go. No problem.'

No problem? *No* problem? I feel hijacked. I feel I have no choice.

'God, I always forget how crowded it gets in here.'

'We could always have walked but I thought you might prefer a slightly drier *rowt*.'

'A what?'

'*Rowt*. A drier *rowt*.'

'Oh you mean route.'

'Yeah, *rowt*. There's a seat over there now look. That guy with the afro's getting off. Go on. You'd better be speedy or that fat guy'll get it.'

'Nicholas. Hush. You can't say that!'

'Who's going to hear? We can hardly hear each other.'

'Even so...'

I leave the argument where it is and instead opt for a stab at securing the seat but instantly change my mind. The woman next to me is swaying with the rocking rhythm of the metro as it hurtles through the tunnels. With her left hand she is supporting a dirty sling just below an ample bosom, and black curls creep from under a deep red, cotton headscarf wound tightly around her head. She clings to the bar above us with her right hand, knuckles grey-white with the effort. The sling wriggles and she nuzzles down into the faded paisley fabric where a tiny head is just visible.

'*Madame*,' I gesture towards the precious seat. The brakes scream and the train flings itself around a final corner before we slow into the station.

She shrugs at me as the fat guy makes a lunge for the seat. We smile and I shrug back. Paris.

'Too slow, Sloane, just too damn slow,' Nicholas smirks.

If there's one thing I've learnt since my young days in Paris, it's that the metro can be unpredictable. I don't just mean timetables, breakdowns, that sort of thing. I mean things that happen. You expect just to get on, wobble about a bit and then hop off when you get to your station. But what happens in between can be unexpected and sometimes even change your life.

Take, for example, the first time my exchange partner, Elodie and I went into Paris alone. It's quite a long way from Savigny Sur-Orge into town. You have to take the *RER* and then pick up the metro for wherever you want to go. The trains on the regional network all had names and I imagined them with different haircuts and skin colours – *Mona* was a pale-skinned, bobbed blonde, *Bali* was an olive-skinned beauty, her hair black, long and wavy with a bright pink orchid tucked behind her ear.

The train was stuffy that day and by the time the two of us arrived in town, the fluey symptoms I'd been trying all morning to ignore had really taken hold. Elodie grabbed my arm and shouted something inaudible, urging me to run with her down the crowded platform, jostling shoppers, weak with the weight of spoils from *Galeries-Lafayette* or *Printemps* as we went. When finally we leapt into the crowded metro carriage, ramming ourselves into the narrowing gap as the hissing doors closed tight, my head was pounding and my flared jeans were clammy and scratchy against my skin. My sweater was glued to my armpit and I wriggled, feeling my flesh peel from the wool, sticky with the effort of catching the train. Leaning my head against the cool glass of the door, I juggled to remove my coat, and glanced down as the tall black man by my side nudged me in the ribs.

At first I thought what he held in his hand was a rolled up newspaper or some handle jutting from a bag. I had never seen a penis before and certainly not a fat, black-purple one. My mind tried to make of it any object other than what it so surely was.

As I fainted, I heard the man say *merde* just under his breath. I would have fallen to the floor but wedged in sideways as I was, Elodie's support kept me upright. I can still feel the vomit rising in my throat, bitter in my mouth, swallowing its sour acid as I willed it not to burst down the front of some stranger's coat. I fixed my eyes firmly on a sign on the door as I floated in and out, dizzy and dazed: '*Ne pas cracher,*' it read; do not spit.

What became of the man I cannot tell, and I never knew if I was faint from flu or shock. Nor did I ever let on to anyone what I had seen. It was a guilty secret, this penis *à Paris*, unobserved by anyone but me. It was as if it was only there for me, as if I had asked it to be there that day on that train.

Later, I was sad that this was the first manhood I had ever seen, that it wasn't in some lovely boudoir with a *Mills-and-Boon* lover in some fairy tale tryst. My first penis made me faint, but not in the way I'd have liked. But somehow it sealed a pact with Paris, a place so exotic and deliciously dangerous in my otherwise tiny world. And it wouldn't be the only penis that Paris and I would share.

Chapter 3

Nicholas

Dear Em,

First of all, let's get this straight; I never wanted to write this and it's not my idea. She says I have to do it. She says it will sort things out, make things clearer in our minds and do something to take away the guilt. Jesus, am I supposed to pick away at every little action, every tiny thought?

I'm not so sure. No, damn it, I *am* sure; sure that it's a complete waste of time and, hell, I want nothing to do with all this junk about guilt. And how do I know that she'll keep it all in? In this account, that is. What's to stop her changing things? Not telling them exactly the way they were? Damn it, Em, what's to stop her doing anything now that we've got this far?

I guess I really don't have a choice, Em. I guess I'll just write and hope that we will learn, all of us, what it is she wants. But let's get one thing straight – this isn't going to be anything fancy. I've spent enough of my life trying to sound right and write right so there's no messing about this time – this is it, raw and ready, just as it comes into my head.

We have to go back to that day; the day that Marcia was ill. I never dreamed in a million years that she'd ask me to go on that trip but it just seemed wrong to refuse. If I had refused, refused to feel guilty enough to go, then who knows how different things might have turned out?

I still don't know if it really was guilt that made me go. Marcia seemed kind of pathetic that day, out of character and out of sorts. And I wasn't feeling all that terrific myself. I had no idea why I'd even bothered to take that job, sort of job. I guess I was tempted by a fresh start, but deep down, I reckon I knew it'd never do the trick.

And then there was the whole temptation of the trip itself. Unload the kids, hang around in Paris. And I'd read about the exhibition.

That was it; the exhibition. I'd like to think that I went to be kind to Marcia but the idea of seeing all those sculptures up close has got to be the main reason why I couldn't bring myself to refuse.

I guess I was still pissed that someone else had got to do the whole Camille Claudel thing before me. That whole mistress and muse scenario was really getting to me. It seemed that everything was always from a woman's point of view. How hard done by the mistresses were, how they inspired these guys selflessly as if somehow it was all some massive great sacrifice on their part. Me, I wanted to see things from Rodin's point of view and I wanted to see for myself whether Claudel's so-called masterpieces could truly sit side by side with Rodin's magnificent work. Here was an opportunity on a plate. But I hadn't reckoned on meeting Sloane.

The driver of the bus was a real asshole. Didn't want to know when I was trying to tell him what we were in for. Marcia had warned me how narrow the street was and that parking that thing in front of the hotel while we sorted out the kids would never be an option. But this guy, he just didn't give a damn. I got pretty mad at him and he listened in the end, but I was still wired. Then suddenly she was right there on the seat next to mine. What a pain. What an absolute pain in the butt. I just wanted, needed to be alone and to get the coach jerk off my back but she kept on making these smart-arse remarks and wouldn't let it go. So what if she'd not been asked to lead the crummy kids herself? Though why the heck she'd want to had me beat. The other guy, Pete, I could tell he wanted to be team captain too, though he didn't give me a hard time like Sloane. No, she was out to get me, right from the get-go.

She was kinda snooty in a duchess way and she had this habit of looking at me like I was something off her shoe. Did it pretty much to everyone, but I didn't want any hassle, for Marcia's sake as much as mine, so I played real nice.

What the heck am I saying? I was nice. I am nice. It wasn't some kind of act. And she attracted me. There, I've said it. She attracted me, goddammit, with her bouncy hair and her sparky eyes, her outright ambition. She wasn't scared of saying what she thought, especially about me. I admired her guts.

I was mad with her when she made me go clear up some girl's vomit but I liked her for it too, the way she was no pushover. Marcia would've just quietly got out her Kleenex and left me to my thoughts, but not Sloane. She was in for the kill.

I'd seen her around, of course, like you see people from a distance across a corridor, playground or assembly hall. She used to hang around with Cathy at break, looking efficient with lists and notices for the Upper School. My office was way over in Lower School, which was crazy looking back. I used to get soaked to the skin on a near-daily basis when I needed to get to the art room or grab a coffee. Still, that's English schools for you. Nothing made too easy for your average American boy.

Sloane led assembly one time just before the Paris trip. I remember seeing her up there on the stage, waxing lyrical about some love song with a moral to the tale. It was maybe Valentine's Day or something and she'd done this big display with heroes and heroines and why they were prepared to die for love. I thought it was pretty lame but the kids seemed to like it – and to like her.

Anyway, there she was next to me on the bus, pretending to read a magazine, just flicking through, this way and that. All the time I felt her thoughts puddling themselves over me. Like she was working out what to say next; planning my humiliation. And all the time my skin so close to hers, my chest so tight with my breath like I was afraid to breathe out and disturb the air – as if allowing the air to ripple would force space between us where I wanted there to be none. I wanted that closeness, already I wanted her close.

I knew for sure she was pretending to read when she stopped at this page that had *orgasm* splashed all over it. She knew I'd seen it. Hilarious, the way she shut it and dropped it like some red hot potato, plop into her bag.

But it was in the restaurant that I knew that there'd be no going back. You know when you feel something so strong that it gets between each beat of your heart. Sounds like an exaggeration, like something some wet college boy would say, but I was no college kid and at thirty-five I knew enough to know that this was something different. Something heart-stoppingly, ball-crushingly different and that I didn't want to let this one go.

I'd been there before, to *La Joconde*. It's this cool little restaurant that I'd been to with the guys from the *Sorbonne* when a bunch of us from Harvard went to Paris this one time. Didier and Jean-Luc were your regular post May 1968 intellectuals. I'd never met anyone like them, willing to do battle in the *Quartier Latin* because they believed the government was wrong, uncaring and discriminating in a way that we'd treated as pretty much okay in the US of A.

When I was twelve years old, these guys were there, on the spot, wielding batons, storming that university, forcing the occupying police to retreat. Jean-Luc had a scar on his forehead, wore it proudly, testament to his *gauchiste,* lefter than left soul. He was still angry with *les flics*, the police force, corrupt, guilty though untried according to Jean-Luc. Guilty of planting agents-provocateurs among the crowd to up the ante, he said, burning cars, inciting violence, causing harm in a malicious and self-satisfying way, getting their own back. They were outside the law themselves, he said.

Didier, well now, he was gentler, had more of a philosopher's spirit, I guess. He'd always be quoting Voltaire, Rousseau, Descartes, those great and famous thinkers. He brought those names in books to life for a student whose interest in French had begun with a pretty teacher and a thing for fancy food. God, what wouldn't I have given for the chance that these spoilt little Brits had? To be shipped off to Paris and dropped in the lap of some middle-class family, to get the chance to soak up the language, the culture, everything French?

Yeah, I know, Em, it really didn't make any sense for me to study French, or the art thing – that came a little later, a kind of extension of all that stuff. But this was something I could be good at, unlike the all-hallowed field of sport. I never did get all that baseball and golfing junk, and my dad never got why. Nor did he get why I could possibly get a kick out of languages and art. Business man through and through with a whole load of swagger on the side, that was my dad. I guess I was embarrassing to him faced with all the jocks in the clubhouse boasting about who scored what, when and how.

When I stayed on at Harvard, my folks reckoned I was just avoiding having to earn a real living in the big wide world. Looking back, I guess they could've been right. But it was nothing to do with the work and nothing to do with the pay. It was the not wanting to be like them.

So *La Joconde* was my place and I wanted Sloane to discover it through my eyes and I would've been disappointed if I hadn't seen what I was looking for in her face as we walked through that door. This place is priceless – French with a capital F.

I saw what she saw as she saw it; the green-blue walls, the fishing nets, the oak tables, craggy old tops, stained with red circles from years of *vin rouge*, 'like the kiss of lipstick, where secrets have been spilled and sorrows shared,' she said later over supper. Real poetic, I thought.

I caught that sensuous prick of garlic as I watched Sloane inhale the terrific waft that grabs at your senses, and I could see that she got it. She got that restaurant all right.

The menu had scarcely changed in all the time I'd known the place and I made a secret bet with myself what Sloane would choose.

'Okay with a *Vouvray* and a *Luberon*, old chap? Think we should have one of each, don't you?' Pete says.

I'm not going to argue the toss. *Vouvray* is way too fruity for my taste but who cares? My mind's on other things. Pete calls the waiter, the wine arrives and we all say *cheers*, like we've known each other forever, like old buddies catching up at some reunion. Except the woman sitting across the table from me is not my buddy.

Sloane sits opposite me, slightly askew. She shifts around in her seat, taking in the pyramid of dusty bottles and the faded drapes. I like that she bothers to get to know the place. The firm curve of her breast just offers a chink of lace where the button and loop of her cream, silk shirt don't quite meet. It's all it takes to make me want more. A buddy is not what I have mind.

'How do you know this place?' she asks, 'it's amazing. And how come it just happens to be across the way from our hotel?' *She finds it amazing. Big tick. So far so good.*

I explain to her about Jean-Luc and Didier and she draws her hair back from her face. Her slender fingers run through its shine. She holds it high on her head while she listens to my tale.

It's as if the others aren't there, Cathy and Pete. Like I've zoned out their chat and all I can see is this young woman, her sea-blue eyes, her full lips with just a smear of pink and the slight inclination of her head — her interested but not too interested pose. I give her the rundown on the menu while we wait.

'Yeah, now this one's good. They do the lentils with *lardons*, you know, those little pork pieces with shallots and this creamy sauce. And this one here, see, this one comes with *couscous* and the sausage is real spicy. Oh, and the snails are incredible. Where could you get snails at this price anywhere else in the world?'

She smiles. She has a kind of energy about her. I want to absorb it, as if by some weird osmosis I can grab a hold of it for myself.

'Well, seeing as you ask,' she says, 'there're a fair few in the garden at school.' She lets go of her hair and the candlelight catches the colours. It's like almond strands speckled with gold. She tosses it back and catches it up again, untangling it as she slides her hands through its length. Jesus, sexy or what?

I find myself staring at her neat hands. On the middle finger of her right hand she wears a simple band of gold with three tiny stones set on a diagonal. Diamonds maybe? In my head I see her pale hands on my flesh and I feel a tight pulse between my thighs.

'*Vous avez choisi, M'sieur, 'dame*'? The waiter flourishes a pad and pen. He turns first to Sloane.

She goes for *La soupe de poissons*. Got that one wrong. I'd have sworn she'd have the snails – didn't have her down as a fish soup kind of girl. Then *Le navarin d'agneau*. Wrong again. Why the hell eat lamb when you can eat steak?

She ate with gusto that night, not afraid to mop the deep plates clean with French bread, so damn crusty that one false move and you've cut your hand on the spikes. *Saucer*, they call it, sponging up the sauce, savouring every last mouthful like you'll never eat again.

Maybe this was the last meal we would share. Maybe it was the first of many and Em, I wanted to know where this would go, where the hell it would lead. I'd spent so much time doing what I ought to, worrying about the old man and what everyone thought. What made this the moment that I began to stop to care?

I stood outside the restaurant that night, impatient for the morning, wondering what the hell I was doing there, what the heck I was playing at and how things would pan out. Not just with Sloane, but with the whole mess at home. I stood there on that March day, an ordinary, chill day with nothing in particular to mark it out and I felt the first drops of rain on my head as the Paris skies began to open. I looked up and there she was, darting back from her window.

She'd been looking at me, Em, and thought I hadn't seen. My mind went back to that moment as we ate our food and I'd challenged her to try mine. Not a serious challenge, mind you. I was kind of playing with her to see how she'd react, but she surprised me then as she would surprise me a hundred times over.

She tried my *rillettes*. 'Great,' she said, but the slight wrinkle in her nose, the way she dove for her wine, it gave her away. She didn't like them and she knew she wasn't going to. So to me that begs a question. Why did she let me put my fork in her mouth?

Jae De Wylde

Chapter 4

Sloane

'I wasn't being slow, if you don't mind. I tried to get that lady with the baby to sit down but the other guy just barged across.'

'The fat guy, you mean?'

'Nicholas!' He grins.

'Jeez, it's hot in this damn metro.' We are pressed together and I feel his breath as it expels with a rush, 'Phew. How can you stand that coat?'

I glance down at the tweedy red and beige coat and a thought goes through my mind. How curious it is that when you're not concentrating on how hot or how cold it is, you can be completely unaware until someone makes you focus. Suddenly, my skin is prickly hot and I can feel the heat rising in my face. I somehow feel the need to explain my clothing choice but have not the faintest idea why.

'I always pack a coat for this time of the year. Paris is so unpredictable. I could never wear something like that,' I nod at his leather jacket. 'I'd be frozen. I'm the sort of person who wears thermals all year round and has a hotty-botty until the summer term!'

Oh my God. What did I just say? My words trip over themselves as they pile out of my mouth, heaping themselves uselessly onto my embarrassment, 'I mean, it gets pretty cold in the flat and I have this sort-of rule about not turning the heating on 'til half term and…' Hell, he's going to think I'm just some stupid kid. And if it's not bad enough to offer an image of me in thermals, I have to say *hotty-botty*. Oh hell.

'Relax, Felicity,' he interrupts, 'strange though. I'd have kinda thought that all in all you were pretty damn hot…'

The comment dances in the heat of the carriage, in the heat of that frozen moment in that hot carriage in Paris where I am standing with this man that I do not know. He called me Felicity. My parents called me that when I was naughty. He said I am hot – or did I not hear him right? Perhaps I am hot. Perhaps I will be naughty.

'Come on. Let's get off here. It's crazy-crowded. Let's get some air.'

I don't have time to think or analyse what has just happened. Nicholas leaves me no choice. As the train draws into the station, he hooks his arm through mine and steers me from the train onto the platform, elbowing us through the crowds.

The smell of urine is unmistakable and I wonder how the buskers can bear it all day. A guy, hunched and worn, eyes blank, unseeing, not wanting to see, strums at a guitar. The unkempt strands of his beard tickle the edge of the battered instrument, which bears the scrappy, picked-at stickers of his travelling times. It is faintly out of tune but still the Jacques Brel song soars in the echo of the arched cavern of the bleak, tiled corridors. I thrill with recognition, *Ne me quitte pas, ne me quitte pas, ne me quitte pas*. Will you leave me, Nicholas Bride, I wonder?

We surface at Châtelet-Les Halles. It's drizzling with that wet in-the-clouds kind of rain that rapidly soaks you and turns everything grey – unless something has happened to add colour to your world. Something such that everything appears triumphantly bright and what is to be, feels so much more alive than everything that has gone before; a world where suddenly the future fizzes with lively potential whilst the past is dead and hushed with regret.

'Quick, in here. The coffee'll be good and we can wait for the rain to stop.'

'No, let's walk,' I reply.

'You're kidding me.'

'I want to, no, I need to walk.'

I remember this place, Em, from my visits long ago. It's weird to think that I'm now bringing kids here – to this place where I was a kid, putting them through the same strange process of being thrust into the core of a French family. Sink or swim. Speak or starve. Fall in love or hate it forever. I fell in love. The sing-song of conjugating verbs: *je mange, tu manges, il mange, elle mange, nous mangeons, vous mangez, ils mangent, elles mangent*, (at least I never went hungry with such a command of the verb *to eat*), the nasal vowels, the buzz, hum and crash of the city, the shrug and the *bof* of the aloof citizens of this vibrant place, I fell in love with them all, although maybe not so with *Les Halles*.

This is the place they called *le trou de Paris*, the gigantic scar where they scooped out the innards of the city in the name of progress, the old market making way for this faceless shopping mall. It was a scandal *par excellence* when the building work stopped, and Parisians were left to stare in woe at the deep and rotting wound that festered until money was found to make it whole. Despite the money, the building, the schemes and ideas, the great hole of Paris is not whole, I reflect. It has just lost its heart.

Afterwards, Em, looking at that moment with Nicholas on the train, I found myself questioning if it had ever really happened. I wondered if it hadn't perhaps been some daydream that my mind had conjured in the warmth of the carriage, that my brain might somehow have created its own strange reality from the desires of my subconscious. But then again, we were in Paris, a city of promise, a city where the improbable was nonetheless possible.

Pretty damn hot, Em. That was what he said. Could it have been more corny? Did it make me wary? Not a jot. I should have said something and not let the comment cast a blush on the rest of the day, but somehow the words wouldn't come and everything I wanted said was left unsaid. The moment was condemned to play like a film on a loop in my head.

I've had other moments like this. Those moments when you think you can't possibly have heard what you are certain was said. Those moments when you wish you could find the words to counter an outrageous remark or snide comment, or worse some mortifying deed, which shapes how you think and what you are from that moment on.

After the penis on the train, Elodie never left my side. I think she felt guilty about not realising just how ill I was – or how ill she thought I must have been. She wasn't to know that a tall, black stranger had added fever to my brow. She chatted endlessly away whilst I, sponge-like, drank in the language and lilt and finally, as it always does, the conversation turned to sex.

We were sitting on the sofa in her bedroom – more of a den really with its stereo, TV and couch. Elodie had everything I'd have liked in a room myself.

The bookshelves, lined with classics – *Sartre, Camus, Mauriac, Zola* – seemed out of place since this skinny girl next to me had so far been anything but bookish. Her hair was cropped short and messily, like she could have stepped into the cast of Oliver and not looked out of place. Her nails in contrast to mine were bitten ragged and although she wore a flimsy skirt, it was all but covered by a mannish sweatshirt, a maple leaf emblem across the chest from some visit to Toronto the previous year. Somehow it managed to be stylish, adding colour and form to the sofa whilst my denim skirt, rigid and structured jutted uncomfortably from the soft grey velvet on which we sat. We leaned back against the gnarled mahogany arms at either end, her legs, tanned from lazy weekends with *Grandmère* by the sea, curling into her body, mirrored by my own bleached white limbs.

Elodie reached down and drew a pile of magazines from beneath the box pleats of the sofa valance. Bringing her finger to her lips, she glanced furtively at the door, '*Chut!*' she said, unnecessarily since I was already quiet as a mouse.

'*Regarde-moi ça!*' Elodie opened the glossy, thumbed pages towards me and I looked to where she was pointing. I had never see such a magazine before; bodies, naked, displayed in this pose and that. Part of me knew that Auntie Jean would not approve; part of me could not resist the illicit thrill; could not look away from this new and curious knowledge.

Elodie giggled, turning the page first to where two women lay, their breasts thrusting, their legs entwined, then to where a man lay naked, tied by his wrists to a bed. Astride him, a woman, her red hair hanging loose, blew a kiss to the unseen camera. My mind took its own photograph, storing the image in a brand new compartment in my brain.

'*Ça suffit*,' she said, clutching the magazine to her chest, as if by seeing more I might somehow blemish the precious cache. Hurriedly, she stuffed her haul back out of sight, sat back up and smiled at me, her head to one side.

'*Tu es vierge?*' she asked. Yes of course I was. I was only thirteen; far too young to have had sex. I didn't ask her the question back. Maybe she wanted me to, I think now.

'*Mais ta tige? Ben oui, tu as sûrement perdu la tige?*'

She often made that curious little noise that the French make, which sounded like the *baa* of a sheep with a blocked nose – *ben*. I found myself imitating it after a while. I punctuated my sentences with it, upping my French-ness, losing my English 'um' and earning a linguistic badge of honour to show off when I got back to school.

But I had never come across that word, *tige*, and I wracked my brains to think what it could possibly be that she was sure I had lost if my virginity was not in question.

Sorry, Em. I know I am digressing but you need to understand what made me the person that I was when Nicholas came into my life. If we are going to be honest – and there's no other way to tell this story or it will all be in vain – then I have to let you see into the girl that I was and the moments in time that shaped what I was to become; the moments that Paris gave me, preparing me for the Paris moments to come.

These are the moments that stick with you like the penis on the train; moments which make you question, was it real or was it just a chimera of the night? The moments of pure joy that change you forever and moments of deep and stabbing pain when it hurts so much that your chest is crushing with the effort of a breath. And there are moments of utter bewilderment; moments when you are confronted with someone so much bolder, wide open, willing to risk conversations, ideas, actions that, in my world, would never have shifted into view. This was such a moment for me.

Elodie went for the dictionary, determined I should understand. *Cane, stem, shank, shaft...* the dictionary translations of *la tige* meant nothing.

'*C'est de l'argot,*' she explained – slang, I got that. '*Regarde,*' I looked down to where she was pointing as she unfolded and spread her legs.

She pulled the elastic of her knickers to one side and I saw her, pink with spikey hairs, not unlike those on her head. My fascination seemed to slow down time and, closing my eyes, I am back in that moment right now as I tell you my story:

The air, tense around us, has gone still like we are frozen in a painting or moulded into clay. In my mind it seems to take forever, but the movement is swift.

With her left hand Elodie reaches out and takes my right hand in hers. She grasps my middle and index fingers, holding them together as if tied with twine and she draws them towards her. I have to lean into her to follow as she holds my fingers firmly in hers. I shift my balance further onto my thighs, rolling until I am perched slightly at an angle, and my face comes close to hers as she guides my fingers into her.

I can hear her breath, shallow little intakes of that still air. I am not aware that I'm holding my breath until I feel the pumping in the back of my throat, forcing me finally to breathe out. She is in control but part of me buzzes with curiosity and the tingling between my legs mounts as I feel the smooth, gliding shape of her. It is like turning someone inside out. I don't know what to do with this feeling of inside-ness.

I look at her face, the fierce freckles and the snub nose, and scrutinise what I see, looking for a clue as to where we are going. Her hazel eyes dart with mischief. Is she loving her role, holding this little English virgin hostage with the first stirrings of sensual pleasure?

I don't know what to do. Shock and fascination vie for attention. This surely cannot be right. Maybe I should call for help. Tell someone – her parents, my teachers? But I am in awe. Her control is absolute and I do nothing in the end to betray my education. Then it is over.

She draws back and my fingers are returned to me and I smell for the first time the dark perfume of sex.

'*Voilà,*' Elodie says, a smile on her face, conspiratorial, knowing, '*ça, c'est perdre la tige. Tu l'as perdu, toi?*'

No, I hadn't lost mine. So far mine was intact.

'Okay. So we're here. Pretty damn wet, but we're here.' Nicholas gives a little shiver. *Not so hot now, eh?*

'Where?'

'Here.' Nicholas swings his arm to the side and bows with a smile, indicating the entrance to a supermarket I'd never noticed before.

'And there's a café. For Christ sake, let's just take a moment for a coffee. Look, this is dumb. You're wet through.'

'It was your idea to come all the way here. I tell you, the wine'd better be good – and cheap. Pete and Cathy won't want to spend a fortune, you know. You should've said how far it was, not just dragged me off in the rain.'

'Come on. Sloane. That's not fair. I absolutely did not drag you off. You were the one who wanted to walk.'

'Yeah – but not across the entire city.'

'That's a gross exaggeration and you know it.'

He has me there. He's right. God, I have no idea why I am being such a brat. It's hardly his fault that he was put in charge – and why do I care so much anyway? It's all Marcia's fault and I'm just taking it out on him.

I have this impatience in me, this kind of high achieving middle-class girl thing that taps me constantly on the shoulder and tells me that I should be progressing in my career – or in something at least – so the tiniest sleight at work, the faintest criticism or vague suggestion that there's room for improvement, everything becomes just one more blot on the career horizon. God, I am pathetic with a capital P.

'Fine. Let's have coffee. Fine.'

It's more of a little bar than a café, just wedged in amongst the groceries, just enough room to allow customers a breather from the rows of stinky cheeses, rich wines and herby, meaty pâtés.

We shed our coats. His leather jacket glistens with raindrops. My woollen coat is misshapen, arms wet and crooked, bumpy where I have held them around me in the downpour. I wanted to get wet and to wash away this weirdness that's settled itself on me since I boarded the coach and since I had seen that bottom in front of my face. I shake myself and my hair flings left and right like some spaniel come in from the rain.

'What's your poison?'

'Sorry?'

'What would you like to drink, Sloane? You are gonna have a drink, aren't ya?'

Is it my imagination or is he over-americanising his vowels again? Nicholas orders the coffee, both black no sugar, and sits opposite me. He pulls the red-checked paper tablecloth straight, teasing it this way and that until it is perfectly symmetrical on all sides then runs both hands through his dripping hair, plastering it back like a French politician – Mitterand or Chirac.

His hair is strands of dark honey. I can see drops of water gathering, wallowing up and spilling finally onto his collar and I feel sorry to have caused his near-drowning on a wet March day in Paris. Bizarrely, I start to giggle.

'What's so damn funny?'

'Nothing. You. This.' I look around us at the Parisians straight from their taxis, snug, dry and sporting trench coats, their collars up, umbrellas neatly stowed and coordinating to the point of irritation; perfect examples of the cliché of French chic. They coolly pluck delicacies from the shelves whilst we, dishevelled and imperfect are bundled, discarded rags on these too-small chairs. I can almost hear their disdain, that little shrugging sound, *Les Anglais, bof,* that means *'huh, these English, they 'ave no style.'*

'What is this place anyway?'

'This, Sloane Ranger, is Monoprix, the go-to store for anything and everything you could ever want in Paris.

'They have terrific cookies. I'll treat you. Used to come here all the time when I stayed with Didier, especially for the wine – and they even give you these cute pink striped plastic bags so the rain won't make the labels peel off and Pete and Cathy'll see, no problem, what bargains we got for them. So you see, Sloane, you're in good hands.' He spreads his fingers before me and for an instant I see them on my skin. 'So there's no need to have any doubts on that front. Trust me; I know what I'm doing here.'

So he knows what he's doing. But does he know what he's saying? Does he know what he said?

I'd have kinda thought that all in all you were pretty damn hot…

Monoprix, Em. A single price. But we all know that there never is a single price to pay for things we want in life. It's what they want you to think, but it's never true. You, at least, have taught me that.

Chapter 5

Nicholas

So, if we're going to continue with this farce, Em – hah, like I have a choice – I'd better tell you what happened next. I want to tell it my way, not her way because I think you'll understand that from a guy's point of view – and let's face it, what kind of guy is generally into that whole horoscope crap – it all needs to add up. You need some sort of context to make it all make sense.

You know now about my dad and what he thought about art, languages, anything that wasn't directly related to dollar signs popping out in front of your eyes. I guess that had kind of made me wary about sharing stuff. Personal stuff, I mean.

I have no idea where the hell I thought I was going with Sloane but to be honest, I wasn't thinking that much with my brain. You know what I mean. At least not until it happened, and then when it happened it changed the way I saw her. And it began to change the way I saw myself. It made me think that in some crazy way, there may be more to this whole damn thing than I thought. Made me think that maybe this life I'd been living was not going to be this dismal, grey affair, not forever like it seemed. Made me think that I was here on this trip for reasons I could never have known, never have predicted.

Maybe I was just making excuses for my animal instincts, giving them some higher, noble motive, maybe I'm doing that now, but then that's for you to judge. Because that's what it's all about isn't it, Em? Judgement?

We were so wet through that day in Monoprix that my underwear was sticking to me under my jeans. It was pretty damn uncomfortable, I can tell you, and it was all I could do not to get mad with Sloane and hang the fact that I fancied her rotten.

She was the one who insisted on walking through the rain, God knows why. She had this plum in her mouth and poker up her ass and I just felt she was looking down on me like some princess. I guess I fancied her but didn't like her a lot. I think that's possible for a guy – or maybe I just like a challenge.

I never mentioned what I'd said on the underground. I don't even know why I said it. If I said it was out of character, you'd probably think I was just saying it to save my ass, but I know we have to be honest here so I'm telling you, Em, it was not like me – and I knew I was way out of line. Maybe I just wanted to shock her, to see if the iceberg would melt a little if I said she was hot. And she heard it all right. She just didn't choose to reply.

Anyways, there we are in this little café and I want to strangle her when she just starts laughing, this crazy, high pitched laugh. Then she snorts, just like that.

Well now, I can't control myself when I hear Miss Goody Two-Shoes snorting so then I join in too and before we know where we are we're there like two hyenas laughing and yakking away.

That's not it though, not the thing I need to tell you except you need to know that by this stage we're not like enemies but kinda friendly. She starts leafing through this magazine that she's got out of her bag. Makes me a bit antsy at first – I think that she's not paying attention to what I'm saying but then she starts reading her horoscope out loud, like it's something real important.

'You're going on a journey that will set you on a whole new pathway. This is a chance for you to turn things around and take a fresh look at life. Romantically, things are going to get a whole lot more interesting for Librans,' she reads.

Sloane looks up from her magazine and blushes. Her pupils are large and limpid and her lashes are like spiders' legs, long and separate. They curl upwards towards her brow. Not like the falsies they wear back home, I decide.

'What?' she says. I shrug.

'You're smiling – so, what?'

'It's just… you don't really believe all this stuff do you?'

'Why? Don't you?'

'Come on, Sloane, this is just entertainment, surely you don't think…?'

'Oh you don't think it's possible then, that the place of our birth and where the moon and stars are at that particular moment can possibly have an effect on how we are, what we're like?'

'Yeah, but…'

'Even though the moon has a clear effect on tides and on menstrual cycles – and did you know for example, that women living together start having their periods all at the same time and that's down to the moon and its cycle…'

Here she goes again. She seems not to have noticed that she's talking about periods so I'm not going to notice it either.

'…and that it's a proven fact, Nicholas, that…'

'Just hang on. I'm not saying that all the scientific stuff can't be true, I'm just saying, you can't honestly believe that these horoscopes can possibly fit all the people that are that one star sign. Libra, for example. So you're a Libra and you reckon that all the other Libras will have the same things happen to them? And call me Nicky, please…'

'That's not the point, Nicholas. They don't predict a particular happening – it's more of a trend because of where the stars are in relation to those people who are all born at the same time of the year.

'It's like people will have certain characteristics according to their star sign. Take me, for example. Librans have to weigh up decisions, balancing them out,' she holds out her hand and turns it palm up then palm down, ' they can seem indecisive but that's not it. It's that they want to make sure everything's fair and that they see everyone's point of view. Make sure they've looked at every angle.'

'Okay then. What star sign am I?'

'What?' Sloane wrinkles up her brow and, puts her hands on the table and leans forward like she hasn't heard me right.

'What's my star sign?'

'That's not really a fair test, is it? I hardly know you and…'

'Come on, Sloane. We sat together all day on the bus, we sorted the kids together, we ate together, spent the morning in and out of the rain together. So come on. Grab the challenge – what star sign?'

'You're crazy. What's the point?'

'The point is that one of us gets to prove the other wrong. Tell you what? I'll give you a point. You guess right and I'll take you to dinner. Not just any dinner but something awesome, something that'll really hit the spot.'

'That's stupid. Ridiculous. Why would I want to have dinner with you anyhow? And what if I get it wrong?'

So goddamn crazy of me: I reach over and put my hand on hers and turn it over so I am cupping it, her palm up. It is cool and soft and it uncurls invitingly as I trace the lines gently with the fingertips of my other hand. It looks tiny and fragile. Like the hand of a child. I shift my gaze from her hand to her face. I love how she looks petulant, her chin up, her eyes glaring at me, defiant. But she leaves her hand where it is and I feel the little jolt of its weight as she relaxes it into mine.

'It's win-win, Sloane. We do dinner either way. No Pete, no Cathy. Just you and me and dinner,' I glance back at the palm of her hand.

'Come on, now. It's you that believes in the stars.'

Chapter 6

Sloane

I never really got over having my fingers inside Elodie's body. For the whole of the rest of that holiday, I couldn't bring myself to look her properly in the face.

I've lost count of how many times I've looked for *perdre la tige* in a dictionary. It's not really the sort of thing you can just ask some arbitrary French person, is it? Never found it – which in itself is frustrating because I wanted to see it written down, concrete evidence of what Elodie had done.

If it was slang, it must have been local, some cool language that only her gang would understand – but not finding it made me wonder whether she had laid a spurious linguistic trap to teach me an altogether different skill.

Perhaps, Em, this helps you to see that I am not really that kind of girl. It was years later that someone came along and finally found inside me what I had found inside Elodie.

I was a virgin for so many long years while girls at school boasted of doing it in the back of cars, down alleyways, in their parents' beds and behind the bike sheds at school. It wasn't that I was unattractive, not at all. They used to call me 'bonny' whatever that meant. Now it sounds as if it means healthy and plump, like an over-fed baby, but back then it sounded like a compliment. I suppose that the opportunities just weren't there. In the early days, Mum and Dad would always make sure I was picked up from school, either by them or by my auntie Jean, who lived not far from St Joseph's. She'd give me tea and look after me while we waited for my parents to arrive.

Auntie Jean told me that men were only ever after one thing but she never actually told me what it was. I used to think maybe it was a telly or a car. Who would have thought that the clue would lie in the actions of my Parisian *correspondante*?

When my parents died, it was my auntie Jean who took me in, so boys were completely off the cards. She wouldn't have let me go near them and I was so busy being sad that I wouldn't have let myself. I liked her a lot but it wasn't like having a mum and a dad.

People were very nice to me though. I went on school trips for nothing after that — some special fund for kids like me who'd been orphaned at an early age, and I got free dinners at school — oh, and the bus pass came free too.

Auntie Jean let me have my mum and dad's bed at her house. After the funeral, she asked me what I wanted and that was it. She seemed quite surprised at my request but I thought I could smell them somehow in that bed and it comforted me to know that at least some of their cells had to be there. Some of the dust mites must still be lingering, I thought, at least I could share them. It was something that besides me they had left behind.

I could tell which side of the bed was which, just from the mattress where the hollows had formed casts of their bodies, as always side by side. It was like their forms had melted away, leaving only the mould of their beings, lonely ripples of nothing, like they still slept, silent and invisible in the cool, white sheets.

My dad made more of an imprint than my mum but my mum's was a different shape like she'd been lying on her side, and I swore I could trace the curve of her stomach, ample as it was. I would lie right in that hollow and feel her arms around me and hear her voice in my head: *It's okay, ducks. You'll be okay.*

The funeral was another of those moments you never forget. Not the funeral itself maybe, but the burial. They dug the grave doubly deep, so that Mum could go on top of Dad – or maybe it was the other way round. Shit, I don't know which way round it is and now there's no one left to ask. Anyway, one went on top of the other.

The first coffin went so far down that the blokes who were holding the rope almost overbalanced into the hole. It was like they were putting them into the bowels of the earth, as if maybe they could keep warm from the heat of the earth's core. I was obsessed with the idea of them being cold after that so I liked to think that maybe there was some kind of heat down there.

Leaving my parents there in the earth seemed all wrong and I didn't want to just walk off and go back to my auntie's that night but everyone said I should. They said that was what Mum and Dad would have wanted so I let myself be led back to the car and this kind of party we had. 'Celebrating their lives,' the vicar said, but I didn't feel like celebrating at all, just like burying myself with them and staying there forever and not having to face school, homework, other kids.

As they lowered them in, Mum and Dad, everything became so dark. It wasn't that late – about half two or three – but the clouds were so black and the sky was so full. When it burst, it exploded into hard and fast raindrops, then into gritty, biting hail. It sent people scrambling for umbrellas even though the vicar was still saying the prayers. I remember thinking that it was rude, all this scrambling and scrabbling and that people should just listen and not move. This moment would be gone forever and my parents with it and the vicar's prayers would be swallowed up in the flurry to stay dry. Maybe God wouldn't hear the prayers either and not know that my parents were coming.

I didn't notice whether I was crying or not. My face was wet and cold and my hands ached with their clenching. Later, I noticed a little ridge just inside my mouth – a little row of ulcers where I had been biting my lip and, running my fingers along, I was pleased to have at least some physical wound from what happened that day.

Everyone started picking up clods of earth and chucking it in the grave so I thought I'd better do it too but then Auntie Jean gave me a deep pink and white rose – a *Nicole* rose, she said it was. She told me to throw that in instead. I remember thinking what a shame to waste something so beautiful and so alive, that I would rather take it home with me and put it in a vase. But I threw it in and it disappeared into the ground. I thought, if I ever get married, those are the roses I'll have.

I never knew what happened to the car. I heard Auntie Jean saying it was a 'write off' several times that day but I didn't know then what that meant. She kept telling the story over and over about how they'd been coming to fetch me and how they'd tried to overtake but it looked like Dad had misjudged how far away the oncoming truck had been and then gone into it head-on.

I didn't like to think of it being my dad's fault so I tried to close my ears and my eyes but I kept on seeing the truck and my mum and my dad and the look on his face and him realising that he was about to kill my mum.

Chapter 7

Nicholas

I swear I have never had an instant moment like the one I had there and then. It was like one of those god-awful movies where they behave as if some electric current shoots through them and they're all loved up from there on in.

When Sloane took her hand away, I got this real weird pull inside of me, as if I was losing something, like letting her go was a big deal. I had only spent a few hours with her and already she somehow knew me. Like she saw the bit inside that I'd always tried to hide, the bit that was never macho enough for my Dad or big-handsome-son enough for my mom.

With my mom, it was all about the *Schadenfreude*. She could have a real good time just picking away about other people's miseries and she never really liked that I wouldn't join in and look down my nose in that superior way she had.

It wasn't as if she was really anybody; just a woman who'd lucked out and married the boss. She was the kind of woman who'd say *now you know how I feel* if her best friend succumbed to an illness or was widowed after her. She'd say it very crisply, in impeccable East Coast style, mind you, her pearls just large enough to be noticed but not so big that she'd fall into the ostentatious camp. *My Lord, Nicholas, have you seen the size of Patsy's mother's solitaire? Just so vulgar, don't you think? So much classier to be a little restrained, but then I guess that's what you expect from her. You know, Cynthia told me it came from some market in New York City. Now that wouldn't do for me…* It was never really about the other person, only about how it related to her – and to her next move into the upper reaches of society's high wire.

And that's the biggest joke of it all. That accent, those pearls, none of it came naturally to her – any more than that whole preppy upper middle class thing came to me. Oh, I might *say* I'm from Boston but between you and me, that isn't quite strictly true. Not that Mom would want to let on, of course.

No, Em, us Brides, we aren't from Boston or any other fancy place. My daddy's daddy and his daddy before him got their money quite literally out of the earth. Marble – cold, clean, pure and simple. Ha – never thought that maybe that was where my interest in sculpture came from – never thought that maybe my daddy was to blame for that. And when you come from the wrong side of the tracks up the highway in Vermont, you'd better make sure you keep that one quiet. *Hush, Nicholas, you mustn't say 'wanna' – what will the neighbours think, for goodness sakes? Now, Nicholas, you need to make something of yourself like your daddy did. You do know that, don't you?* Fit in or move out. My parents moved right in and up.

There was this moment when I was a kid. It was around about my second year away from home. I guess my dad thought that boarding school would put a little polish on me and toughen me up, make me a bit more like him; develop a little bit of that 'ole' man ruthlessness he was so damn proud of.

Like I said before. I never was any good at sport. My coach had no real hopes for me but I guess he gave in to my dad, who was probably due a payoff from all the cash he'd endowed the school. I liked the place just fine and the teachers were neat, but my dad expected me to slot in one end as me and come out the other a kind of miniature him. Like the school could somehow remove the things that made you *you* and magic them into what your parents really wanted and squirt you out the other end with *Son of My Father* stamped on your butt.

Anyways, the coach, like I said, keeping my father sweet, let me play in field that day and everyone was there and watching – my mom and my dad, our next door neighbours with their daughter who I hung out with when I was home and loads of my dad's fraternity buddies – that was the worst of it all.

So there I am, my big moment and this ball comes right for me. It's classic. The sun's right in my eyes and I stagger around a bit, praying that the ball is going to somehow land in my glove even though I can't see a darned thing. So of course I miss it and I am in the biggest disgrace.

Well, there I am and I'm trying not to cry. I had this buddy, Josh. He was in the same dorm and he preferred arty stuff too. He got that kind of pressure that you feel when you are just no damned good at the one thing the whole world wants you to be good at.

Well, Josh comes over and he gives me this great big bear hug – nothing weird, just a little guy being nice – and my dad, well, he comes over and he shoves Josh right to the ground and he grabs me by the shoulder and marches me off the field with my mom running behind to keep up. Her high heels keep getting stuck in the grass and she's yelping every now and then,

'Elliott, wait for me, Elliott, think what it's going to look like,' at the top of her voice.

So we get back up to school and he sends Mom to the car and he drags me down the corridor to where the Dean of Students has his office and tells me to wait there for him. So I wait and I wait. And I wait.

Now, I know that I missed the ball alright and I know that my dad's pretty mad with me for that, but I have no idea why I'm there waiting around for my dad. I figure I must have done something else pretty wrong. It's all beige and grey and cold in that corridor and there's no one around as they're all still out there down at the field having a barbecue, dousing their wounds with a few cans of beer.

There's this clock on the wall and it makes this real loud ticking sound and I find myself counting the ticks, concentrating real hard on not shivering. I pick away at the skin on side of my thumb until it starts to bleed and I can suck it up and taste the blood. I am absolutely not going to cry just in case. If my dad gets back and finds me blubbing then the trouble'll really start.

Finally, a couple of hours later, Mr Barker, my Head of Dorm, comes to get me and takes me to this other dorm where I find my stuff chucked on the bed. My paintings are all kind of screwed up and this real neat book on *Rodin* that Josh gave me from France is nowhere to be seen. Turns out my dad's insisted on me changing dorms and sleeping anywhere where Josh isn't. Well, you can imagine what all the other guys made of that and it wasn't long after that Josh left the school.

My dad never showed up all afternoon and it turned out that he'd left just about straight away. My mum didn't come to see me either, so I never got to say goodbye to them that day.

I lay down on that new bed and it felt unfamiliar and cold and I wished I could've had a brother or sister – someone else who could have made my parents proud. But then looking back, I wouldn't have wanted to sleep more than once with my father either.

My point is that those are moments I do remember whereas there are so many moments that I don't. My dad, my mom, my head of dorm, the looks on all of their faces. The way the guys in the new dorm avoided me. Like I had a contagious disease. Like they'd been told by their folks that if they went anywhere near me then they'd be crap at baseball too. These are the sort of things that play around in your head and make of you the person you become.

So Em, when I'm here and I'm supposed to be telling you the whys and the wherefores of everything that happened, I have to relate it to the things that were meaningful for me, to the things that made an impression and changed the way things were.

That moment, when I touched Sloane's hand and I curled it into mine; that was a moment like no moment I could remember. Moments are usually attached to other moments so that together they all make sense, a kind of a pattern that makes a whole. But this moment was like a whole pattern of moments that made sense all on its own.

I don't know if I'm explaining it right and I know that a lot depends on making this all clear. That moment imprinted itself on my brain and just wouldn't let me go. It felt like I was accepted, that I didn't have to be anyone else but the person that I was. That was the moment that made me want more, more than any of the moments that had gone before, though back then I had no idea what moments were yet to come.

Chapter 8

Sloane

I am going to be brutally honest here, Em, which I didn't expect when I decided we had to record these events. I am still convinced that telling this story is our only hope of making things right, making it all stop, and I pray every day that I am not wrong.

I need you to know that when Nicholas took my hand, I knew exactly what I was about to do and the lie that I was going to tell. Maybe lie is too strong. It was really more of a trick. I was so delighted at the very idea of fooling him that the consequences of falsehood didn't even enter my head.

My hand is in his and, despite my conscious effort his touch shifts a gear in me. I am playing with him now but I am not aware that I am losing myself in the game.

'Okay, okay. If you want me to tell you your star sign, I will.' I remove my hand and sit back. Dinner with him? Who does he think he is? He is smiling and I look up to the left as if contemplating my move.

He grins. He is sure that I have no idea. That I cannot possibly divine his star sign and pinpoint the month in which he was born to arrive in my life on this day, in this café, and to make me feel that no one has ever held my hand before.

Miserable, hopeful people read horoscopes. Those who have given up on life don't bother and those who are happy with their lot have no need, so I must come into the class of miserable-hopefuls. But on this day I am glad of every stupid horoscope book I have read and every penny I have spent in the pursuit of the right job and the right man. At least I can teach a lesson to Mr Wrong.

'I don't think you're a Pisces. They are too dreamy and I'm not getting that from you. And you are definitely not a Libran as I don't think you're remotely interested in what's fair.'

Harsh, Sloane, very harsh.

'There's no way you're an Aries as they are way too loud and you don't strike me as a bull-in-a-china shop type either so that rules Taurus out. You are quite contrary so Capricorn might fit, but somehow I don't think so.'

Nicholas is sitting up now, tense, alert. I have him spellbound. I am in control and he is hanging on my every word. What is it about men that makes them so weak, so susceptible and just so vain?

He is curious, torn between wanting me to be wrong, to lord it over me and wanting me magically to know him, to be a witch able to conjure his fate. And I want to be that witch, to be able to cast a spell and then to cast him aside and to laugh in his face.

I tick the star signs off one by one, knowing that so far I am right, that I haven't yet picked the right one. Now it gets trickier. We are down to two.

'Okay, so that leaves Leo and Virgo.'

Now I have to do this right. This one has to be a guess but I hesitate before I mentally flip a coin.

I think back to what, as a miserable hopeful, I have read. I consider the time on the coach, how he needed the coach driver to pay heed, to make sure that everything went to plan. How he fussed a lot with the papers and had to have it all in order and how he cleared up the sick without fuss. He's not noisy either. He's self-contained in a kind of enigmatic way and he's definitely not a man's man with all that art and stuff and according to my book, Leos are real rugger buggers and pretty loud. So not a Leo, not a Leo...

'Virgo. You're a Virgo.' I hold my breath and fix my smile.

Em, I could tell by the look on his face that I was right and that the impact I had made was everything I'd hoped. He was hooked by my witchery and I had him in my grasp. I had played a trick and had gathered all the cards. What I could not tell, though, Em, is where my trickery would lead.

Chapter 9

Nicholas

I feel like I am falling. Like something is opening up and swallowing me whole. Like there is no air. Everything around me is silent and light, bright like I have never known before. *Jesus Christ, what's happening to me?* And then I breathe.

The shoppers are still here and the rush and clang of the café is still all around us. If anything the store has gotten manic while Sloane has been taking me apart. Piece by piece, bit by bit, she has told me what I am and what I am not and it's like in some strange way she's seen into me. Like I've become transparent with all my guts and garbage hanging out for all to see.

What the hell? I don't know what to do with this. Don't know what to do next. What the hell am I doing? Like I really believe in this star sign crap?

Okay, I know the basics and yeah, I've read that whole thing about Virgos and their meticulous ways but I always thought that that was kind of a fluke. Jeez, there have to be gazillions of meticulous guys out there. But she has it there, bang on the money like she really knows me or something. Or something.

Hang it, I just have to go with the flow. I can't let her see that in biblical terms, she just cut off my hair.

'Well, I guess that one way or another you just earned yourself a meal at the *Le Procope*.'

'I'm right aren't I?' She has her chin right up now, her eyes blazing, imperious and mischievous all at the same time.

I am saying nothing. She looks away before I do, her eyelashes flutter down and then she speaks: 'Never heard of it. What is it again, *Le Procope*?'

'Yeah, but I'm not giving anything away. You'll have to trust me on this one.'

Just like I'm trusting you...

Chapter 10

Sloane

After Nicholas left that morning, I went straight to Cacharel. I know, ridiculous, expensive, but I'd read about this outlet that did end of lines and overstocks, that kind of thing and it popped into my head when my senses popped out. Suddenly all the clothes I had brought on this trip just weren't going to be right. If I was going to have dinner with Nicholas, I would have to have something new.

I honestly just meant to teach him a lesson, although I had almost lost sight of the reason why. I still think now, Em, that my pride had been hurt and he was just someone on whom to take it out – someone who just happened to be there. But he was also someone who had an attractive bottom and who made my skin tingle without a single touch. I didn't want to own the feelings he made me feel and lashing out was easier than letting in. That he was vain enough to think I cared so much that I could read his star sign was laughable, that I felt uneasy and ashamed at what I'd done, less so. He was visibly shocked that I'd been right. I was horrified to see the shine in his eyes, like he was almost on the point of tears, and he was holding his hands tight around his coffee cup, as if afraid they might shake.

My triumph vanished the instant I felt its glow. I felt my face flush, I had to look away and I covered my cheeks with my hands. He recovered quickly, sort of turned the page on the moment but I had seen it there in his eyes, the sadness and the fear and I had no idea what they meant.

I managed to dodge Cathy at the hotel, grateful not to have to explain my morning away and in no mood for school talk or girly chats. I liked her a lot, she was good company, but I was in my head on that day, if you know what I mean, Em, and I didn't want to let her in or any of my thoughts out.

Nicholas had said he would take care of the evening, booking it, sorting things with Cathy and Pete. I have no idea where my brain was. It never occurred to me that Cathy and Pete might need us at the hotel or might wonder where we'd gone. It's not like I'd not done this all before – the trip, that is. It's all very clear, that we takes turns at being in the hotel, or if we all go out – like to a restaurant in the area we are staying, we let the guy behind the desk know where we are going to be.

To be fair, I'd only been around at the end the year before to help take the students back home and we'd stayed in a different hotel, further out, near the Porte de Clichy. It was a seedy dump, and we'd all agreed that for a few pounds more it would make sense to be in a more decent place. This was certainly that. This hotel was elegant with its chandeliers in the hall, its plump, red cushions and its gold brocade but none of that had gone to my head in the way that Nicholas Bride had done. Nicholas said he would sort things out and I just blindly carried on, like a schoolgirl about to enjoy a first date.

I bet you think I was a virgin, Em, but I will tell you here and now that I was not, although in truth I might as well have been. Stuart and I met at Wall Hall. He was doing a straight teaching degree and I was doing my Post Grad. And yep, I had got through the whole of university and (unlike Elodie) without managing even to *lose my stem,* mainly courtesy of living still with Auntie Jean, and a serious lack of suitable beaux.

It felt like Stuart and I were the only ones in the whole college who didn't have an 'other half'. We found ourselves hanging around together, kissed a few times and eventually fumble turned into sex but the sex never turned to passion. Not for me anyway. And really the sex never got much beyond the fumble stage – more of a practised fumble but predictable. Start with the top half, unhook the bra, play around a bit there, move down below, play around a bit more, climb on top – him, not me – and then five minutes later it's done and we're off down the pub.

He was a nice guy, wanted to get married, but one day I found myself looking at him and thinking, is this really the sort of person you would magic up if you were choosing a mate for life? God, that seems so brutal now but I promised you honesty and that's where we're at. I was twenty-six. I wasn't a virgin. I had no particular ties and I was playing with fire.

The dress I bought was way more expensive than I had intended. It was pale blue, which I knew brought out depth in my eyes. Why was that important? I wanted Nicholas to see in, and I wanted him to want more. Was I conscious of that at the time? Probably not, but rather than lie, I shall say that I do not know.

The confection from Cacharel was what I'd call *Empire Line*, lace at the collar and cuffs, buttons down the front and a cascade of tiny flowers in pink and green hues. Looking back, it sounds naff but it shouted 'romance' and it was as anti-eighties as you could get. I was drawn to its soft cotton folds, having spent far too long in shoulder pads and chains. And it wasn't without a *frisson* that I checked that the buttons actually did undo.

We do these things, Em. We go out and buy dresses, gilding our lilies and giving off scent and then we stand back and pretend not to know what has happened and why. We are deceitful creatures, our messages as clear as the written word. Yet we do not own them so that when we are accused we can declare ourselves not guilty – that whatever attraction occurred was accidental, no intent, no purpose and we are not at fault. When I was getting ready that day, donning my dress and dabbing Dior behind my ears, I was not getting ready for me. I was getting ready for him. For whatever it was he might want.

He is already there, browsing through art books on the stands outside Hachette. I watch him as I make my way along the street and past the fountain. Kids are playing tag in and out of the tourists, around their parents at the café on the corner of the Rue Saint André des Arts. I've been killing time in the poster shop, this amazing shop that has been there for as long as I've been coming to Paris – much longer, I am sure. I was tempted to buy a poster by Mucha, they are all the rage. But then I left it, deciding not to clutter the image, not to detract from the impression I want to make when Nicholas sees me arrive.

An icy, unforgiving breeze is coming off the Seine, but in the way that we wear heels for effect despite the pain, I have no sense of regret that I have not chosen a warmer dress. I turn the collar of my denim jacket up, skirting around the kids and past the fountain, not wanting Nicholas to see me too soon, clinging to the delicious anticipation of the moment, so I can register his reaction, good or bad.

He turns just as I arrive and without a word he reaches out his hand and I put my hand in his, and there it is again, this flash of excitement, this shudder of something new.

He gives a little nod, taking the whole of me in. There's that corny expression, *undressing me with his eyes*, which I have to say he really didn't do. I just wanted him to, Em. I just wanted him to want what he saw.

'It's a little early to eat, let's just go walk,' he says.

We cross the road, dodging out of the way of a *Deux Chevaux*, which toots in annoyance at our audacity to cross when the sign says to go. Nicholas slides his hand out of mine and tucks it behind me, a light brush on my spine as he steers me safely to the other side. He takes my arm and I am surprised at the home-ness of his touch. I do not know this man and yet I do. It is as natural as breathing to feel him by my side. We walk in silence, him steering, me full of wanting in a way I'd never been before.

'*T'es pas frileuse?*' Nicholas asks, French rolling neatly off his tongue. *No, Nicholas, I am neither cold nor frigid, whichever it is you mean.*

I shake my head. He has fractured the still air between us and I find that I have a voice – too much of one, in fact – and I prattle on about my visits to Paris as a child.

We find that we both love the Pyramid at the Louvre and hate the Pompidou Centre. We have neither of us been to the *Cimetière* Père Lachaise, where Edith Piaf and Jim Morrison are both buried, along with La Fontaine and Molière. Already I had visions of an outing *à deux*, 'No, I've never been there either,' I say, 'Can you get there by metro or what?' Was I frantic to see the graves of those famous singers or authors of renown? Did I even care? At that moment I'd have probably dangled naked from The Eiffel Tower if it had been what Nicholas wanted me to do.

The smells of Paris drift in and out as we go; *crêpes* smothered in chestnut purée, heady with vanilla here, the Italianate waft of oregano, garlic and onion on thick, doughy pizza slices there, the rancid tang of the city's discarded detritus in stark contrast on another corner of the street. Nicholas shifts conscientiously from left to right and back again, making sure I am never on the traffic side, tucking me safely away from the kerb, as if in another era where some horse and cart might splash my cloak. High-pitched sirens scream in the distance and a street walker stops to light a cigarette, hitching her tights and patting her hair. We move silently past, both knowing, neither commenting on, what this evening will bring for her.

There is that feeling of separation in the air, that we are not part of all that is around us, that we are in a bubble of whatever it is we are in, like when you are a child and shut your eyes, believing that if you can't see them, they can't see you.

Em, you have to believe me, I never meant to keep it going, but once we were at the table, I found myself carrying on the whole charade; the idea of knowing his star sign, this unexplained knowledge of who he was, which he didn't seem to question. I didn't know what to do.

I played willingly to the crowd of one and never said a word. What in my mind had started as an apology swiftly followed by confession, was swallowed in a sense of self-loss and a need to be whatever it was that this man needed me to be. If he saw me as a witch, then I was willing to oblige. It was an unfamiliar role and all the more inviting as a result.

Chapter 11

Nicholas

I didn't mean to remind her about anything to do with school but it just slipped out that I had bumped into Cathy and Pete. All I wanted was for her to love where we were, the food, the wine, the atmosphere and maybe me.

'God, I'd forgotten all about the kids – and the tickets. Bloody hell. What did you say to Pete?'

She's not exactly beautiful in a classic way. Her nose is a little too big and her eyes are quite far apart but her mouth, now that's perfect. I love the way she dances her hair back and forth when she speaks, all expressive just like the French. I wonder if she's picked up that habit from being here as a kid.

The candlelight is tripping over her face and the quiver I feel inside is almost unbearably good. She likes this restaurant too. Another tick. At least I have gotten this right.

'Relax. He was fine, really happy with the wine we chose. It was Cathy who was all weird. She seemed pretty put out about something. Guess she'd just had a bad day – but then I figure that any day with 'Petey' isn't exactly gonna be great.'

'Nicholas, that's so bad…'

'Sorry, he's just such a teacher.'

'And you are?'

'Me? I'm passing time until things work out.'

'Things? Like what things?'

'Like a few issues I need to clear up. Like the book I'm gonna get published.'

'What sort of book? I thought you were an artist and a teacher. Now you're suddenly a writer?'

'No saying you have to be one without the other, now is there? If you must know I'm writing a novel – part of the reason I agreed to come to Paris, matter of fact. There's an exhibition of Rodin's work, along with Camille Claudel's. I'm writing this kind of counter-story to the one that's in the film. Fiction but kind of putting Rodin's point of view rather than everything through the eyes of the poor old, badly-treated mistress.'

'I take it you don't approve of mistresses then.' Sloane looks me straight in the eye as she says it. I take a slug of water from the glass on the table and find myself straightening the knife and the fork either side of the table mat, evening them up so there's just a half inch gap either side. Sloane's gaze drops to my hands and I draw them back as she grins.

'Virgos,' she says, 'can't resist perfection.' *Jeez, what is this girl up to?*

'So tell me about this place – why's it so special?' *She's curious, that's a good sign, right?*

'My dear Ms Sloane, you are sitting where the revolutionary guys sat – Robespierre, Danton, Marat, this is where they met and this is where Voltaire would drink forty cups of coffee a day. This place was the hub of the gossip-factory, scandal mongering, that sort of thing, but intellectuals too, they'd sit here for hours on end philosophising over this and that. Don't you think that's neat – the idea of all those great guys right here where we are now? The food's pretty awesome too.' *God, I sound like a salesman, don't even know if I'm getting my facts exactly right. What the hell?*

She smiles and studies the menu and I just have to ask about the star sign. I know she didn't see my passport so how the hell could she find out?

'So come on then. How d'ya guess?' She ignores me. The sommelier arrives with the wine. We seem to be having bits of conversations and getting nowhere fast.

The whole thing with Cathy and Pete was insane but I wasn't about to tell Sloane over dinner. Sloane and I went our separate ways when we left the Monoprix and we agreed to meet later at the *Pont St Michel*, by the fountain, at the bookshop across the road. She was going to check out some clothing store she'd heard of and I just wanted to get some air and walk off this feeling I had that I'd somehow been turned inside out.

Neither of us had thought for a second about what to tell Pete and Cathy that evening so I thought I'd better head on back and make sure things were okay. But some parent had called about this kid who'd been real homesick. So not long after we'd left, Pete had gone off on the train to check him out, make sure that there wasn't any other problem, like with the family or his room. That meant Cathy had spent the whole day at the hotel, manning the phone alone and she didn't look too pleased.

Turns out the family were all very nice, he said. Just this kid had never been away from home before so Pete gave the kid's parents a call and sorted it out. I felt bad that I hadn't been around. I was supposed to be in charge for Christ sakes and all I could think about was this girl who had my brain – and other bits of me – on fire.

I made some excuse about how bad the rain had been and not wanting to drag Sloane through it all and Pete was real cool. Said he was fine about fetching the tickets for the boat trip and that he and Cathy could do that too if we didn't fancy going. The French parents would be there anyways so there'd be no problem with the kids.

'Sloane sends her apologies,' I said. 'She's a little beat after the journey and the late night last night. Think she'll most likely have an early night.'

Already, Em, I was telling lies. She says it's important that the lies are 'unveiled'. The story needs to know its lies.

'Okay, old chap,' Pete said, 'she did seem rather whacked out yesterday. Distracted at dinner, not at all like her, I said as much to Cathy, isn't that right? She's usually right on the button, at school anyway. Always very organised, professional. Nice girl, Cathy, wouldn't you say?'

Cathy was going along with it all but she seemed twitchy. She kept walking to the doorway, looking out then coming back, like she was expecting someone to arrive.

I wasn't the only one who'd noticed. There was an olive-skinned guy behind the desk. He watched her walk back and forth and he caught my eye and shrugged, a little twist on his face. Every now and then he'd turn and tap the heavy metal keys firmly into the pigeon holes labelled with the room numbers, like they'd somehow escape a little when he turned away. *Virgo*, I thought, and then mentally I shook myself; *C'mon, Nicky. You're acting crazy too.*

Just as I was heading upstairs, Pete called out after me. The mahogany bannister was polished and smooth and the shiny surface made this farting sound under my hand as I swung around to face them. I squeaked my hand again, made it obvious – just so they'd know I wasn't being impolite.

'No, it's nothing,' Cathy said and she gave Pete this stare, like she was didn't want to give something away. I shrugged and turned to go up the stairs but not so quickly that I didn't hear her half-whisper to Pete.

'Why should you tell him? He'll find out soon enough.'

Jae De Wylde

Chapter 12

Sloane

I have been stuck on this bit, Em but I suppose I will just have to get on and tell it as it was. It's how to tell it and make it real so it doesn't sound like some fantasy or made-up scene from a book. Nicholas has done well. I have read what he has recorded so far and I believe it to be a true record of what occurred to that point. I will continue to be honest even though I am not sure it is in my favour to portray it as it was. I cannot judge so I must leave that to you.

The meal may have been wonderful – probably was given the reputation, the place and the cost, but honestly, I couldn't have cared less if we'd been eating dog food – and I'm pretty sure that Nicholas felt the same way.

He told me about the exhibition at the *Musée Rodin*. His eyes sparked as he talked of sculptures that I had seen in books, of Camille Claudel, and of what he wanted to write. How incredible to be so confident – to allow yourself to dream that there is hope for your hopes, however hopeless they seem. I am a writer clothed in a teacher's skin but I did not share that with Nicholas. He was in full flow. I listened yet mostly I was watching as he gestured this way and that, describing figure and form, his hand caressing the air where the sculpture he spoke of was present as he saw it in his mind. All I could imagine was that hand caressing me. By the time he paid – you see, I have included that chivalrous detail – we both knew what was coming next.

There is a knock on my door. He knows the number of my room – of course he does. I was the one who told him and I must not hide that fact.

We, neither of us speak.

The room is arranged in such a way that the bed is close to the window. The curtains are open and an orange-red light casts its glow across the covers, chintzy drapes of blue shot with gold. I am still wearing the dress that I have chosen for this man who is in my room. At my invitation, though I have known him just forty-eight hours. We must not forget this fact when we are judging what has happened and why and who exactly is to blame. Where, Em, you may ask, were the days and weeks of foreplay, the sparring wits, the barely touching hands and the over-aching bodies? Where indeed? But maybe there is no need for what comes before if what comes after is ready to be served.

I am still wearing the dress but, testament to my expectations of what will transpire, I have removed my tights since I wear them under my pants. How mortifying for the man I want to love to find me sausaged into nylon, flesh dented and splayed in an ugly sack. I must be hard on myself if I am to be hard on him too. We must decide where the balance is fair and where it falls down on the side of guilt. If it is to be me so be it. If it is to be him then my tale is of use. Either way, exorcism of the truth is a necessary part of the process we must endure and I will not tolerate an untruth. No neglected fact, no on-purpose forgetting, absolutely no lies.

We are in the room with the orange-red glow and I can barely breathe. He goes to turn on the light and I still his hand. I want to feel and I don't need to see. No, I want to see him but I don't want him to see me. That is it. That is where the balance lies.

Why don't I want him to see? Disappointment – I don't want him to feel it, like I might not add up to the sum of what is in his mind, the sculpture he imagines under this pale blue dress with its sprigs of green and pink. Like when you see the film of a book. It is not how you imagined but impoverished in the chasm that exists between what you see in your mind and what turns out to be on screen. That is why, if honesty is to prevail and prevail it must.

I am the one who makes the first move. I lead him to the bed, guide him down and for the first time I kiss him on the mouth. He kisses back. I expect it to be more firm but his mouth is delicate in its seeking, unexpected, unrehearsed.

It is the balance of control that I do not understand. I am in his grip and yet he seems to be in mine. I don't know how that works but maybe this will all come clear.

Now he moves. He runs his hands around the lace at my neck, bends and kisses me gently behind my ear. Sometimes when you stop what you are doing and focus on your fingers, on your hands, you can feel a rushing sensation, the pumping of blood as it courses through your arteries and veins. This is what I feel now except I feel it everywhere and not just in my hands.

He undoes the tiny buttons of my dress and slides his hand inside and softly into my bra.

My auntie Jean, she always said not to go out without matching underwear in case you got hit by a bus. She stopped saying it after Mum and Dad were killed by a truck but today I was glad of her advice. I knew that what Nicholas would find would match and would thrill. Did I always heed my auntie Jean? Not a bit of it. My bras and knickers were usually mix and match except very little did the matching and most of it was grey. I had bought those frilly bits of nothing that he found that very day and I had worn them just for him. So if I wanted a get-out clause, I could have told a lie. But I haven't, Em. I have stuck with the truth.

He does not undo my dress *expertly* as you would read in a great romance. He has to tug a little now and then, to release the buttons from their holes. I do not move to help.

I am on the other side of the room, watching this happen.

I am looking down from above, staring down on the man who undresses the girl, watching and waiting for what will happen next.

I do not want to be here, the sensation too vital, intense, like the essence of me is being lost, but as he removes my bra and his mouth closes on my breast, my mind is sucked back to my body and the two become one.

This is something new.

I am the clay beneath his sculptor's hands as he moves them over me, finding those places that make me gasp, those places that only I have ever found before.

Chapter 13

Nicholas

Em, I swear I wasn't gonna go up to her room. I thought maybe it was just the booze talking like it does when you've had a heady evening and that she'd forget her invite when the night air hit home.

She looked great, knockout. I just couldn't work her out – or how she'd worked me out. Never did tell me how it was she saw in me what others didn't. In fact, she didn't say a lot and I found myself talking about me.

Not me exactly, more my book idea and the exhibition that was on in town, the way I'd been trying to cover the whole Camille Claudel story but put more from Rodin's point of view. Okay, he wasn't exactly married to Rose, but they had got a kid and he'd been with her a heck of a long time and yeah, he'd had mistresses, but there wasn't a single other mistress that unhinged him, impacted dramatically on his work and life.

I'd been mad when I found that that big French movie star was making this massive film but then I thought, what the heck, everyone's so obsessed with what happened to Claudel and her work that everyone forgets this guy who, let's face it, had to put up with all her crap.

She was crazy all right, at the end, and she just wouldn't leave go. And then she starts accusing Rodin of stealing all her work and her ideas. I'd seen her work before alright, but just bits of collections, like when there was some in the *Musée d'Orsay* this one time and then a few bits in New York and to be honest I wasn't that impressed.

But this time it was his work and hers – together at one go. Now this for me was something. This whole story haunted me and I needed to prove myself right – not for anyone but me, since despite my swagger, I didn't believe that publication was on the cards. I'd been pipped to the post on that one and it had made me real sore.

Sloane said she'd come with me to the exhibition the following day. Pete and Cathy were sorting the trip with the kids and we neither of us fancied the tourist-packed boats. I guess we were too busy fancying each other – well I was for sure, and I knew she was too when she came right out with the question that knocked me for six.

She looks at me with her hair just covering one eye, Bambi-like, doe-eyed I guess you'd say, and in her cool, British accent she just asks me straight out, 'Let's go back to my room. After.' She brushes her hair aside and looks at me dead-on. 'Do you want to come back to my room, Nicholas? Is that what you have in mind?'

Shit, I hadn't had anything but on my mind. But it wasn't just the prospect of sex. Yeah, you may laugh but you can save all the jokes about guys thinking with their dicks and no, I wouldn't have been human if I'd not been thinking just a little with mine, but this girl had really gotten under my skin with her mumbo jumbo star sign stuff.

I pay the bill. It's a fortune and the food and wine weren't really all that terrific, but it's been the kind of evening you don't easily forget, not unlike irresistible invitations from pretty Brits. I hardly remember walking back. It's cold alright and I have her wrapped up with half my jacket around her as well as me. You're gonna think it strange that we could walk like that, like we'd been a couple together for years but Em, that's just how it was.

We reach the hotel and she puts her hand on my cheek. It's warm from her pocket where my face is cold from the wind. She goes on tiptoe and I think she's gonna give me a peck, like a quick kiss goodnight. I may be disappointed but it's nothing I didn't expect.

'Twenty-two,' she says, breathing it out, hot on my cheek, 'Room twenty-two. Just give me ten minutes.'

And then she's gone, through the door and up the stairs. God knows, we never gave Pete or Cathy a thought.

It is midnight when I knock at her door, though I don't know how I dare, and I can't think of how things might be the following day, in the light of day, but I guess this is Paris and strange things happen here.

Just before she answers I am convinced I've got it wrong. Did I even hear right? Was it just some sick joke?

But there she is in the doorway. There's this red light behind her and I can make out her curves in its glow. She won't let me turn on the light and takes me straight to the bed.

Afterwards, I am glad it was dark, that she couldn't see the look on my face, which she might've misread as pain. My jaw ached with the bursting strain and the sweet agony of being inside her – and I knew I didn't want this to be a one-off.

I like to think I can stay a course, but it didn't take me that long to come. She made me want to hold my breath, to hang on to the moment until it just wouldn't hang on any more.

She was just so fresh and soft in my hands and slipping into her was like bathing in velvet. She smelled spicy, and I could still taste her on my tongue when I got back to my room. I was ready to go again when she asked me to leave. There was still so much I wanted to do – wanted her to do – but she showed me the door and it wouldn't have been polite to try and stay.

Jesus, Em, I knew this wasn't right but then it really didn't feel at all wrong. And after all, she was the one who invited me.

Chapter 14

Sloane

I am not going to read what he has written again. Not until we reach the end. If I read it and I find he has lied then I will be tempted not to go on – and then you will never know, Em, what it is you have to know and what I need you to know to make the story complete.

After he left me, I still wanted more but I was scared that I would drive him away. No, I don't know if that's right. Perhaps I was scared he might not want more and that somehow I had not measured up. Maybe if I offered him the quickie one-night stand and left it at that, I would risk less of myself, be able to hold on to more and extinguish what he had woken up in me. But even as he left I knew that this was not a flame without a fire.

'My goodness, Sloane, you look rough. Nicky said you were all done in.' I look wildly around for Nicholas, sure that he has somehow given us away and then realise that Cathy and Pete are alone. I don't know what it is about this foyer but they clearly prefer it to their room.

'Golly. Are you okay? Do you need some tablets? I've got some codeine somewhere in here...' Cathy drags a black, drawstring bag from under her skirt and begins ferreting around inside. 'Here,' she brandishes a crumpled foil packet and I take it from her hand. I don't have a headache but it's easier than explaining what it is that ails. 'That should set you right,' she says.

'Good job you're not coming on the trip. That's right isn't it, only Nicholas said…?'

'Stop fussing, Pete, of course that's right. You look dreadful, Sloane. Don't even think about it, you're going straight back to bed.'

Except bed's the reason why I look quite this bad.

I feel I have it written in bold across my face, *Sex Last Night*, but it appears that neither Pete nor Cathy can see the sign.

So, it's not like in films, when the heroine springs out of bed, daisy-fresh, with make-up on and radiating health and beauty in her new-found love. Nope, I'm the one who looks like shite and makes everybody think I'm ill. Please God, don't let Nicholas arrive. I had no idea I looked this bad.

'Had a phone call yesterday, by the way, while I was stuck here all alone,' she glares at Pete, which I think is a little unfair. It's more like my fault that she never got to go out since Pete was on a mission to a homesick child.

I help myself to coffee from the machine by the desk and raise my eyebrows in response.

'From Marcia…'

'How's she doing?' I sniff at the coffee and it smells nutty and dark. I take a sip and it's like taking a low down deep breath as the caffeine makes an instant impact on my brain. I am asking the question, although in truth my interest is nil. I have never liked Marcia nor do I ever expect to warm to this cold fish of a boss.

'She's okay – going to be here tomorrow. She reckons it was just a bug.'

Oh joy, the boss is on her way...

'Don't know why she has to bother. It's not like there's a problem and there *are* four of us here. What's the point of five? Why doesn't she just hang on and do the stint at the end?' I ask.

The system goes like this; four teachers go out with the group of exchange kids and stay for however long we all decide. Four more come out to change over with the others so there's one night in Paris with a party of eight – and that becomes the languages staff Christmas 'do' – only we have it at Easter in a French restaurant, which sort of makes sense. The second lot spend the rest of the time in Paris and then get to take the kids back home.

Sometimes, if not enough staff are available, you get to stay the whole two weeks – that's if you don't care about having no Easter break, because when push comes to shove, you are on duty and need to spring into action at any time – like last year when one of the kids broke his leg. Besides that, and the odd outing with all the kids and parents, it's a free trip to Paris with very few strings – and who wouldn't risk the inconvenience of the odd child-centred drama for that? The key is to make sure someone is always around to man – or woman – the phones in case any of the kids staying with their host families has an emergency. Apart from that you have practically nothing to do with the kids in the whole time you're in Paris. Genius!

I am a starter teacher, like last year. I got to bring the kids out and the others are bringing them back. Marcia is down to do the whole two weeks – no doubt a perk of the job.

'You're not still upset at not being put in charge? For God's sake, Sloane, Pete's got over it and so should you. It's daft.

What's the difference? Pete sorted the problem yesterday,' Cathy interrupts herself with a sniff, 'and you told me Nicky cleaned up the sick. Don't tell me you wanted to be in charge of that?'

'I still don't see why it wasn't one of us.' I am whining. I know I am whining. I really just need to buck up.

'Sloane, I think she was just being nice and not disturbing us at a stupid hour. She's really not all bad – I don't quite get what it is with you and her but please don't make things unpleasant. This is Paris, after all.' Cathy make a flourish with her hand, encompassing the foyer as if it represents the capital itself.

I am in a bad mood – lack of sleep, lack of self-esteem, a bit of both? It is not often I take against a person so what is it with Marcia that so gets me down?

'She's just always so prickly and stuck up, like if you try to chat, she's always somewhere else as if she just can't be bothered. Never really looks at you, like she's always got something better to do than to listen to what you have to say. And she never ever offers a word of thanks or praise.'

I am a people pleaser. Always have been and I doubt it'll ever change. I want to be praised, it's what makes me tick but Marcia reacts like a sponge and never bounces anything back, like you shine a light in and it's all absorbed into some dark space, which never offers a chink.

Good results? She just soaks them in and spits them out when it's time to take the collective departmental glory. Extra hours? She takes them for granted. Problems? Forget that, if you try to complain it just ends up working against you. If you have problems with the lower sets, she just gives you them all the more – at least that's what happened to me.

In a private school, your time is not your own and a little thanks goes a pretty long way. Once, early on last academic year, when I had been there about five minutes flat, the Head got all the newbies together, and said precisely this: 'During term time, you belong to Hazelwood, and I expect you to be available at any time, night or day for any reason and without complaint. Any time that is your own, you should count as a bonus. And if we need you at any other time, holidays included, you are expected to be there, no questions asked. No exceptions, no excuses, understood?'

We all nodded, dogs on the back window of the car, going along with the rhythm and expectation of it all, selling our creative souls to be moulded into whatever the school wants us to be, forgetting what we were or could become.

'Give Marcia a break, Sloane. We don't all have to like everyone, you know.'

There's that glare again but Pete ignores Cathy and carries on; 'We know her a little better, Sloane, she's got a lot on her plate. She probably wouldn't like me to say, but if she's been distracted, it's not entirely her fault. Why don't you cut her a little slack? Better for us all, wouldn't you say?'

'*M'sieur, 'dame, c'est pour vous!*' The desk clerk brandishes the phone.

Cathy hops up to take the call. I listen in for a bit and then slip away, satisfied that the call does not spell pupil trouble. I am glad of a chance to retreat.

What made me think I could possibly lead this trip? Why would I even want to? Do I even want to teach?

There is only one thing on my mind and I can still feel the tease of it between my legs. I will see him again in just over an hour. I wonder how much make-up will disguise the bags, whilst still falling short of a painted-lady look.

'Just take a look at this! This was what she did when it was Alfred Boucher who was teaching her at the Colarossi.'

'What's the Colarossi?' It's not that I really want to know. I want him to consider me bright.

'Gee, sorry, I was forgetting you're not into art. It's the academy where she trained, before she went private with Rodin.'

It's not that I'm not into art. It's just not a subject I know much about. Should I protest? But then the moment is gone.

'You know, I've got to hand it to them, this exhibition is pretty neat. I've seen some of these pieces before, but laid out like this, it's the progression that really gets you, and I can see what they mean about the hands. Look how she sculpts them, lifelike and so expressive – but then you take a look at these earlier ones of Rodin and he just doesn't really have it down.

'They say she did all the hands for him in the end but how do you know if that's true? But when you look at these, it sure does make you think... But hey, look at this now. You know *The Kiss*, right?' Nicholas points to Rodin's famous statue. Even I know about this one.

'Yes, of course. I've seen it before actually. I came here with Elodie and her mum. I used to do exchanges with her when I was at school. Think I mentioned her on the coach? I'm supposed to be meeting her tomorrow, morning I think, unless...' *Oh God, careful, Sloane, much too keen.*

'Anyway, he did this one originally for *The Gates of Hell* but then decided it should be a separate piece. I even know who the lovers are,' I add.

'Okay, Miss Smarty-Pants, fire away.'

'It's from Dante's *Divine Comedy*, fourth level of the *Inferno*, as a matter of fact. I can't remember their names

(*God, I really wish I could, I so want to impress*) but it's this woman and her brother-in-law, I do know that, and they read the tale about Guinevere and Lancelot and they realise they are in love.

'They have their first kiss – hence the sculpture – and they promptly get killed by her husband, stabbed if I correctly recall and the idea is that they get to wander eternally through hell. Am I right or am I right?'

Thank God for Liberal Studies lectures. They do say that knowledge is never wasted and hey presto, here's the proof.

'My, my, Missy Sloane, you do know your stuff.'

I like his teasing now. In my mind it is but one tiny connection of a synapse from teasing with his words to teasing with his tongue. I feel a shift within me. I want him right now.

'Just so you know, and I don't want'ya to think that I'm teaching my grandma to suck eggs, it was *Francesca De Rimini* and *Paolo Malatesta* – and did you know they were real – real thirteenth century lovers that Dante actually knew and that Rodin depicted in *Le Baiser* or *The Kiss*.'

No, I don't and no, I didn't. Appropriate as it is, I can't help focusing on the fact that *baiser* means both to kiss and to fuck in French.

'He was twenty-four years older than she was, you know. Imagine being accused by someone twenty-four years younger of stealing her work – a great master like Rodin. Unbelievable.'

'Why unbelievable? Age doesn't necessarily bring creativity – wisdom, maybe, but life evolves – so maybe Camille was more evolved than Rodin so more able clearly to see the beauty and passion past the form, express things in a more challenging, emotional and less cerebral way?'

'And look at this stuff. I think her work is far more exciting than his. His is all traditional and perfect but look at the movement in this.' I point to a sculpture entitled *Sakountala*. Its edges are rough and furious in stark contrast with Rodin's perfect lines.

Crikey – is this me talking? What the hell am I going on about – it's like I've swallowed an art book or something. Three cheers for the sixth form's fine art module – I must have learnt something by osmosis.

'But that's precisely what I mean. How can she say he copied her when this clearly copies *The Kiss*?'

I see he may have a point and decide to concede.

'This one is really beautiful. Haunting,' I point to a bust of a little girl, her hair in a single plait down her back.

'That's 'The Little Mistress',' Nicholas replies, pointing to the brass plaque, '*La Petite Châtelaine*', it reads, and he sweeps his eyes over my body. I blush.

'So how exactly does this book of yours work?' I ask.

'Oh, you know, it's fiction but with some truth woven in. I just wanted to write from Rodin's point of view – how it was for him coping with Camille and being accused of stealing her work. How she just wouldn't leave him alone once the affair was done, what with him and Rose having a child and all. He married Rose in the end – on his death bed, matter of fact. I guess he wanted to make sure his kid inherited what he was due.

'And another thing; I don't see how anyone can make that much difference to another person's work. That whole muse idea – to me it's like women freeloading off some famous guy and getting all this attention for being nothing in particular except someone's person to fuck.'

Wow. I am stunned. The delivery is pretty venomous but it's the F-word that throws me right off course.

'Sorry, Sloane. Didn't mean to offend. Bit of a raw nerve. I'll maybe tell you some day.'

Now that's not really fair. It's like when they end a soap opera on a cliff hanger every week. I want to know what he means, but I don't know this man well enough to pry. I know him well enough to sleep with him though, and I have a fluttering awareness of the ridiculousness of that concurrence.

'Why don't we go back to the hotel?' I hear myself say.

I have heard of *l'amour l'apres-midi*, the kind of love making that lovers do in the afternoon illicitly, avoiding discovery, or just because they can. Just because they want each other so much so, that night time seems a lifetime away.

Stuart would have laughed in my face if I'd suggested getting sweaty between the sheets any time before the ten o'clock news and, on reflection, I can't say that I was ever moved so to do. But it is that kind of afternoon that I have in mind and I am counting on Nicholas wanting that too. He does not disappoint.

We steal into the foyer separately like kids hiding from their mum and dad. Fate is once again on my side and I am relieved that Cathy and Pete have left their afternoon vigil at least long enough for me to begin mine. Then I remember they are out on the *Seine* enjoying a trip down the river with the kids. The place is our own.

I need to take it fast but he removes my clothing with aching care. Standing as we are in front of the bed, the balcony window ajar, I imagine that from the flat across the street it would not be hard to make out the couple that we are, and a little bit of me thrills at the idea of being seen in our naked state. His hands linger over my body and he shuts his eyes, the better to see.

His touch makes my nerves judder, he holds me rapt; a silent agony of a statue. I am marble, onyx, terracotta and bronze. I am anything he wants me to be. He motions towards the bed and I allow myself to be lowered in his arms. I want this to be special and I try to make myself compact, so the movement does not dislodge the moment and we are the perfect lovers I want us to be.

He urges my head down to his belly and below. The musk of him is potent and I am giddy with wanting and delight. I have never made love before and yet I have. How can two experiences described semantically in the same way be so diametrically opposed?

If I say *he enters me*, it becomes an action like any action in a cheap romance. He does enter me but I am dissolving into him as he dissolves into me. Soluble bodies that have no need to ask for what they need.

There is no thrust and plunge. Once high inside my body he holds still and the wave of wanting is more than I can bear. I arch my back and push myself against him but he resists. Then he moves, slowly, slowly, then he holds still, each by turn, and so it is that he takes me to the highest point that I have ever been.

Suddenly I am inventive, wanting to be the witch that this man has taken me for. My mind sieves its store to find some clue to being that person; the person who will make him forget anyone who has gone before. Here at last is a man I want to impress. The index in my brain slows as it flicks through the Paris moments I have known, and then it clicks to a halt with the vivid form of Elodie, her head to one side, giggling over the pages of a glossy magazine.

I look around for something, anything to use, and then I am tying his hands to the bedposts with my tights. His face is contorted in only the way that a face contorts when the pleasure is too great, when you are on the edge of the chasm and it is all you can do not to launch into descent, to let yourself fall despite yourself. It is there that I am keeping Nicholas whilst I fasten between and around his thighs, one side of his penis and then the other, securing the knots on the bedstead below. His back arches in anticipation of what I might do.

He is wide open, breathless with pleasure as I allow myself to go astride and do what he has done to me. I lower myself a fraction and enjoy the power as he struggles for more. Three pairs of sacrificial tights are all it takes. I have tied him well and the bonds hold fast as he pulls them taut.

How wonderful to be unexpected for a man who expects so much.

Paris is far from our thoughts though it is Paris that has brought us together. I know I don't want Paris to be the end, but then again, there is much I do not know, which will shape what there is to be.

Chapter 15

Nicholas

Jesus Christ, Em, I didn't just know what had gotten into her. One minute we're making love, the next she's rooting around in her bag and then wham, she's tying me up. She grabs my hands and knots them together onto the bed post with pantyhose, of all things.

She takes me completely by surprise and I haven't a clue what's coming next, and then bam, she grabs a hold of my legs and pushes them wide apart. I tell you, Em, it was all I could do not to come there and then. She loops these pantyhose around my thighs and under my balls, so she's got my dick prisoner and kinda on display, like it's the only part of me she wants. I feel exposed, you know, and it's such a frigging turn on. Maybe I shouldn't be saying this to you, but just thinking about it now, Em, has me hard as a rock.

Anyway, she gets on top of me and she's like teasing me – takes me right to that point and then stops and I think I'm gonna burst. I'm telling you Em, this girl was a witch and I was completely in her spell. I had no idea what she was going to pull out of the bag next. I'd had good sex and I'd had great sex, but sex like that? No way.

If I want to be in that moment now, all I have to do is close my eyes and I can see her clear as day, her hands brushing softly over me, feathering me with that wicked look in her eyes, bending over me as she pushes me inside her. The warmth of her and this wanton need, her breasts, small but with full, dark nipples and her hair just brushing over my face in a to and fro rhythm – I tell you, Em, I was hooked.

Later, I am holding her in my arms, just basking like two loved-up kids in that crazy afterglow, when it's like nothing else matters and it's just you and that one person in the whole, entire world.

Except something else did matter. It mattered a lot.

I'm there with her in my arms. Running my fingers gently over her breasts, I feel an appreciative intake of breath as I take back control. I know in minutes I will be back on top and my whole body is firing up for whatever we can invent.

She has made me feel at home, inside and out, and I know this is a woman who is not afraid of where our minds might lead our bodies. In some ways it freaks me out. I am losing myself in her. No woman has ever made me lose myself before.

I know what I have to say but I just can't find the words. They come climbing to the roof of my mouth, push themselves forward and just as I'm about to let them out, they're gone again.

Maybe I am just a fling. A getting-over Stuart fuck. Oh, yeah, she told me about Stuart on our way back to the hotel. Like I really wanted to hear all about some other guy when we're gearing up for a siesta ourselves! He sounded a real jerk. He must be if he couldn't hang on to a woman like Sloane.

Can I imagine calling it a day when we go back home? Never feeling her curves and those glorious, welcoming places of her body again? Picturing her at school, walking on past without a second glance, now that would really hurt.

Jesus, she's so young; twenty-six, and a young twenty-six at that. Where the hell did she get that idea? At her age I'd have been happy with first base. Boy, she was something else.

Wherever it was and however she did, I was sure as hell glad she had. I didn't think I had fallen in love, Em, I knew. Not having her was not an option. I just needed her to agree.

Chapter 16

Sloane

Later, sitting in the café, I studied the features of this man who had made me a woman. You'll laugh at that, Em – like I wasn't a woman before? I suppose what I am trying to tell you is that I knew I had all these working parts, *private parts*, as Auntie Jean would say. I just thought that with Stuart that's all they were ever going to be; private parts, that I occasionally had to share because in a relationship that's what's expected after a time.

Did it now feel like my virginity had been thrown carelessly away on Stuart; that I should have saved it for this moment when I wanted to make my private parts mutual? For this moment when I wanted someone to own my woman-ness along with me?

At least by knowing Stuart in all his bland and flaccid glory, I could recognize that *sex* was just three letters that could encompass a whole and varied range of truths.

Not knowing the difference would have brought a far greater danger than the discarding of a membrane way past its sell-by date. Had I not opened my legs and welcomed Stuart, I might have presumed that the act which Nicholas and I enjoyed was the only version of sex there was. In doing so I might have been careless and let him go, believing that this passion – the word has to be said, deficient though it is – could be achieved with any other man.

Nicholas felt like the part that was meant to slot into me to stuff out the hollow that I had discovered was there just through the contrast of feeling it full.

He looks at me, his mud-blond hair still tousled from our afternoon of love. There, I have used the word: our afternoon of *love*. His eyes are deep blue in the half light of the alcove in the café where we sit, creating a world within a world where we are the only two alive.

He is rarely still. Even now he is picking at the paper on the sugar cubes, placing them this way and that, lining them up, making them level and neat.

The word *Ricard* is written on each cube and I wonder fleetingly why an aniseed apéritif would want to paste its name there, instantly conceding that they have a perfect rationale for their advertisement. I can already taste the ice cold liquid in my mouth and order two the moment the waiter comes by.

Nicholas, on the other hand, advertises nothing. Besides his book, he has given little away and I am keen to know more.

Don't misunderstand me, Em. I wanted him just as he was and for that moment at least, whatever he gave was enough, but I do think that we cannot help ourselves. Whatever it is we have, eventually we will thirst for more, and especially so for what we cannot have.

'Tell me about the States. I've always wanted to go.'

This is not strictly true, Em, so must be earmarked as a lie. Outside England, my map consisted mostly of France, and that was by simple accident of the school trips to Elodie that preceded and continued after my parents' death. There is far more for an orphan to dream about than foreign climes.

'Come on, Sloane, you surely don't want a lesson in geography?'

'I just wanted to know what it's like, where you come from. What was it like growing up?'

'Well now, that's pretty hard to say. I grew up mostly at boarding school some ways from where I lived. Interlaken, that's where it's at.' He says Inter-*lay*-ken and it makes me smile.

'You mean Inter-*lar*-ken, but I thought that was in Switzerland. It's where the ski trip goes. Although, maybe you wouldn't know that seeing as you're just a visiting *Harper* person – you're not really that involved in the school are you?'

'You're right, I'm not really that involved but honey, it's Inter-*lay*-ken, I promise you, and it's in Connecticut, USA, well, actually on the border of Connecticut and New York State, which makes it kind of interesting.'

Not sure what I think about the 'honey' but I let it go.

'Oh, why's that?'

'Well, the opening hours in the two states are different, so if you want late night liquor, you gotta go over the state line to get it. We used to have fun watching the teachers come back to school late. We knew exactly where they'd been.

'You're also not wrong, by the way. Interlaken *is* in Switzerland and it means between lakes.'

I know that but I don't say. He is smiling, his eyes are smiling, and I am hanging on his every word, even if they are mispronounced.

'The school was great. I mean everything you could possibly want in a school. We used to go to the lakes some weekends, Wononskpomuc and Wononpakook.'

'Gosh, weird names. What about your parents? Where were they?'

'Oh, they weren't that far away. Little place called Dedham, just outside of Boston. They've got this great old clapboard mansion with a wrap-around deck.'

'Wow.' I imagine the archetypal New England family and try to place Nicholas in amongst it, the Thanksgiving of Hollywood films springing readily to mind.

'What about yours?' Nicholas asks.

'Dead,' I say. 'Car crash. My aunt brought me up,' I look down, anticipating that awkward silence that always follows taboo subjects – death, sex, religion. Mostly I spare people the detail – just wave it off with an *oh, they're not around anymore* but I want Nicholas to know these grim aspects of my life without embellishment or colour.

Nicholas barely misses a beat. 'That's too bad,' he says. 'Must have been tough on you but at least they can never disappoint you or judge you, ever thought of that?'

I open my mouth to query his comment but he flows straight on, my question hanging in the ether, unasked.

'Mom's the queen bee of the neighbourhood, regular little Martha Stewart – she's like the doyenne of domesticity in the US – home baking, church on a Sunday, lunch on Thursday, that kinda thing.

'Dad, well he should be retired but he's big into business, investments, corporate stuff. Wanted me to take over but it's not for me. Could see what it did to him and didn't like what I saw.' There is a tone in his voice that I don't recognize; bitterness or regret?

'You don't have brothers or sisters?'

'No, just me, no idea if they wanted more or not, but me is all they got. Think that's maybe why they sent me off to school. Get to know more guys of my own age. There weren't a lot of kids round our way – just the kid next door...' His voice trails off.

He looks at me, his brow pleated a little, like he's trying to work something out or read it in my face.

'Hell, you're beautiful. You're really something else. How did this ever happen, eh, Sloane?'

'You started it, with your comment about me being hot.' Instantly I blush. I hadn't meant to let him know that I'd heard.

'Hell, I'm sorry about that, Sloane. It's not like me to make that sort of caveman remark. You were just so...'

'Yes, Nicholas, I know what I was being and I'm sorry too. I was being a brat. I realise now that I should've been grateful. If it hadn't been you sitting next to me on the coach, it would have been Marcia instead.' I pour the water into my drink and watch it turn from clear to opaque as the two become one. Had I known then what was to come, the irony would not have been lost. How often is judgement clouded by the fusion of two people seeking love?

'So here's to you saving me from her.' I give a broad smile as I raise my glass to his, but he does not smile back. I have gone too far. 'Sorry, I shouldn't have said that. She's the boss and I should know better than to do her down. She just seems to bring out the worst in me – maybe I bring out the worst in her.' I try another smile. It doesn't work.

'Never mind; I've decided to make a big effort once she's here. I don't think we should be too obvious, do you?

It might not go down too well. Maybe we could just take her out somewhere. What do you think she might like? Maybe if I can get to know her a bit. She's always such a cold fish – oops, there I go again.' I try another smile.

Shit, I am clearly making this worse, prattling on.

'She's coming tomorrow, by the way. Cathy got a phone call to say. Seems a bit silly to me, when it's all under control over here, though I suppose I'd take Paris over Peterborough too.'

Nicholas is staring into his drink, his mouth set firm and his eyes are dark.

'Come on, cheer up, we've still got tonight – and who cares really if she does find out. There's nothing she can do.'

Still he does not look up from his glass. Still he does not smile. I am puzzled. I have got something very wrong.

Chapter 17

Nicholas

Hell, do we really have to go on with this farce? Picking apart every little detail as if it's gonna make anything change? What has happened has happened, there's no way that some freaking analysis of the past and what we did is gonna make a cent's worth of difference. She thinks it will and I guess that leaves me no choice. But I just wanna say here and now that I don't want to carry on and I just want the pain to stop.

God help me, Em, I knew I was wrong right from the moment I sat with her on the bus. Knew where it was going to go. That chemistry, like I was on fire or something. But there was a moment when I could have made a difference and I just didn't have it in me to find the words.

She was just so cute and so bewitching, goddammit. I just didn't want to break the spell.

This was something I'd always thought possible. I knew it was out there – it was all there in literature, Baudelaire, Flaubert, all the French poetry and prose I'd had to digest – wanted to digest. I loved this stuff but never thought that the aching, breaking, breath-taking feelings they described could ever be felt by me. Just thinking about it makes my heart pound like it's trying to find the exit from my chest and even now with this god-awful task still ahead of me, I am compelled to think of her body pressing close to mine.

The moments play out like a movie orbiting around me in the air. Coming into focus and then just moving beyond my vision only to come back into focus again with each groaning memory I drag from my skull.

I was in her grasp, Em, and logic didn't even come into the equation – like by denying the inevitable would somehow make it go away. A stupid ostrich with his stupid head buried way deep down in the sand. What a jerk!

It gets more painful now, Em, so I'm just gonna take a breath and get on with it then maybe we can both find some peace.

At first, it doesn't seem to do any harm, just telling her a little about where I come from, school and suchlike, but the more I talk about it, the harder it is and the more real it all becomes.

Then Sloane goes and tells me that the boss is on the way and I just start freaking out, realising what I'm playing at and that I have no right to be here with her. It's all out of control. I don't know anymore where the control lies but I can tell you it sure is not with me.

Maybe when you go to a foreign country, you can pretend to yourself that the things that get you down back home just don't exist – can't touch you in another place. I guess it's only after a while that we realise that the baggage of life darn well hunts you down wherever you are. It just catches you up and catches you out.

I am a coward. I can't control the moment no matter how hard I try. Bravery would be to say nothing – nothing more to injure or abuse – or to tell her everything and risk the result. Maybe I am to blame.

Or does the exquisite intoxication of what she offers mean that the fault lies with her? Already I am asking these questions before the play has played out.

I look into her eyes, where I see hurt, maybe shame. She thinks she has done something wrong but I am the guilty one, although she is guilty of being everything that turns me on and everything I want.

'Nicholas? Nicky? What is it? What did I do wrong?'

This is my moment. Do I choose to take it? The hell I do.

'Hey, baby. Sorry, I'm so sorry. Hey, I like it when you call me Nicholas. I'm Nicky to everyone else so let's stick with the Nicholas, shall we?'

'As long as you promise not to call me Felicity, Fizz, Flissy or anything else you can do with my name.'

Sloane, her name is Sloane. She is everything I want a woman to be.

'How about we settle for 'darling'?' God, she's beautiful when she blushes. She has this cute way of looking up under those bangs, like she's innocent but poker hot all at the same time. Is she jerking me around? I don't think so. God, I hope she's not jerking me around.

She opens her eyes wide and she gently bites her lower lip as if she's the one that's waiting for the answer.

'God help me. Sloane, I think I've fallen in love with you. Christ, how can you fall in love with someone in two days flat?'

'I don't know, Nicholas,' she says, 'but it must be possible because I think I have fallen in love with you too.'

Chapter 18

Sloane

He said he loved me, Em and there in that moment I knew I loved him too. It was absurd, irrational given how little time we had spent together but that time, that brief flirtation of time, meant more to me than all the good moments of my life put together.

I wonder – if we could take all the good moments and have them in one go and do the same with all the bad ones, what would we choose to do? Would we decide to take the honey of life when we are vibrant and young, hoping that youth will make all those moments that much more dazzling? If we know that everything that's coming later in life is bad, we could opt out at any time knowing that we have enjoyed the sweetness of our early days – youth and good fortune in one delicious basket.

Or would we gamble our youth and ride through the bitter stuff of life first, knowing that we can end our days with fate casting its glorious bloom on our moments – yet never knowing how many of those moments we shall have?

Would I have given up those moments with Nicholas if I had known where they would lead? I think not, Em. I think not.

When Nicholas came to my room that night, I met him naked at the door, not caring if there were unwitting witnesses or deliberate voyeurs. I wanted to be seen with this man whose very scent made me quiver in anticipation and delight. It wasn't just his body, strong and lean though it was; I loved him for his intellect, his appreciation of all things literary and creative, I loved his intangible fragility and the element of him that was still a mystery – the tiny piece of a puzzle which eluded me still. I still did not know what made this man tick but finding out, unravelling the enigma, went hand in hand with exploring his silky body. It was what I wanted and I knew he wanted it too.

He closes the door behind him and kisses me, running his hands gently over my body. His mouth finds my breast. If there is a heaven, God help me, this must be it. I hold my breath, caressing the moment until my lungs beg release. I exhale sharply and the air catches in my throat.

'You okay? Sloane?'

I move slowly to the bed, knowing that I am silhouetted against the amber light from outside, my form mirrored in the admiration and need in his eyes. I motion for him to sit and I lean into him so he has no choice but to take my breast into his mouth as I stroke his head and run my fingers through his hair, shot golden in the half light.

I breathe in and my senses dance to the raw smell of him. I am in control. I am not me, Sloane, teacher, would-be writer, novice and amounting to little more than nought. I am intoxicated, alive, burnt lusty by this new Paris of love and desire. I am his *femme fatale*. I am what he wants me to be.

I unbutton his shirt; Chambray cotton, it is soft beneath the tips of my fingers as I smooth it back over his shoulders and slip my hands between its loose weave and the warmth of his skin. As he pulls me into him, he murmurs my name again and again, a barely audible mantra on his breath. As my balance tips his way, he releases me and pours me from him onto the bed, shrugging himself from his shirt and unbuckling his belt in a breath-taking choreography, set to the rhythm of the tight thump of my heart.

He hesitates, almost imperceptibly, but still it is there, a half a heartbeat between us.

'Nicholas? What is it, Nicholas?'

There is no answer; just a part-sigh, part-groan as he lies down and presses his body next to mine. He sweeps his hand through my hair, holds it back, scanning my face as if it is there that the answer lies. I think he will kiss me and I close my eyes, my full, ready mouth demanding his, but gently he kisses my forehead. Unexpected, utterly beguiling, like I am something small and precious he has unearthed. He brushes his forehead against mine, then holds it there, as if he seeks some transference of thought, some knowledge that I have that must be his. That groan again and he moves back and pulls me up and towards him, over him.

'Tie me up, Sloane. Please. Tie me up.'

'Morning, Sloane. Where did you get to last night, eh? Cathy tried your room a couple of times. We went to that place around the corner – the one with food from Alsace. Fantastic *choucroute*, loved it. You really missed a treat.'

Ah, Petey, I had a treat all of my own that I somehow think surpassed the delights of a concoction of cabbage.

'You feeling better now? You look a lot better than yesterday, I must say. You looked pretty rough. Cathy and I were worried – thought you were coming down with something, but you look much better now.'

Pete pats the sofa next to him. I ignore the invitation and perch lightly on the mahogany table; my edge-of-the-desk teacher-pose.

Pete doesn't miss a beat as he leans forward and pours coffee into two white, china cups; 'Trip went okay. Kids loved it, parents were fine. It wasn't a bad day for it in the end. What did you get up to? See much of Nicholas? We didn't see him all day. Think he wanted to do some exhibition or other.

'Anyway, Marcia's on her way. That'll keep him on his toes.' Pete chuckles, mercifully not requiring an answer to any single one of his questions and he passes me the coffee just as Cathy lopes down the stairs and into the foyer, flopping with a thump into one of the burgundy striped chairs.

'Phew, that was exhausting.'

'What was?' I ask, not especially interested but glad of a retreat from Pete's assault.

'Oh nothing really, just had to explain a load of stuff in French about this kid's diet, and you know how you think you're fluent and then you realise that there's no such thing? It's not like it doesn't all go in the info to the school. They're just so inefficient over here. God, I hate telephones.'

'Coffee?' I lift a cup and wave it towards her.

'Please. What say we leave the men here today and hop off and do a little shopping? I need some bits and bobs for my goddaughter. It's her birthday next month and I promised Mira something from Paris, though God only knows what.'

Oh no, what do I say? There's only one person I want to spend my time with and he's not here to rescue me from the shopping trip from hell.

I am being unfair. I like Cathy hugely and any other time I'd have jumped at the chance rather than being stuck in the hotel just in case the phone rings – but the thought of a day less with Nicholas…

'Mira? That's an unusual name.' I am stalling, hoping for some miraculous excuse to pop into my head.

'She was named after her Nan. Yugoslavian, I think, or maybe German? Not sure.'

'We should get one of those phones, you know.' Pete says. 'Kevin has one at school. We wouldn't have to be stuck here then.'

'Kevin's is a car phone, stupid.' Cathy is unwrapping a pastry from a paper napkin, licking her fingers as she peels near-transparent tissue from some gooey, part-eaten cake. I am guessing it's what's left of last night's dessert. I am shocked at the semi-insult and there is an edge in her tone. I hope she's not upset with me. I have been so absent, but then, do I really care?

'No, Cathy. It's not.' Pete's tone too is clipped. 'He used to have a car phone but now he has this other one – you can take it with you anywhere, although I don't think it works in the States. He was saying that he'd had a problem with that. It's brilliant actually, you can…'

'Don't be stupid, Pete. It'd cost a fortune and the school would never in a million years foot the bill. There are worse things than being in a hotel with me in Paris, you know.'

Cathy dunks her cake into her coffee, draws it out, holds it up and looks at it. 'Mmm,' she says, '*J'aime tremper.*' Did you know that if you pronounce it ever so slightly incorrectly, just rounding your mouth a little too much that you could end up saying that you like being unfaithful, by mistake?'

Pete and I look at one another. Of course we both know that.

'And isn't it funny how 'to dunk' and 'to be unfaithful' could almost mean the same thing?' Cathy continues, '*Tremper* and *tromper*; curious.'

She stuffs the rest of the pastry into her mouth and sits back, chewing. If it's possible to chew angrily, that is exactly what she's doing now, her brow knitted together as she over-masticates the mouthful of sugary mess. She wipes her face with the back of her hand, sending a whoosh of sugar up her cheek, screws what's left of the napkin into a tight ball and thrusts it into her drawstring bag.

I try to think of some witty retort but it is Pete who saves us from the awkward silence.

'Anyway,' Pete says, 'you can't go anywhere yet. Marcia's due any minute and it would be rude not to at least wait to say 'hello'.'

Cathy shrugs, walks over to the desk, leans over and speaks to the concierge.

'*Vous permettez, Monsieur Jacques*?' She picks up the newspaper and raises her brows. No idea how she knows his name but Cathy's good like that. Makes the sort of effort with people that I'd like to be able to make, but somehow can never be bothered.

He nods without looking up from his files and she folds the paper in half, stalks back across the clip-clop floor, tucks herself back into her armchair and straightens the folds of her long, red and blue corduroy skirt. With one explosive shake, the paper is open and she disappears behind it, instantly absorbed.

Pete coughs to fill the silence. I am hovering without purpose. I slide from the table and turn to go back to my room, an excuse forming on my lips.

'Oh, there you are.' Pete stands up as Marcia humps an overlarge suitcase over the tiled threshold. It is a suitcase that shouts 'first class' with its gold buckles and deep brown hide, despite the battering of its travels.

Cathy looks up.

You see Pete mouths at us. He shoots over to Marcia. 'Let me,' he says as he hoists the suitcase from the spot where Marcia has lost the battle with its weight, only to dump it again in front of the desk.

Marcia tosses back her long, dark hair. She draws the poker-straight lengths back and up into a pony tail only to allow it to cascade down through her fingers where its sheen lies gleaming over the *Hermès* scarf around her tall, designer neck.

She smiles at Pete with her mouth, since Marcia does not do smiling with the eyes. Her skin is fair like no sun has ever dared kiss it and she has a tip-turned nose, delicate and ladylike in a way I could never be. It is what the Germans call a *Himmelfahrtsnase* – literally, a-travelling-towards-heaven-nose, but I just think the slope of it makes it easier for her to look down on people, and most especially down on me. It is only on second glance that the furrow between her bright blue eyes betrays that she is more than a teenager, but all else – that slender form and dainty gait, the skip and hop of her – all else belies her thirty-five years. All else besides her pig-headed arrogance, that is.

'Thank you so much, Pete. How kind you are.'

'You're welcome. Let me help you with your coat,' Pete says, and sticks his arms out, hands palm up, offering himself as a human coat stand.

Marcia unhooks her red leather handbag from her shoulder and balances it on her case. She unwinds the belt of her camel-coloured trench coat. It is impossible not to notice that it is wrapped twice around her tiny waist. She slips the coat smoothly from her shoulders, and catches hold of the scarf, drawing it up the sleeve of the coat to keep its precious silk safe. She deftly turns the coat lining out, displaying its bold burgundy checks and plants it across Pete's eager outstretched arms. Finally she plucks her bag back up and tucks it under her arm, a ballet of coordination and charm. Pete gives a little half bow.

'We were just all saying how glad we are that you could come after all. Rotten business, these bugs. But still, you're here now and...'

I tune out Pete's sycophantic ramblings and plant my nose in my coffee cup. He appears not to have noticed that he is still holding Marcia's coat, arms outstretched like a misplaced sleepwalker. I wonder if he plans to stand there all week.

Marcia shifts her attention and nods first to me and then to Cathy.

'Sloane, Cathy,' she says, a high priestess acknowledging her subjects.

'How was the journey? Did you get any sleep on the train?' Cathy asks.

'Actually, I didn't come by train. Someone I know, some friends, they were coming to Paris anyway. They just dropped me off outside.'

Ha! That explains the perfect hair.

'Super, super,' Pete says. 'Let's get you sorted, shall we? Now where's Nicholas got to?'

Just what I was wondering too. Excellent, Pete has saved me from having to ask. Last I saw of Nicholas he was sliding from my bed as dawn slid through the balcony window. He left without a word and my stirring gave way instantly to my contented drowning in sleep. How kind of him not to wake me, I thought.

'Someone call my name?' Nicholas asks. He drops on the tips of his toes from one step to the next as he comes down the last few stairs. I notice that his feet are small, for a man at least. Just proves that what they say is not always true. Amused by my idle thought, I mentally tuck my observation away to share with him another time.

'Oh, Sloane, you're here. I thought you were heading out to see Elodie today?'

'Oh my God, you're right. I completely forgot. Oh, Cathy, I'm so sorry. I didn't even ask. Of course I can't go shopping.' My face is hot. Look what I've done now. I've even managed to show myself up in front of Marcia. She's going to think I don't give a fuck about the kids. For once she would be right. Nicholas has wiped my mind clean. I check my watch. Not too late. It's not far from here. I can still make it on time.

'Good morning, Nicky.'

'Jesus, Marcia. When did you get in? Hell, you're early — surely you didn't travel overnight? You should have let me know. I'd have met you from the station if I'd known.'

'Cathy knew. Didn't she say?' Marcia frowns and turns towards Cathy and her handbag slips out from under her arm. She just catches it but not before a lipstick escapes, falling to the floor with a clatter. It rolls away and Marcia bends gracefully to scoop it up, plopping it back into the bag, which she shuts with a clunk.

'Well, Nicholas?' Marcia says.

'She's only just got here, old chap. No problem. We've been taking good care of her.' Finally Pete drops his arms and dangles the coat in the crook of his elbow. Now he looks like a waiter, cloth neatly folded over his arm, ready to pop the cork.

Nicholas seems rooted to the spot, held in Marcia's gaze.

'Nicky?'

'Sure, yeah, let's go. I'll get your bag.' Suddenly Nicholas is in a hurry and scoots across the foyer, grabbing the suitcase by its gold-buckled handle and begins dragging it towards the stairs. His senses appear to elude him and I look around to see if anyone else has noticed the obvious, but apparently not.

'Hang on, Nicholas. She's not even checked in. Give her a chance.'

Nicholas swings around, his face a contortion of ...what? Pain? Horror? Confusion?

Marcia smiles with her mouth. It is Cathy who speaks first.

'Don't be silly, Sloane. The rooms are all double – Nicky's already checked Marcia in with him.'

Pete laughs a big, bellowing harrumph of a laugh.

'Oh that's hilarious. No wonder you were upset at Nicky being in charge. You had no idea, did you?'

'What? What did I have no idea of?' My fingers are tingling with the possibility of what might be coming next. My mind floats away like it wants to separate itself from my body to delay the moment, another of those moments that leaves you with a scar that will never heal. I look from Nicholas to Marcia and back again. Surely I cannot have been so stupid, so blind. Surely Nicholas cannot have been so cruel.

Marcia opens her mouth to speak but it is Nicholas who delivers the blow.

'Marcia's my wife, Sloane. She's my wife.'

Chapter 19

Nicholas

Jesus, Jesus, that moment, Em. I didn't expect Marcia to get there at that time in the morning. Christ, Em, do you really think I wouldn't have set the record straight if I'd had time? Of course I should have told her. Of course I should. Do you think I didn't know that? And I was going to, of course I was.

I knew Sloane was out that morning with Elodie, worked out that Marcia couldn't possibly get there much before five, so there was still time. Jesus, if I'd known she was coming by car, don't you think I'd have played it differently? How was I to know that her freaking priest and the la-di-da Mrs Priest would be driving to Paris? Who the hell drives to Paris? Who the hell drives at night? And the priest, Christ! I don't know what I was thinking.

It's like Marcia wanted to catch me out or something. It was only five minutes since we left England and there she is already in Paris when she's supposed to be so darned ill that she can't travel. It was all such a goddamned mess. I honestly thought that Sloane knew about me and Marcia – no, shit, that's a lie and we have to tell the truth. She will know if I don't tell the truth and you will know and you will judge. Hell, what am I saying? Jesus, I must be going crazy. Like you can judge anything? Hell, I'm beginning to believe this stupid crap.

Okay, I need to go on. I know I have no choice so let me remember it as it was – not how I'd like it to have been.

What is true is that I never thought she didn't know, didn't even occur to me, not at first. Just thought she was kinda – well, you know, kinda available, if you get my drift. And I know I shouldn't have gone there, but I did and that's that.

But after a while – I gotta be honest here – I guess it became obvious she had no idea. Thought I could handle it, and then, Christ, it was getting serious. That whole jazz with the star sign had me all fired up and suddenly it was all too late and I didn't want to say. I didn't want to break the spell.

Her hands on my body, the whole darned feel of her, that quirky way of looking up under her bangs, I guess I got so carried away and then just couldn't find the moment to say what I should've said. And I need to remind you, Em, that whole tying up business had me hooked.

Yeah, I know you'll find that curious but let me tell you, it was just so darned sexy. If we're being so damned honest here, I have to tell you, it reminded me of stuff me and Josh used to do. Nothing weird, you know, just kid stuff – like this one time I was crying, homesick for Mom and Dad, though Christ knows why, and Josh, he just held on to me for a while; said why didn't we play a little game – cowboys, some crap like that, help me get over myself a little.

We're playing around and then he just lassoes me like I'm some piece of cattle and he ties me to a chair and starts stroking me. I knew deep down it wasn't supposed to be like that but then it sure felt good.

Anyways, we start doing this stuff, experimenting like kids do. Makes me wonder now if that's why he left school. Maybe he did it to some other kid and got found out but I don't think so, Em. I think what we had back then, it was special, just our own games, him and me.

Marcia, she wasn't at all experimentally inclined but Sloane — she just saw right into me — knew what I wanted before I knew myself. Jesus, Em, what's a guy supposed to do?

But it wasn't just a stupid fling. I promise you, this was truly something more. All the crap with Marcia — it had all taken its toll and I was so ready to be loved and to love. You have no idea of the effect Sloane had on me. She was young, nubile, so sexy. It was like I was a kid again, like I could reinvent myself and forget everything that had gone before. Truly, Em, if I could have done that there and then I would have. I'd have walked out there and then with Sloane and never looked back. I swear to you, Em, I was in love.

But I was also in a panic. My chest felt like it was going to explode, and then all I could think of was getting Marcia as far away from Sloane as possible. But I knew Sloane had seen it all in my eyes. What did she see? Jesus — embarrassment, for sure — goddammit, I didn't know where I was or what to do. I just thought for God's sake, Sloane, say nothing. Indecision, she saw indecision for sure because like I say, for two cents I'd have just walked out of there and never come back. Did she see the pain? I don't know. I guess the whole pain of not being with Sloane hadn't hit me at that point. But she can't have missed the love. Yeah, I know it sounds corny but I swear to you, Em, it was real. I wasn't faking. It wasn't about just getting laid for some cheap thrill. I swear to you it was real.

What I can say to you is that I meant to make it work, with Marcia, that is. I'd made all these promises that I truly meant to keep. So in between all this confusion and indecision I found myself making this pact with God. Yeah, you may well laugh. I just remember saying, 'God, please don't let her find out'.

At that moment, in the foyer, I swore, Em. I swore I'd make it right, as long as Marcia didn't find out. That I'd get back on track and be the husband she needed me to be – that I'd promised to be. So in the midst of all this mess that was happening in my head, I sort of made a decision. I just didn't realise that the decision would not be entirely mine.

Chapter 20

Sloane

So here we have it. I just started off as a cheap lay. He's as much as said so. Sorry, I know I wasn't going to read what he's written until the end, but I couldn't resist – story of my life. God, now I know for sure I was right to do this because it could still not be me to blame. Do you see, Em? It could still not be me.

I cannot stop the tears from falling as Nicholas drags Marcia's bag behind him, and I watch my arrogant bitch of a boss following her husband up the stairs. Her tread makes barely an impact on the plush carpet as her feather-light form disappears from view.

Pete still has her coat over his arm and, suddenly realising, he makes a dash for the stairs.

Cathy and I are the only players left aside from the concierge who is busy still with his papers. There is a charge in the air that only the least sensitive would fail to miss. Cathy is not one of them, and she moves in swiftly, grabbing me under the arm and marching me towards the door. I do not resist and am glad of the damp, cool air on my cheeks as the Paris morning hits my face.

Do I think of Elodie? Not a chance. Elodie and our meeting have evaporated along with my stupid schoolgirl notions of love and romance. I am a dunce; a stupid, worthless dunce who has been played for a fool. But am I angry? Am I resentful? No, I am a whimpering, simpering mess. At least, I am at first.

'How could you not know? It's completely ridiculous. Dry your eyes. Here, have another hanky. What do you expect from a stupid stunt like this? Stop snivelling. People are watching. I can't believe you didn't know. But then, Sloane, you don't always see what's in front of your face, do you?'

'God, Cathy, what do you mean by that?' Already, I am in bits. Is she going to take me still further apart?

'You're not the only one who's had an affair, you know.' I go to protest. In my eyes I have had no such thing since I cannot be accused of being the mistress if I do not know my master has a wife. But Cathy waves her hand in dismissal as I open my mouth, a sob catching in the back of my throat as I try to do as she asks.

'Where do you think Pete went on the first day?'

I think back, wracking my brains even to focus on when the first day was. It seems impossible that it was only three days ago.

'There was some homesick kid, wasn't there? Third former? Christopher Blake?'

'Full marks, Sloane. Thought you were far too besotted to notice.'

'Don't tell me you...'

'Don't be ridiculous, Sloane. How could I not notice? All that eating off the same fork business. Pete and I might as well have not been there. Not that he noticed, mind; far too busy with his own pathetic little agenda, no doubt.' Cathy doesn't offer pause for comment. She is picking furiously at a napkin in the café where we sit. Our coffee is untouched, as if taking a sip would somehow be rude given the intensity of what is happening between us.

I am there to be mended and soothed, not to be accused. I could walk out at any time, so why do I choose to stay and hear the bilious thoughts of a person I thought was my friend – well, sort-of friend?

Maybe I think I deserve them; that in some way, I should have known that Nicholas was too good to be true, too perfect to be unattached and to want me for me rather than for the pleasuring moments I offered to his hungering body. Except it wasn't hungering, was it? He had a wife.

'I rang the parents,' Cathy says.

'What?'

'Christopher's parents. To check if they'd heard any more. Pete was taking so long and…Turns out the kid was never homesick at all. They had no idea what I was talking about – thought I was bloody mad.'

'That doesn't mean anything, though. Have you asked Pete? There could be all sorts of explanations.'

'No, Sloane. You don't get it. I know he was having an affair. I know for sure. He went to a funeral and met an old flame. How crazy is that? He admitted it but he said he was sorry. That it was a silly thing to do and we agreed we'd give it another go – and we *were* giving it another go, until now. I know he met her here. I just know. Gut instinct, whatever. I never asked any more about her – for all I know she could live here in Paris. So stupid, so stupid. And you messing around with Nicholas doesn't help. It's like suddenly it's okay for all husbands to fuck off with someone else.'

Oh my God, I have never heard Cathy swear. Ever. Well, crikey. What about good old Petey then? Have to say I didn't think he had it in him but now is not the moment to share that with Cathy. How can I have such an inappropriate thought when I feel like someone has wrenched out my guts? I steel myself to demonstrate sympathy when all I want to feel is self pity.

'I'm so sorry, Cathy. I had no idea. You always seem so happy, so…together.'

'We were happy. Until *she* came along. Thing is, I'd had a miscarriage and it was all a bit much. Didn't fancy, well you know, just didn't seem right, and I kept getting angry with Pete.

'It wasn't his fault, course it wasn't and we both really wanted the baby but I just kept on pushing him away, like if I couldn't have the baby, I'd make sure I'd have no one. But I didn't mean to. And I do still love Pete. It's just…

'So you see, Sloane, you messing with Nicholas, it could kick off a whole chain of events. You are just being plain stupid and selfish, and thoughtless, and…'

Cathy is crying now. We are both crying. I take her hand across the table and squeeze it, expecting it to be whipped away but she doesn't pull back. She looks up at me with her cow eyes and huge tears plop onto the chipped melamine table as we sit there, each as fragile as the other.

This is a person I have shared a class with, organised assemblies with, had the odd lunch with. This is not a person I have cried with or shared deep, dark thoughts with. But here we are, in an off-route café in Paris, thrust together with our sack loads of baggage. I had no idea. I genuinely had no idea.

How did all this happen to this over-ordinary, jolly hockey-sticks of a teacher? And when?

As if she reads my thoughts, Cathy speaks: 'You know when I was at the Sixth Form conference?'

'Yes. September, wasn't it?' I remember covering lessons right at the beginning of term – so many bottom sets when you haven't even had a chance to learn their names – and being resentful.

'Gosh, Sloane, I'm sorry. It's my fault that Nicholas didn't tell you she was on her way. I did it on purpose. I never told him about the phone call from Marcia, that she'd phoned to say she was coming. I was mad with Pete and could see it all happening with you – I wanted to teach Nicholas a lesson. I am so, so sorry. I should have said, should have warned you. He could have warned you. I am so sorry…'

'No, Cathy. It's not your fault at all.' The full impact of what she has said hits me. 'You told me yourself that you'd had a call from her. I knew she was coming. And I told Nicholas. He just chose not to tell me that Marcia is his wife.'

It was midday by the time Cathy looked at her watch. Neither of us had given a moment's thought to the task of phone-manning back at the hotel, perhaps in a subconscious decision to leave it to those we considered the guilty parties. Except I was guilty too, wasn't I, Em? Guilty at least of not asking the right questions before I invited Nicholas into my bed. There were so many questions I could have asked, should have asked. Easy to say that with the hindsight of two hours with Cathy but I still don't know, Em, I still don't know if I would have changed a moment of that time.

'*Eh bien, te-voilà!*' Cathy and I look up, our thoughts abruptly shattered by the sing-song voice.

'Elodie! How on earth did you find me here? I am so sorry. I didn't mean to…'

'*Ben, assez facile, quoi.* It was easy,' Elodie glances at Cathy and switches to English, and her breathy, nasal rendering of the language takes me instantly back to our teenage days – except now she is rather better at it than she was then.

Cathy gives her a weak smile and I quickly introduce them.

'*Cathy parle français, si tu préfères?*'

'No, it's okay, I stay in English. Is good to practise. I wait for you long time and you are not coming so I worry and I come to the 'otel. The concierge, he tell me that you go without coat and that you are in great distress so I think you are not far et *voilà!*' Elodie demonstrates that we are in fact here by sweeping her hand in our direction. Her olive skin peeps out between black, leather gloves and the sleeves of her long, black raincoat. Around her neck is an artfully arranged pashmina, also black, perfect attire for bereavement, I reflect, for that is how I feel, and I am at least qualified to judge.

I do think that what they say about grief having hooks is right; how when tragedy strikes it drags along with it all the bad moments that life has ever brought you, digging them up from their grave of near-forgotten memories to make them as vivid as ever they were. To make you feel them all over again, as if somehow the pain of the now is not enough and we must cruelly revisit the pain of all our yesterdays. At this moment, though, yesterdays are all I have since it feels like tomorrows are out of the question.

'I'd better get back,' Cathy scrapes her chair back as she stands. She brushes her skirt, dismissing phantom crumbs and offers her hand to Elodie. I go to protest but see that her mouth is set firm. I wouldn't want to be Pete just now.

'Let's walk.' Elodie unwinds the pashmina and envelopes me in its folds. 'Here, you must not catch cold. It's not raining now but it does make wind.'

'Oh, come on, Elodie. Where's your English gone? It doesn't make wind – it's windy, for God's sake.'

'Is no matter. We walk and you tell me what it is that has wounded you.'

I hold the wrap tightly around me as we walk into the bracing Paris air. My body is cold with longing and shame, a strange balancing act of contrary emotions. Pounding heavily in my head is the unbearable thought that I cannot have this glorious man that I have found only to lose in Paris.

'So tell me. I do not understand how you cannot know that this man he is married. In any case, to me, is not a problem.' Elodie shrugs her shoulders, a kind of conspiratorial shrug and I see that she thinks I am holding the moral high ground in some bid for propriety in her eyes.

'Oh no, Elodie. You don't get it. I really had no idea they were married. None at all. I hardly knew him – he only arrived last September and I'd maybe seen him a few times but never to speak to. I…'

'But is not possible. You work in the same school, no?'

'No, I mean, yes, we work in the same school, but on a split site. There are loads of staff members I don't know properly – apart from to say hello and goodbye. We're all too busy, unless you're in the same department, but even then most of us just want to get away from school and get the marking done and crap like that. I only got to know Pete and Cathy properly from this trip last year and Cathy more because we do a lot together – exam timetables, stuff like that.'

'But Nicholas – yes, is correct?' Elodie pronounces his name *Nicola*, without the *s*, and I think that it sounds even more romantic in French. My stomach lurches, a renewal of his betrayal, which for split seconds I have forgotten, distracted in my story, only for it to hit me full force, a tidal wave of pain and regret.

'Yes, that's correct,' I reply.

'But *Nicola*, he is married to your boss, no?'

'Yes, Nicholas Bride is married to my boss, my super-bitchy, ungrateful boss.'

'You know, Sloane, sometimes we hate the people who challenge us.' I ignore her and she continues. 'So, how you not know that he is her husband?' Elodie makes a massive effort not to neglect the *h* on *how*, *he*, *her* and *husband* and it comes out like she is huffing steam on a mirror prior to a shine.

'I know what you're saying. I've wracked my brains and at no point did it ever come up that she even had a husband. Honestly, Marcia just kept herself to herself out of school.

'And anyway, she was at school a whole year before he got there. Cathy told me all about it. They don't even have the same name. It's all so complicated. It was all arranged by the Harper people to try and save the marriage, they're all involved. Christ almighty! God, I'm such an idiot. The Harper people. Oh my God, Elodie, Marcia's name is Harper. Our lecture theatre's called Harper – and Nicholas is giving the Harper lecture funded by the Harper scholarship. Why did I not see the connection? I just never put two and two together. Oh my God, no wonder Cathy thought I was going insane.'

'Come, let's sit. Is not so cold here.'

We perch side by side on the fountain wall. I have hardly noticed that she has led me into the Jardin du Luxembourg, not far from the Café Rostand, close to where Elodie works in some high powered secretarial post, PA to some big wig in the parliament. The splendidly chichi café is where we should have met some three hours earlier, a meeting I had seen in my mind as all smiles and laughter, not all sadness and tears.

A pale bloom of sunshine is dappling the grey-white sky, a backdrop for a million tulips in as many shades, an oscillating ocean of colour on a dank, dark day. Elodie undoes the top buttons of her coat and peels the gloves from her slender hands. Her fingers make me think of mine and a question burns on my tongue until it bursts into life.

'Elodie?'

'Oui, *chérie*.'

'Are you gay?'

'Sometimes gay, sometimes not gay.' She cuts off the end of the word, pronouncing it *à la francaise* so it becomes *geh*.

'I mean, are you a lesbian?'

'Why? You are lesbian? I thought you like this *Nicola*.'

'No, yes, I do like, no I love Nicholas (I feel here I need to emphasise the *s* and do so) but I just wondered about you…'

'Why do you ask that, *ma chère*?'

'Well, you know, you were always such a tomboy, and then there was this time when, I don't know if you remember it but you, you know…' I know I have turned red. I can't bring myself to say what I have been dying to say for over a decade. Elodie looks at me and bursts out laughing.

'You mean when I ask you about…'

'Yeah, *perdre la tige*. I looked it up. Couldn't find it.'

'Eh bien, *ma chère*, only you would go to the *dictionaire* for such a thing. It's just what we used to say. My friends and me.' She laughs again.

'Well?'

'Okay, okay. No, I am not lesbian. I do it for bet.'

'A bet? What bet?'

'My friends, the boys and me, we experience a lot when we are young, we try this, we try that. They say you are virgin and cold, that all English girls are cold and I say no, you are different, you are warm; you are my friend. They tell me they want to know, they will discover, you know, and I say no, they must not be unkind to you, so they bet me you do not experience something with me and say if you do that, they leave you alone.'

'But that's completely crazy, and I think you mean experiment, not experience. For God's sake, Elodie.'

'Eh, *ben*, we were young and the young do foolish things, but you must not worry. It was good, no?' Elodie's eyes are shining and she cocks her head to one side. Her hair is still cropped as it was all those years before, but the cut is precise and it stylishly frames her elfin face.

'Oh my God, Elodie, what am I going to do?'

'What do you want to do?'

'I don't have a choice, do I? I'm going to have to leave school. Thing is, I don't even know if I even want to be there, regardless of all this.

'Auntie Jean, you remember, she wanted me so much to make something of myself and to her, being a teacher was as good as it got. Security, long holidays, a good pension, status – that's a laugh – everything your parents would have wanted for you, Felicity, she'd say. I know why and I don't blame her. She just needed to feel she'd done a good job of bringing me up all those years – and quite honestly I think I was just too exhausted with missing Mum and Dad to even think about it much.

'But now I just can't stop pushing. Pushing to be better, putting myself forward, hoping to be noticed, praised, like some stupid puppy dog. Like I'm trying to prove something but God knows who to. That's why she makes me feel so bad. Marcia, she never notices any of the extra stuff I do. And now I've gone and slept with her husband. Fuck, fuck, fuck. '

'*Bof*,' Elodie shrugs her shoulders. 'That's up to you. You can leave or you can stay. But your boss's husband, that's another question, *ma petite* Sloane. Or should I say Felicity?' She digs me in the ribs and I squirm out of the way.

'You know I don't use that anymore so stop it. God, I feel so stupid, so fucking wretched. What am I going to do?'

'You want to know?' Elodie asks. I shift my position. The stone beneath me is suddenly hard and cold through the fabric of my jeans. I draw the pashmina further around me, feeling the chill wind needling through my clothes. Elodie seems far away, staring at an invisible canvas of what? What scene is playing out in my penfriend's mind?

'*Ma chère*, Sloane. What I think is this. You do nothing and you be clever.'

'For goodness sake, Elodie. What are you talking about now?'

'We French, we fight for love. *L'amour, c'est la folie*, it's crazy, madness. If we love, we love hard, we love selfish, we let nothing get in our way. Nothing. What is a wife? Pouf,' she snaps her fingers and opens her hand, raising it, allowing the vapour of a wife into the air. She turns to me, her hand still aloft and she smiles like she is sharing some secret.

'You must be clever, *ma* Sloane. You must be everything she is not. You hold the strength, *ma chérie*.'

'I hold the what?'

'The strength, *la force, ma* Sloane.'

'Oh, *la force*. You mean the power, Elodie. It translates both ways, remember.'

'*Oui, c'est ça*. It is not the wife who has the power, *ma chérie*. It is the mistress who keeps him wanting more.'

Chapter 21

Nicholas

Dear God, Em, I thought it was all over. Not that I wanted it to be. God no. I wanted her so much it was like my dick and my brain would explode.

It wasn't just about the sex, I swear to you. It was everything. After Marcia, Sloane was just so gentle but so strong, this weird kind of mix. She just got right under my skin – not in a bad way. I knew all about getting under your skin in a bad way, Jesus Christ, I knew.

You gotta understand where I was coming from, Em. Marcia and me, we were all shot to pieces, the miscarriage, the lies, all of it and we should have just gone our separate ways. But the family, hoho, they weren't having any of it. Not the precious Harpers for sure, and not my mom and dad, my socially climbing, money-grabbing, pathetic excuse for parents. They saw to everything, didn't they?

Marcia, she was the girl next door. To be fair, she was on a hiding to nothing because she shouldn't have been a girl. Oh no, she should have been a boy to preserve that precious Harper name, carry on the great family traditions, the English connection, the big business and all that. Not that she didn't have the chance to take over the Harper empire – it just wasn't what she wanted and this was one area where she wouldn't budge, and I kinda respected her for that.

I was on a hiding to nothing too. There's no two ways about it, after the Josh thing, my dad, he's convinced that his only son is gay, right? So it's his job to bash that right out of me. So he's there, every weekend, at the school, getting me to try this and that. 'How about basketball, son, you'd like that. What about soccer? Now, have you thought about soccer, son?' Shit, I'd thought about just about everything you could imagine but I knew this stuff wasn't for me. He just didn't want to let go of it, like if he tried hard enough it would make me into the kind of son he wanted. Mom, she used to just stand there and watch this all happen, a kind of bleating pity in her eyes. He'd never have let me get away with doing languages or art if it hadn't been for my teachers – convinced him that I was no good at any of the other stuff he wanted me to do. They finally got him to agree to my studies because I was good enough to go to Harvard.

Gotta hand it to the school, Em, their big fat endowment from my dad was on the line for a while there – he just really didn't want to hear that his only son was never going to make the grade in everything he thought the school should have taught him. Christ knows what would have happened if I hadn't made Ivy League. I guess a gay son is okay so long as he brings glory on the family name. Except I wasn't gay, Em, just experimenting a little, you know how you do and I just wasn't really into girls.

Well, my mom and dad, they soon took care of that; fixed up for me to take Marcia to the prom. She was over from her posh school in England, where all the Harpers had gone since big granddaddy Harper had done the whole Oxford thing on account of his education there. They took their English ancestry real serious.

Jesus, I remember this one time when I went to tea at Marcia's – tea, note, Em – and her mom had it all laid out, dainty cups and saucers, bone china, little cute silver teaspoon, these cut out paper things on the plates, doilies she called them, and we had tea and scones, which she pronounced, *scohnes*. And there were these little cubes of sugar, all different colours; blue, pink, green and she tells me that she has them sent from this place in England, Fortnums, which even I had heard of.

It's like crazy stuff, this England obsession. Marcia, she was even born in England. Can't say for sure if that was a deliberate thing, but her daddy, he does business all over the world and when he wants to be somewhere he can be there, especially if it means a dual passport for his little girl. Now that's taking your heritage seriously.

Mind you, they paid the price for it all; Marcia got the chance to travel, fell in love with Europe and most especially with France – at least we had that in common. So she became a teacher instead of a corporate chief, one in the eye for daddy, a knife in the gut of the man who didn't father a son.

Old man Harper, he gives all this money for this building at his old school – Marcia's school – to be named after him. I guess that if you have no son and heir to carry on your name then you might as well have a building, and I think that's pretty quaint but it's also kinda far away and has nothing to do with me and then, boom, suddenly I'm engaged to Marcia and the whole world changes and I'm part of all this society stuff and my mom and my dad, they're real proud.

They've made it, see. My dad, he's the American Dream guy, he's made it with the money and all, but you can't buy status, son, he says, you can't buy status.

And Marcia, you can't blame Marcia because now, she's in love with this other guy she's met out on the Vineyard (oh, did I mention that the Harpers have property on Martha's Vineyard too?) but he's into music and stuff, which doesn't go down too well with Daddio Harper. This dude writes all these songs about her but he's not good enough. Oh no, he's just some lowlife who wants to seduce their little girl. He ends up with a degree from UCLA and starts a rock band, pretty famous, so just as well they split them up because that wouldn't have done for the Harpers, no Siree.

So it's in their interest to go along with this whole Bride and Harper stuff, get the kids together. Pretty neat if you think about it; my parents can stop worrying about me being gay and Marcia's parents can stop fretting about their little girl with some drug-taking loser.

So every holiday we're in each other's pockets and the families are like, how sweet, aren't the kids lovely together, why don't we just leave them alone for a while, give the kids some space.

But Marcia and me, we have no idea what to do with the space we're given and we just, you know, mess around a little because it's kind of expected, when all she wants to do is see her rock guy and all I want is to be left alone with my art.

It's not that I wasn't into girls. I just wasn't really into Marcia. Christ, she was like my sister so it was like putting your hands in your sister's knickers, and the stickiness I found there just made me want to throw up.

Suddenly I'm a Harper by marriage and boy, that's some hard work. Maybe if Marcia couldn't have her music man it didn't matter who she married, I don't know. We've talked about it, sure, especially after the affair, but I guess we never really know what's going on in people's minds.

Were the regrets real? I can't say. All I can say is that after she lost the baby it seemed like we were maybe getting a second chance so I was willing to give it another go and of course, the families, they sure didn't want for us to split up.

Jesus, my dad, he set so much store by this whole Harper connection, propelled them so far up the social ladder that they almost had vertigo; my mom and her designer dresses, my dad with his ever-ready contracts, dealing with all the big sharks. Even had grand ideas about me taking over as the big cheese one day – as if I'd want the Harper business if I didn't want my own dad's.

Divorce was just not on the cards, especially given the whole Catholic thing that Marcia and her folks had going, so we separated for a bit to let things calm down. To be honest, I just didn't have the energy to make a big thing of it all. Sure, I was upset but things were just so out of hand that I needed to just take stock, concentrate on my work and get together research for my book. Thought maybe that would make me some decent money of my own.

So I move out for a bit, thinking that maybe it'll just be a few weeks, get a flat over at the college and she stays home with the in-laws. Oh, I guess I didn't mention that, Em. We were still living there, in this lovely big annexe for sure, but still there in her folks' house with my folks next door; all very cosy, like we're one big, happy family.

Then she calls me to say she's got this post at her old school. In England, for Christ sake. And I think okay, now it's over for good but Mr and Mrs H, they're having none of that. Yeah, they organised her to go alright to give her a little space to 'get things out of her system' but then they're on the phone to her day after day, to me too. 'Now, why don't you two lovebirds just use this itty bit of time apart to count all those blessings that you two share and then just see if you can't just try again. Marriage wasn't made to be broken, you know. What the Lord has created, let no man put asunder,' or something like that.

So the folks, they all get together and Harper, he hits on this idea. After all, his daddy started the whole scholarship so why not take advantage? And if he can get his daughter a Head of Department post straight off then he can sure as hell get his arty farty son-in-law into his own damn scheme – and it's not as if his son-in-law's making a name for himself in anything remotely important. And there's no way my parents are going to argue with that.

You know, Em, now it makes me wonder at how the two of us, Marcia and me, could just let our futures float away, allowing other people to steer the ship.

I had no argument for them faced with the power of the sanctity of marriage. Which is how I found myself on this stupid Harper scholarship programme, living in some god-awful dump. Yeah, we could have taken some Harper money and blown it on some great apartment somewhere and I've only got myself to blame for that. Let Marcia persuade me that if we were going to do this thing, we should do it for ourselves, stuff the trust funds and the crazy money, just give things a try for ourselves. Like that somehow was going to make it all better.

When she got sick, I thought, okay, let's just do this thing for her. Go to Paris, have some fun away from all the pressure of trying to hang on to this dead-in-the-water marriage that I need to keep going, and get a little research done at the same time, no harm done. Jesus, Em, no harm done?

Anyway, I guess you're getting the picture. Christ, maybe this is all too much information at once? I just need to keep this going now, need to get the story told, am scared of what's gonna happen if I don't. Just have to keep on…

So now I'm thinking okay, this is all over with Sloane, you just need to sort yourself out, just carry on and do what the family wants you to do, be a good son and a good husband. For sure, I'm never going to be a father and that's real hard to swallow, especially since none of that was my fault. Not that I ever really wanted kids. It's just the way it all happened that pisses me off.

But there I am, dragging around after Marcia, this shop, that gallery, another monument, passing time. All I can think of is Sloane. The places we went, the light in her eyes and the shadow across her shining skin, the brush of her hands across my body, the tense pulse between my legs when she straddled me, me there, raw and open; she opened my mind and body to places I have never been before and will likely never go again.

Sloane is somewhere in Paris, confused and hurting, hating me most likely; Jesus, I hate myself, what's not to hate? Knowing she is in Paris but that I can't be with her – worse, I need not to be near her, certainly not if Marcia's around, it's like ripping my skin from my bones. How can my wife not smell the scent of lust in the air, on my breath?

But I swear to God, Em, I thought it was all over, I meant for it to be all over; a moment's oasis in my desert of a life. Which is why, when I got the note, I could scarcely believe what I read.

Chapter 22

Sloane

At first I think I've got it all wrong and then I realise I did hear her right; 'It is not the wife who has the power, *ma chérie*. It is the mistress who keeps him wanting more,' Elodie said.

On our way out of the gardens, Elodie waves her hand towards the Palais du Luxembourg, the seat of the upper house of the French parliament and bends down to whisper in my ear, 'I have the power and he has the power, if you know what I mean.' I raise my brows, questioning her cryptic comment. She shrugs her shoulders and bends in to whisper again: 'It is my secretarial duty, *non*?'

With a flourish, she whips the pashmina from my neck, kisses me on one cheek and the other, then again on the first and she is gone, leaving me open-mouthed at her admission of mistress-ship.

Was it good advice delivered so adeptly by my friend, so French and so much more experienced than I? Or were they the words of just another young woman, herself snarled in the confusion of forbidden love? Perhaps just two perfect clichés, one egging the other on to drown alongside her in the depths of eventual desolation.

Oh, Em, I had read all about the folly of heart-stabbing, all-consuming love, the soul mate version where one can't breathe without the other, but why would I have ever thought it could happen to me? Everyone I had ever loved in my life was gone – my mum, my dad, Auntie Jean and now Nicholas. But Nicholas was at least not dead.

Elodie slips out of view. I have no coat, little cash and a great deal of thinking to do. Walking seems the solution to all three aspects of my immediate future and I set off, hoping that a more distant future might come into view. Sometimes it's possible to drive or to walk and to be unaware of anything beyond the thoughts in your head. Maybe this could be one of those times.

There is no way I am going back to the hotel to fetch my jacket. Bumping into Nicholas and Marcia is not an option. Funny really – I should feel guilty but deep as I dig I cannot find an element of shame. I hadn't known about Marcia and although my intense dislike has softened a fraction knowing that she's had a hard time, I still feel no warmth, no sense of loyalty. I am not quite owning the fact that I would have wanted Nicholas no matter what – that I would have slept with him even if I had known about Marcia, that I still want him on any terms. But the flicker of recognition is there if I choose to tune in, a tiny flame fanned by the intimate confidence that Elodie has shared.

One foot follows another as the mechanics of my walking move into autopilot. I am just aware of the damp beneath my feet as my ballet flats allow Paris puddles to seep between the seams. I welcome the sensation, lifting me as it does from the dark chamber of my mind where I have been betrayed and see no escape.

Where is the anger? Where is the violence – since I know that somewhere in the depths there should be outrage, rage? God, yes maybe it is God who must take the blame, for thrusting Nicholas under my nose only to whip him away the instant we declare love.

The rain falls slowly at first kissing my skin through the loops in my pale cotton sweater. As I breathe in the syrupy smells of pancake and chestnut, the flashback to our first day in this city is at first sweet but then the aching begins. How could I have wasted precious moments with this man, scoring points, holding grudges, useless, meaningless grudges when I only had a fraction of the whole? Is this what we do? Waste time on the nothings of life when the somethings are staring us in the face?

My foot catches the edge of the pavement and I stumble into the road, nudging an old man crossing from the other side. His angry face meets mine as he scoops to retrieve the battered, washed-out blue cap that has fallen from his head, '*Oh pardon, Monsieur, je m'excuse.*' I say. He mumbles something, completing his complaint with a spat-out expletive: '*Putain!*' he says. Oh my God, perhaps I *am* a whore.

I lift my face up into the rain. The sky is black-grey with thunderclouds. A loud crack ruptures the unremitting blare of traffic. Upriver, Notre Dame is blazed in a split second of light, her flying buttresses bathed in the instant wash of lightening. So I am here, yards only from where our lovers' tryst took place. Not lovers then, lovers-to-be. We both knew that it is what our bodies would dictate and that our minds would yield to the rainbow of sensations we could each offer the other.

The eye that is in my mind craves his image, and it conjures Nicholas standing there, thumbing the books in the store, alert for my arrival, yet nonchalant enough to seduce.

My hand goes up to my head and I shake the water from my hair. Lightening again. Is it in my head or has the sky become my ally as it erupts once more? I have to leave this place, move on. He is everywhere, outside the store, in my mind, in my body, cleaving a scar between my breasts. My breath becomes shallow with the strain of trying to breathe as my hearts pounds and my head swims with the reality of my day. He cannot be gone, he cannot be gone. How can I not feel those hands on my body, those lips on mine? How can I not have a lifetime of sitting in cafés, laughing, sharing stories, talking books, art, life? Talking everything and nothing for surely that is the art of true love and completeness, and I do not feel complete without him.

I am running before I know my feet have moved, pushing through the crowds and umbrellas on the *Pont St Michel*. I cross the bridge, the angry eddies of the Seine swirling below, and run harder still along the *quai*, my ribs burning. My cotton jumper clings, soaked on the one side by the sweat of my efforts and on the other by the unrelenting rain.

Finally I come to a halt, the majesty of the cathedral before me. Looking down I see *Kilomètre Zero* directly beneath my feet. *Kilomètre Zero*, the spot from which all points in France are measured. How fitting that I find myself in a nowhere place as if somehow standing here would bring me back to nought and offer the chance of some other outcome. Nought. That is where I am. Self-pity in all its disgusting glory flows over me and tears fall unchecked. There is no one to see, no one to care, so why should I care?

There comes a point when you are so wet that any further downpour will make little impact but I do not recognise that this is where I am. Nor do I recognise that my mind, too, is at saturation point. A maelstrom of emotion, trapped in its own vortex that has nowhere to go except around again on the same loop. I still think I have a choice.

As I enter through its huge, ornate doors, the cathedral draws me in but stops me dead as the sound fills the air around me. Lilting and lulling, the nuns are singing in one voice, pure, edge-of-knife clean notes that wrap themselves around my broken spirit and gently pull it upwards into the cavernous height above my head. To my right is a tray of candles, their long spindled legs streaked with jewels of wax as their flames sputter with the ghosts of a chill church draught.

I fish in the pocket of my jeans, breathing in to allow my hand to probe, and as I feel my own hand push against my flesh, the memory of another hand twists at my senses. I draw out a few coins. There is enough for a candle, several candles, and I wonder if just the one will suffice for all the people I have loved and lost.

The coin rattles in the slot and I pluck up a taper and hold it in the flames of another. Whose soul is joining with the souls of those I mourn as those two flames become one? I hesitate to consign my candle to a spike, eking out my prayer in case it has not quite been heard, not yet sufficiently fulsome to be answered. Finally with my parents, my aunt and my love in my heart, I find it a home, burning brightly amongst the spirits of others who have died. Did I die this day or is there more life to come? If Nicholas is not to be part of it I want none of it.

When I leave Notre Dame I pay direction no heed, a route march through the roads and paths of Paris that I have loved but that has let me badly down, and I feel my love affair with her drifting away. I negotiate the intersection at La Bastille, and pick an arbitrary road. Keep walking, keep walking. Maybe if I keep walking my head will clear or I will wake up and all this will not have happened.

Panting now, bracing my legs as I trudge uphill, I glance up at the street sign: Rue Du Repos, the street of rest. So this is where my feet have brought me. Ahead of me is the *Cimetière* Père Lachaise. I remember the conversation we had, the visit we had planned. Nicholas and I should be here together.

I go to cross the road but stop short as I recognise a familiar figure in a doorway on the opposite side of the street. Under his arm is a package. I duck into a doorway myself and watch and wait. His collar is up, scant protection against the rain. He makes a dive for it, hopping from one doorway to the next, hoping to outsmart the grim Paris day, until finally he disappears from view. Crossing the street, I peer into the shop window where he stood. So this is Pete's secret, which no doubt, sometime soon, Cathy will share.

Edith Piaf – that's whose grave I want to see, and I stride towards the entrance to the famous burial ground, the singer's celebrated song running through my head: *Non, je ne regrette rien*. Do I regret nothing, I wonder?

My breath catches in my throat and I pause at the gate. What was it that Elodie said? *It is the mistress who makes him want more?* What am I thinking, for fuck's sake? This love does not deserve to be a rotting corpse consigned to history. It deserves to sit up there amongst the great loves. Why shouldn't I fight for it, fight hard and selfishly as Elodie advised?

I fish in my pocket and pull out a tissue, wipe my eyes and blow my nose loudly. I turn on my heel, resolve injecting a spring into my step. Maybe I will visit this cemetery one day — but if I do, it will be with Nicholas on my arm. I will not be beaten. I will take Elodie's advice. If it's good enough for her, why shouldn't it be good enough for me? And it's not as if Marcia's my friend, she's never once been nice to me. She can't be a very good wife if Nicholas can fall in love with me just like that – no, she cannot possibly love him as do I.

So tucking away the comforting thought that Marcia does not deserve the husband she has I head back to the hotel. I need pen and paper and Cathy.

Jae De Wylde

Chapter 23

Dearest Nicholas,

I know you will not expect this message since I did not expect to be writing it, but I love you and find I have no choice.

I have tried to understand why you didn't tell me about Marcia. I know you knew she was coming since I told you myself, there in the café before we made love - and it was love, wasn't it, Nicholas? I must believe that it was real or I shall know that I have gone mad.

You have no idea how many times I have turned this over in my mind, but no matter how I see it, I cannot believe that you thought I knew that you were married – worse, that Marcia was your wife – certainly not considering all the unpleasant things I said about her. You could have jumped in at any time, defended her, let me know it was your wife I was insulting. But you chose not to act at any point, which is why I have reached a decision.

My darling, if given all that evidence, you were unable to tell me the truth, then it can mean only one thing; that you could not bring yourself to tell me, that the truth was just too painful to bear and that it was only at that moment, when Marcia appeared out of nowhere, that you were faced with the awful reality – that there was no hope for the love we had only just discovered, the joy of being together, physically and emotionally. I know it's crazy and we have been together for just a fraction of time, but Nicholas, that time has meant more to me than any other time in my life, and I pray that you feel the same.

Make some excuse, my darling, any excuse or wait until she is asleep, but come to my room tonight. I must see you again, must hold your glorious naked body next to mine and feel you inside me, even if it is just one last time. I shall be waiting, whatever the time. My door will be open, as will my heart.

Yours always,

Sloane

Chapter 24

Nicholas

I waited until her breathing changed, until I recognised that Marcia was sound asleep and then I grabbed my robe. Sloane's room was not far from mine and I guessed that at two in the morning there wouldn't be anyone around to see me slip out to pay her a little visit. I hadn't expected to be having sex with Marcia that night and when I got Sloane's note I was going to make pretty sure it didn't happen that way, but then it was kinda hard not to; Marcia was pretty keen on cashing in on the whole romance of Paris and she had other ideas, which was pretty unusual, I can tell you.

The weird thing is, Em, that it was Cathy who gave me the note. No idea what explanation Sloane had given her but I remembering thinking thank God she didn't give it to me in front of Marcia.

The floor is wooden along the landing and gives a little under my bare feet. Here and there it creaks and the sound echoes along the corridor; only my heartbeat sounds louder. I don't stop to think what I'm doing, what would happen if Cathy, Pete or Marcia found me here in my robe about to push open

Sloane's door, to push open her legs and to be inside of her. I just need to be with her. I need her and she is waiting.

As I enter the room, she stirs and turns over in the bed to face me. 'I knew you would come. Darling, Nicholas, I knew you would come.'

She pulls me toward her. Her perfume, familiar, sultry, in her hair, behind her ears, down her throat. I bury my face in her magnificent nakedness. God, she's so damned sexy, so exciting and so deliciously shameless. She pushes me down on the bed and strokes my face, her eyes tender and warm. I expect recrimination but it never comes. A groan rises in my chest and escapes as she kisses me full on the mouth, her tongue and mine in rhythmic harmony between our two mouths. She smooths her body over mine, flesh pressing and flowing against flesh, embracing all that I am. All that we have become.

She draws back and plants tiny kisses on my mouth, my chest, the pits of my arms, my stomach, my thighs: tiny, light-as-air kisses and my senses are alive with the wanting of her. She explores me with her tongue, greedily, like she needs to taste the whole of me. Like she needs to note each flavour and smell and to store it inside of her, an imprint of the very essence of me. Her mouth closes over me. For an instant, I pull back. Jesus, I was in Marcia and now I'm in her mouth, but she sucks me in harder and I let go, allowing her to transport me anywhere she wants us to go. Anywhere our eager bodies will take us.

Afterwards, when we wrap our arms around one another, she whispers to me in an angel-soft voice: 'Darling, Nicholas. We must be together always. Don't worry. We can make it happen. You and I, we are meant to be. We both believe that, don't we,

Nicholas?' I look into the depths of her eyes that look back at me with so much love, so much passion, and for the first time I understand what it truly is to be loved. I kiss her full on the mouth in reply.

She speaks again, gently, tenderly. She understands so much without me even having to ask. 'Don't worry, Nicholas, we can make it work,' she repeats, stroking my forehead with the tips of her fingers. She moves her index finger to her mouth, brushes it over her lips and over her tongue. She presses the finger, moist and warm, against my lips, a secret covenant between us, and then she speaks again, 'and I promise you, Nicholas. I promise that I will never ever ask you to leave your wife.'

Chapter 25

Sloane

Oh my God, Em. There it is. Blame with a capital B. I was the one who wouldn't let go; pushed it further than it would stretch. I consciously, callously, calculatingly offered myself to Nicholas, knowing that he would not resist.

Did I think about Marcia for one minute? No I did not. Did I really believe that it was my right to take her husband because she wasn't a good enough wife? No I did not. Was I just trying to ease my conscience when I told myself that if she was a bad wife, I would be a good mistress? No I was not. I was not, Em, because I had no conscience. I took what I could because I wanted to take it – like taking it would somehow make up for all the things that had been taken from me.

Did I mean it when I said I wouldn't ever ask him to leave his wife? Of course I did not. I was working to instruction. I was being clever, just as Elodie said. I was telling him what he wanted to hear, offering erotic love without strings. As if such a thing exists!

But the strings weren't just attached to him. We were all just puppets, weren't we, Em? In one mad puppet show.

'You *are* joking.'

'No, Cathy, I am deadly serious. It was bad enough trying to avoid them in Paris, but here, it's like I am constantly playing hide-and-seek, except I don't want to seek, there's nowhere to hide and they are every-bloody-where. How does that make sense? And now it looks like they're extending the Harper thing another year. And after yesterday, well…'

'I so do not want you to leave. Who will do the timetables with me? And how do you know about the Harper Award?'

'Oh cheers, friend. Is that my only purpose around here?' I ignore her final question and am grateful she lets it go.

'Don't be daft, I just meant, you know I'll miss you. Miss this.' She splays her hands in front of her. I know what she means. It's a pity we were not this friendly before. That's how I think of it. Before and after. Before Nicholas and after Nicholas. Like my life is divided and the start button was only pressed when Nicholas entered the scene.

'You're right, though, it's weird. We hardly ever saw him before the trip but now he's always down this end of the school. You're not still…?'

I shake my head and put my finger over my lips. 'Don't even say it,' I say.

'Did he ever mention the note?' Cathy dives into her bag and fishes out an apple and penknife. Oh hell, the note. I didn't want this one to come up. Poor Cathy, she thought that she was delivering a *Dear John* not a *come-and-get-me-I'm-yours*.

I purse my lips and suck in my breath. 'No, not a word,' lie.

'Do you think Marcia knows? About you two?' Cathy asks as she peels the apple into the over-full bin. She is paying her task only limited attention and several of the curls of skin land on the parquet floor.

'Shush,' I say, my eyes darting about lest these walls have ears, 'I don't know. I don't think so. I just think it's all part of the same thing. We just don't like each other, we never have.'

'But why would she single you out for getting the marking schemes wrong? We all got it wrong. Not one of us noticed we were working to last year's brief, even she didn't know, I'll bet you. Do you think she has some sixth sense, maybe?'

'Cathy, you're not helping.'

Cathy looks at me sheepishly. 'Sorry,' she says.

'Anyway, it's done. I won't be here next year and to be honest it's a massive relief. I just don't enjoy it anymore and it'll do me good to get away. Try to move on.' I look away. I am being disingenuous and whilst I believe that with Marcia it's fair game, I have real trouble lying to Cathy.

'But surely your aunt's money's not going to be enough to live on?'

'It'll do for now – and I'm going to be writing much more. Even got a few freelance things lined up. And it will at least get me away from *them*.'

What I don't tell Cathy is that I still own Auntie Jean's house in London. I hardly ever think about it. It's a rainy day house – a house that she paid off with the money left by my parents and then she left the house to me. It's been rented out for years now and I have never touched the money. It's like the money belongs to someone else, like it would be bad luck to dip in and smell its seductive scent.

'You'll always have somewhere to come back to, Felicity. It's your nest egg for a rainy day,' Auntie Jean used to say. Perhaps the rainy day has come and if I need an umbrella to see me through then I guess my mum, dad and aunt would probably approve. There is plenty they wouldn't approve of though, I think.

'I don't think they're happy, you know.' It's Cathy's turn to look furtively around. She shuffles to the edge of her chair and leans forward. 'I heard them arguing, yesterday – after all that hoo-ha with the schemes.

'It was her who had the affair, you know. I thought it was him but it wasn't, it was her. Some ex-boyfriend or other. That's how she got pregnant – before the miscarriage. That baby wasn't his. You *were* on the pill, weren't you?' she adds, almost in the same breath.

'Oh my God, Cathy! How the bloody hell do you know all this? This is the first I've heard about any affair. Oh my God!' Why the hell *don't* I know about this? Jesus, poor Nicholas, no wonder he seemed so sad. 'And I'm not entirely stupid, by the way! I've been on the pill for years.'

So I am right. She is not a good wife. I feel self-righteousness welling up inside of me. So I am the rescuer after all. She really does not deserve that man. But why hasn't he told me? I guess there was never a moment, never the right time.

'It was her who told me about the affair – when I told her about our baby and what had happened with Pete. We just got talking. It was like she needed to tell someone, and I suppose we were both in the same boat. I didn't think I should tell you under the circumstances but given you're leaving – we will still get together, won't we?'

'Jesus, Cathy. How could you not tell me something like that? I thought it was me that was your friend, not Marcia?'

Cathy is wounded, her moon face drooping with hurt. 'It's because I'm your friend that I didn't tell you, Sloane. How can you not see that? And anyway, for all I knew Nicholas might already have told you. Don't blame me if he chose not to. It's not my fault.'

'God, I'm sorry. It's just all getting to me. Yes, it's better not to know stuff like that. Just makes it all harder to move on.' Thank God for Cathy. She's a natural born gossip and things just come out in the end. I store away the information, perfect justification for my role in Nicholas' life.

'I'd hate not to see you, Cathy,' I say, and I do really mean it.

Most days I see him across the hall, and the hairs on my skin prickle up. I am on edge, alert, and my body makes ready to receive Nicholas whether or not we have a plan. Sometimes, when there's no one else around, I visit him in his studio, careful always to dress– or to undress – the part.

If there is hesitation, I knock it down with what I know he loves. I sit on the high benches where he kneads his clay and I pull up my skirt, spreading my legs wide so he can nuzzle his face into me, pulling aside my silk cami-knickers, threading his fingers around the suspenders of my lace-topped stockings. I am a good mistress and I never make demands. I have no need. I know just how to make him demand me.

But I too am undone. His touch is the cool waters of a shimmering stream, the quieting glide of a bird through air, the earthy scent of an animal on heat. His touch is fire.

I pour myself into everything that makes him tick. I like what he likes; I draw breath from everything that makes him breathe. How many times have I drowned myself in the story of Rodin's muse, eager to learn what it is that fascinates Nicholas, this man I need to want me. I scan articles, gobble up books, devour the film, such that the harrowed face of Isabelle Adjani has become in my mind the face of Camille Claudel, and the French movie star has in turn become me. I am the faultless mistress. Will I, like her, unravel one day?

Marcia works late a lot, meetings, societies, things that I might be doing if I hadn't already declared my intention to leave. She is hard-working, I'll give her that.

I live too dangerously close to the school for Nicholas to visit my flat, surrounded as I am by prying student eyes. If studio space is not obvious, we are consigned to his car, the occasional thrill of moments shared in a country pub in some hidden village, or to his home on the edge of a sprawling estate a train ride away.

If I take my bike, I can be there in an hour; an hour of sweet anticipation of stolen time with his lean, strong body and his dancing mind, the firm, rocking saddle beneath me welcome, preparing me for what is to come.

What do his neighbours make of this bouncy-haired twenty-something astride a battered old bike? Auntie Jean's old bike is painted red, its straw pannier stuffed with books and files – a little show in case the prying eyes need to make up their own story of who I might be; a student maybe, requiring tutorials, and always on the evenings when his wife is not at home. I do not care, but go through the motions of secrecy, reassurance to Nicholas of my resolve to hold fast to my vow; *I will never ever ask you to leave your wife.*

I'd made that promise to Nicholas and I had every intention of keeping it, just as I had every intention of keeping him – rather some of him than none of him, that's how I had it planned. But we know now, don't we, Em, that things don't always go to plan.

The evening is balmy as we head towards the end of term, towards days when my world will change, into what I cannot yet imagine. Oh, I have my ideas. Wild ideas, some of them, but they all include Nicholas, as I know he includes me.

I lean my bike against the cherry tree at the back of the house, its blossom now spent upon the floor and my shoes collect tiny pink petals as I go. I steal in through the open patio doors.

The frisson of wanting down my spine almost overwhelms me and I am giddy with longing. Nicholas is waiting for me in the neat, sparsely furnished room, a blanket spread on the drab velour couch, our blanket. The room is not romantic but the romance is not in our surroundings, it is in the overwhelming passion that we share. There is no need for frills or frippery. We both know why I am here and we make love hungrily, without performance or pretence, just the thirst for each other sufficient to heighten our senses and fuse our spirits in mutual delight and desire.

Afterwards, he strokes my face gently as we lie side by side. 'Oh Sloane, Sloane,' he says, 'you're the one who found me, who sees me, strips me back, who picked me out of the stars; me, the Virgo non-believer. I guess it's you who has made me believe.'

I float away in his tender words. Part of me is always alert, the urgency of snatched moments never far from my mind, but the part of me that basks in the glory of Nicholas, his body, his love, is quiet for this moment, bathed in the togetherness of two soul mates who have become one.

The mood switches almost imperceptibly. Nicholas lets out a sigh, almost a groan, sits up and swings his legs to the floor, retrieves his chinos and shakes them out. There is a withdrawing and I sense that something hangs in the air unsaid.

'What is it, Nicholas?' I ask. I examine his face and see the knot in his brow. His expression is troubled. I sit up and go to touch his cheek. He turns away. 'Nicholas?' My heart is lifting from my chest. I place my hand lightly on his arm and he turns back, looking into my face, absorbing its features.

He slides from the sofa, scoops his arm under my legs and lays me back down. Nicholas kneels beside me, his eyes suppliant, prayerful almost. He raises his hand, moving it above my breasts, my stomach, between my open legs. There is tension in his muscles as if he fights some invisible forces compelling him to touch my body, which aches for him even now.

'Nicholas?' I say again. His is a portrait of anguish. His hand traces the space above the curves and arches of me and finally, as if he loses some intangible battle, resistance is extinguished and he lowers his hand to my breast, ascetic rendered powerless by the potent temptations of the flesh. Closing his eyes he outlines my contours, blind but seeing, pain still tight on his lips, casting my impression, painting me on the canvas of his mind.

The pressure grows as the tempo mounts and I cannot tell if it is ecstasy or torment that intensifies his touch. He pushes himself up from the floor and lowers himself into me, kissing me hard on the lips. His hands are in my hair, on my forehead. His lips are on my neck, on my breasts, insistent, claiming me. He lets out a moan. 'Oh God, Sloane, forgive me. I'm so sorry, I'm so sorry.' He opens his eyes and I see the tears.

Chapter 26

Nicholas

I have often wondered, Em, why I never told Sloane about the affair – Marcia's affair. Thinking about it now, I guess that Marcia, she was always this girl next door, kind of unspoilt. It was never about the sex with her, more about the kind of way we'd been micromanaged by the families. It gave us this special bond; more about friendship and conspiracy than all the other stuff. In my mind she's always been strangely pure. Yeah, that sounds crazy but she was kind of squeaky clean – clean looks, clean living, no-nonsense.

The affair? Well, I got that in a way. Not that it didn't hurt; still hurts. We were all boxed into this corner and I guess I wasn't really providing the excitement that she needed – and I know I was real hopeless as a lover, compared with the other guy. Like I say, she was like a sister to me and the only other person I'd done any stuff with was Josh – and you can't count that.

Jesus fucking Christ, Em, what the hell am I saying? Here we are condemned to telling the goddamned truth and here I am covering up all over again.

Hell, I sound like the affair was like nothing to me. That's bullshit. Of course I was hurt, mad at this bastard of a guy who was showing me up; showing me up. Yeah, if I'm honest that's what hurt the most. This guy was showing me up in front of my family, her family, showing everyone how things should be done rather than the pathetic attempts of a loser like me.

And she got a kick out of it for sure. Those weekends down on Venice Beach, in New York, Las Vegas; I knew she wasn't with any girlfriend. There can't be that many bachelorette parties in a whole lifetime let alone every damn year.

I knew what she was up to – some kind of groupie hanging around her rock star stud – and I bet she just loved the attention. All those songs about her; as if I was so stupid I wouldn't cotton on. And she goes and tells me that he was never her lover before we got married – too scared what Mom and Dad would have done if they'd found out. *Oh, Nicky, I never would have been unfaithful to you back then. Jake and I were just friends...* Like I believe that one! And why be unfaithful to me at all if you're so damn pure? Don't recall her telling me she was a virgin anytime back then. Don't recall ever asking.

Couldn't wait to jump into bed with him once he got famous, that's for sure, around about the seven year itch. God knows how I put up with it all that time. Sunday after Sunday making excuses as to why she was away again. Sitting there with the folks, saying grace, thanking the Lord for what we are about to receive when I know that what I am about to receive from my wife is a great big fat zero. Yeah, maybe we didn't have the best situation but she didn't have to go and do that. She could have made the best of it, got on with it like everyone expected us to. Jesus, Em, I was patient. Thought it would maybe just run its course, knew what the families would say if we split, and just couldn't face that look in my dad's eye all over again. Failed. Again. *Is there nothing you can get right, son?* Just kept plugging away at the research, the teaching, the book; I guess I wanted it all to go away.

Christ, if it hadn't been for the baby coming along we'd probably still be at it now, the whole goddamned charade. Thank God we kept that one from the parents. It's not as if they hadn't been asking; the little comments, knives in the ribs; *Gee, it would be neat to hear the patter of tiny feet around here, wouldn't it, honey?* Can you imagine my dad's face if he found out? *Well, darn me, can't even get her pregnant, son.*

And Mister Rock Star, well gee whizz, he was married too. What about that now? Pretty little stay-at-home bride with three kiddies all of his own. But that wasn't enough for him. No Siree. Had to go and impregnate my Marcia too. Never did want kids and I sure as hell wasn't going to be taking care of some guy's bastard child. Almost was the end of us, yes it was, but then bingo, one day, just when we've told the folks that it's all over between the two of us, she starts bleeding like it's some damn miracle. I guess it was up to us to take our chance and make a fresh start.

Anyway, Marcia, she takes it real hard. I guess now when I think about it maybe she's counting on this kid to tear Mr Super-stud from the bosom of his loving family so she can set up home with him. Maybe that's being unfair. She never did seem the kind to manipulate. But that's as maybe. She's in pieces about this whole thing. She gets real sick and it turns out she's so messed up down there that there's no question of any more kids. I feel kind of sorry for her, and I wasn't lying – I never could get that girl next door image of her out of my mind. I guess that's what made me want to give it another chance, that maybe I owed her one to make up for being such a disappointment in her life.

Then bam, Marcia's suddenly going to teach in England. Well, I already told you all about that and how I got there and now you know all about the affair.

I am being honest here, Em, trust me. I'm not leaving stuff out. I'm telling it as it was so I sure as hell hope you're taken that into account. I'm scared, Em. I don't mind admitting that I'm scared. I just want to have a fair chance when push comes to shove.

No, I never told Sloane about the affair and I guess it never did have a damn thing to do with how I felt about Marcia. It was all about how I felt about me. Sloane brought my body and soul to life in a way I'd only ever read about in books – and it looked like I pretty much brought her to life too. So why would I want to admit to this incredible creature that my wife had had an affair? Why would I want her to see me as that guy – the one who couldn't satisfy his wife?

Chapter 27

Sloane

After the wedding, Stuart and I didn't bother with a honeymoon. We decided that it was an unnecessary expense, what with me changing careers. My writing hadn't yet brought in more than a little pocket money, so the finances were mostly down to my brand new husband to sort.

Auntie Jean used to talk about 'the one that got away' and I never really understood what she meant until I met Nicholas. 'There's the one you marry and the one that got away,' she'd say and it makes me wonder now who it was in her life that got away, who was the person that made her heart beat faster? Did her heart melt like mine for someone other than Uncle Bob? I scarcely remember him. He was what, fifty maybe when he died, but looking back he didn't strike me as the sort of bloke who could ever break hearts.

I made sure that Nicholas and Marcia received an invitation to the wedding but of course I never expected a reply. So the little note I got from my former boss was quite a surprise: *Congratulations, Sloane. Be the kind of happy you read about in books*, it read. But I knew I would never be that kind of happy. Not until Marcia was out of the way.

When he told me that he wasn't going to stay on at the school, I almost got excited. If Nicholas was turning down the chance of another Harper year then it must surely be to be with me. But the look on his face told me that this wasn't about me at all; that this extraordinary love we shared was to be sacrificed on the altar of duty and honour, discarded in the name of 'doing the right thing.'

'Marcia is leaving too,' he said. We're going back to the US. It's what our families want and I think it's what we should do.'

He said that deep down he loved her and that he owed it to her, brought up the whole the miscarriage thing, said he needed to try to help her piece her life back together and come to terms with not being able to have kids. They could start over again back home, where she had support and where he could get on with his research and his art, where they could live somewhere more comfortably and give things another go.

He was sorry. He felt he had to deny self and do his duty rather than put our love affair first. But what about the fact that he was also denying me?

I almost told him I knew about her affair, wanted to spit it in his face, to shock him, but I decided that the information was maybe better left for another time.

Turns out Cathy knew all about it. She knew there was no other Harper year for Nicholas because she was the one who was getting Marcia's job. All the secrecy, all the subterfuge – God, only in a private school!

I was well out of that one, for sure, and I was able to be genuinely pleased at Cathy's promotion to the ranks. That sort of thing means something to the likes of Pete and Cathy, don't you think? And anyway, there was no point in getting huffy. I had to keep Cathy in my life. She was the only person I could talk to about Nicholas – the only person who knew.

But don't think I was beaten, Em, just because I married Stuart. Nicholas and I were connected. I knew it and I knew he knew it too. His last words to me were the most important words he'd ever said in a precious, pilfered moment on the last day of term. Another of those moments, Em, that pivot your life around; that give you hope, where there was none.

I am walking across the quad and I see him staring through the glass pane of the doorway from the studio, that place where he and I have tasted a frenzy of bliss. I know I look good. It is Speech Day, and I am wearing a pale cream suit, fitted neatly to my hips and waist. A straw hat, trimmed flirtily with feathers and a veil just frames my eyes. I don't want him to see that I have seen. I lower my chin, the brim of my hat scant camouflage as I pass him by, but not before I have caught the wistful stance, the weight of regret in the slight movement he makes towards me. I urge myself to keep walking, to allow the agony of the days that have gone before to settle and not to pick at the wound. He has made his choice, although it is clear that it is not a choice he has made; his moral duty has dictated what his heart is unable to overturn.

I hear the door swing open. 'Sloane, Sloane,' that voice fires up every fibre, every synapse, every cell. Despite myself I turn and as he approaches I see the redness in his eyes. More tears.

'Sloane,' he says, 'Sloane, there is something I want you to remember; I want you to remember this; wherever you are, whenever,' he says,' I shall be loving you then as now.'

The message is carved, an epitaph in my mind. It is a curious message, like he sought somehow to be poetic, impressive; that he feared I would remember it only if it bore some literary clout. But the syntax is unimportant. It is the content that counts.

He turns and he is gone. I will never get over this man, never. But he is not dead, I remind myself. And if he is not dead, there has to be hope.

Stuart was my safe bet. I knew that he wanted to be with me and that he would be pretty easy to manage, fitting in neatly to the humps and bumps in my life. I suppose you think that's callous, Em, but from my point of view, if I couldn't have Nicholas, it didn't really matter who I married, so why not marry Stuart? – rather the devil you know than the devil you don't.

And Stuart was no devil – more of a lamb. He was kind and caring, loving even. Just not very exciting or passionate but then that wasn't something I required. Nicholas was the only man who could fulfil the desire in me. Nobody else stood a chance.

It was Cathy who engineered it all; Cathy who decided that Stuart would be salve for my wounds, although it was an act of fate in the first place that thrust the two of them together. When Cathy finally did go on a Sixth Form conference – for real this time, not some smokescreen to hide tragedy as before – there was Stuart doing a Sixth Form conference himself. What is it they say? That we have six degrees of separation from everyone else we meet? Well these two discovered they had just the one – and that one was me.

To be honest, Em, it was almost a relief not to have to feel everything so deeply. Cathy, knowingly and Stuart, unwittingly, plastered over the surface of my scars and as long as I kept myself busy, the lesions below could be tamed and stilled.

This was familiar territory after all. Did the pain of my parents' death ever truly recede or did I just learn to breathe more shallowly, calm my pulse, to break down the stinging heartache in the months and years between? Even now I can feel their arms around me and hear their voices in my head.

Sometimes I get scared that I will forget the sound, but then in quiet moments, it engulfs me – the lilt and timbre of my mother's soft tones, the depths of my father's bumbling laugh.

I can still hear Nicholas. That is what's important now. I can still hear him like he is there, calling to me, loving me wherever he is, whenever.

When Stuart asked me to marry him, I looked at the options. I looked at this generous and easy, wonderfully ordinary man before me on one knee and decided that in other circumstances, I'd probably consider I was lucky; lucky to have another chance. He was not handsome in the manner of Nicholas's chiselled looks but he had an inviting face. His childhood of teasing about his mop of strawberry blond hair had stood him in good stead and I admired his sense of humour; he was not a person to take himself seriously and I liked that about him. I had had enough angst in my life and the light refreshment of a relationship that could skim the surface of life, instead of plumbing the depths was in some strange way healing.

We were friends. We got on well, and he wasn't part of my past with Nicholas – only Cathy and I shared my secret and I knew she wasn't going to tell. There was a kind of symmetry to it all; losing my virginity to Stuart, losing my heart and mind to Nicholas only to return to where I started.

I decided that it must be fate and I told my conscience to shut up. Being unfaithful in your mind is not being unfaithful at all. I could do this – be the faithful wife of an ordinary teacher in an ordinary life. Until something extraordinary happens, that is.

Chapter 28

Nicholas

Sloane seemed to take it okay and hell, Em, what else could I have done? What kind of a choice did I have with the whole family on my back?

We talked, Marcia and me, back home in the yard, sitting on the porch, looking out at the wooden swings and the old rope dangling from the pink-red maple tree; it looked real pretty, that tree. Made me sad, like I could have made so much more of all the years — you don't get fall colours like that in England. Made me wish we could really start over. Go back to when things seemed sunny, when there was still hope that this all-American guy would turn out to be a proper Bride; *business don't come any better than Bride business, son.*

Marcia, she was so fragile, so alone. The moment she told lover boy he was going to be a dad that was it, he was off; didn't want a tiny thing to do with her once it had gotten complicated. There we were, like two kids, both hurting; her still sore about the other guy, me kidding myself that I could forget about Sloane, move on and do the right thing. Difference was I knew what Marcia's pain was all about. Me, I had to make out that everything about being back in the good old US of A was dandy. After all, I hadn't wanted to go to England in the first place; I could hardly make a fuss about Marcia wanting to come home.

'I do love you,' Marcia says, her head on my shoulder, her eyes all teary, 'Jeez, I'm so sorry about it all, about Jake, us. So sorry that I'll never be a mom, that I can never make you a dad. I'd understand, you know, Nicky,' she says, 'if you want to call it a day – you and me – so you can go have some fun, find someone else, have kids – be a proper family. We're both too old to hang around – you deserve more than anything I can offer you now.'

For one second there I'm tempted. Sloane's supple body, firm skin, her flashing eyes race through my head. Here it is, Nicky-boy, the get-out clause, maybe the sort of excuse that even the old man would buy. Do I deserve something more? 'C'mon now, Marcia, don't say things like that,' I hear myself say. 'We'll get through it. You and me, we'll be okay.'

She nuzzles her silky hair into my neck. 'I'll make it up to you, Nicky, truly I will. I'll start work again soon, I promise. We won't have to rely so much on Mom and Dad. Start over. We can be happy again, can't we?'

She smells clean, like a walk on the beach, and for a moment even I'm sold on the idea, but then it hits me. When were we ever happy before? Hell, the reason we knew for sure that the kid wasn't mine was because Paris was the first time in years we'd made love. That's why she played sick and made me take the trip – so she could get me over there same time as her. Start again; see if we couldn't get Paris to conjure up some kind of a flame. What kind of a marriage is that?

'Hey kids, fancy some lemonade?' Ma Harper shouts us over from the big house.

'Come on, Nicky,' says Marcia. 'Let's go get some. Spend some time with Mom. She missed us so much. Hey, Mom said it might be an idea to get a puppy. What do you think, Nicky? A puppy would be fun, wouldn't it?'

I thought maybe I could handle it. Knuckle down and get back to normal life. But that's just it, Em, nothing was normal after that. I wanted to be good to Marcia, be what she needed me to be but I just couldn't stop thinking about Sloane, at college, in class, in the studio, like I was still in this whole academic world and she was the missing piece.

I kneaded my clay, it was her glorious form I felt beneath my hands; I wrote and it was her critique I wanted to hear; I dressed for dinner, it was in her eyes that I wanted to see how I looked; I took a bath, hers was the body I wanted to press against my clean skin. The only way I could make love with Marcia was if it was Sloane who was inside my head. Oh my God, Em, it was Sloane who was inside my head.

When I saw the invite, I didn't know what to think – Jesus, I was so jealous. This pain just took me over, doubled me up and the aching, Jesus Christ, I wanted her so badly, and the thought of some other guy – this guy Stuart, she'd told me about him, dumped him once already – the thought of his hands all over her, well, I don't mind telling you, Em, it just about crucified me. I couldn't take my eyes off that crumby, cream-coloured piece of shit card:

Miss Felicity Granger and Mr Stuart Bone

Request the pleasure of your company at their wedding on

Saturday 1 July, 1992

11am

At
St Mary's Church, Stamford

RSVP: Catherine Bayes, 77 Casterton Gate Walk, Stamford,
Lincs, PE9 7JN

Jesus Christ, she's going to be Sloane Bone.

I wanted to get on a plane. Wanted to, could barely stop
myself. I had this whole scenario going on in my head where
I'd do that Dustin Hoffman thing in that movie where he goes
and bangs on the windows in the church and runs off with the
bride. Nicholas Bride claiming his bride – yeah that was it.
Why didn't I meet Sloane before all this mess?

So what did I do, Em? Nothing was what I did. Nothing. I
let Marcia just send her some cute little note but I could have
done something, Em, and I didn't. The day of the wedding I
didn't even get out of bed. I wasn't just pretending to be sick, I
was sick; sick in my soul.

Later on that fall, old man Harper pulls some more strings.
Seems like he thought it was high time he took charge and
before I know which way is up, some publishing firm is asking
to see my book. So I take another look at it, think I'll do a little
editing and end up with a total re-write.

You see, now I understand, Em; understand what it is to
have a woman have this power over you, this control, so that

it doesn't matter what you're doing, where you are. You can smell her scent on you, feel her hands on you, like you can never have enough of her. You need her like you need breath; doesn't matter if what you're breathing is toxic – you have to breathe it no matter what. She's in you, around you, outside of you, in your head, her hands on your body, raking through your mind, like magic, like a curse, like something you want and yet you don't want. Something you know that'll never ever go away. It'll never ever damn well go away. In her, out of her, in her, out of her, Jesus Christ, I understand.

And you know what? Here's the laugh; the funny, stupid, pathetic laugh; I spend all that time trying to make this whole story work. To make a little money, cash in on a different angle, write this novel, show the mistress up, just this blood-sucking siren cashing in. But all the time, it's Marcia I'm punishing – Marcia who I saw as this damn groupie, a groupie just like Rodin's mistress and I wanted to write her out, this dumb broad who just took advantage of what she could get; Marcia and the Claudel girl. Dumb broads who just get what they want. But Marcia, she hasn't got much of what she wanted now, has she?

And here I am, you gotta laugh; all my best work comes flowing out and why? You know why, Em, you know why; Sloane has unlocked me. She has shown me places I can go, my work is flying, I am flying and I soar when I take myself back to our moments together. The laugh is on me, Em, the laugh is on me. Instead of writing Rodin's mistress out, I have written my own mistress in.

Chapter 29

Sloane

The good thing about sending wedding invitations to people is that you get to know their addresses.

When I asked Cathy about it, she was hesitant. Why on earth was I inviting them? Was I sure? Did I not think that they were best left alone? But I was adamant and eventually she gave in and passed me a scribbled note, copied from the files that Marcia had left when Cathy took over her job. 'Oh for God's sake, Sloane, do it if you really want to, but I absolutely do not see the point.' *Oh Cathy, no wonder Pete had an affair if you are as naïve as all that.*

I tucked Nicholas and Marcia's address carefully away in the back of my underwear drawer, in between my Cacharel panties and bra. Thank you, Cathy. How very handy to have my lover's address.

I was careful to send my letter in a brown window envelope with a frank mark from school. No sense in stirring up trouble. This was meant for Nicholas's eyes only so no pink scented paper for me, although had Marcia come across it by accident it's not likely I would have cared.

Cathy didn't want to help with the franking at first but I persuaded her that there really was no harm in sending congratulations to someone who's published a book, and no one's going to notice one more piece of post for America in a boarding school full of pupils from overseas.

Stamford, England, 15 October 1993

Dearest Nicholas,

I miss you, I miss you, I miss you. I miss you so much I can hardly breathe. The other day I was standing in the shower and as the water flowed over me I closed my eyes and felt your hands on me in all those places we have shared – that I only ever wanted to share with you. I miss you so much.
I know we promised not to get in touch, but I saw that your book was finally on the shelves and when I read it, oh my darling, you came alive in those pages and I had to let you know that my love for you is as real now as it was two long years ago.

You know that I am married. If I say to you that I believe myself to be married in the same way as you are married I think you will understand what it is that I am telling you. There is a void in my life that only you can fill. I ache for you, Nicholas. The pain never goes away, a constant reminder of what I have lost – what we have lost, my love. I cherish moments alone, away from my husband and the world outside, for in those moments I can focus purely on you, my Nicholas, and the all-consuming love we share. There is only one man for me, Nicholas, and he is miles across the sea.

We agreed we would never again meet, but I am finding that promise impossible to keep; the thought of you now, published (my own attempts have so far been politely declined, although my job with High Travel Holidays is going well), your novel in lights, and not be able at least to hug you and congratulate you in person is a step too far!

Surely there is a place in our lives for one another, however small?

May I suggest a 'grown up meeting' somewhere in the world? Perhaps we could have a meal, a glass of wine or two – whatever you decide. If we are to be friends and nothing more, so be it. That will be enough. It will have to be enough since I find I cannot bear to have none of you, Nicholas. I need to see you. Of course I shall want to touch you, feel your lips on mine. Oh how I have missed your hands on my body and the passion we shared. How I have missed you, my Nicholas. You are my only love, Nicholas, and you always will be.

Cathy will receive any reply you send. Just address it to her:

Catherine Bayes, 77 Casterton Gate Walk, Stamford, Lincs, PE9 7JN, UK

Remember what you said to me that last day of term, the last time I looked into your eyes and felt you close? *Remember that wherever you are, whenever, I shall be loving you then as now.* I say it back to you now, Nicholas, I say it back to you, my one true love.

If I have got this badly wrong, Nicholas, if for you it is all over between us, I will expect to hear nothing.

If you have not replied within a month I will know that life is as you would want it to be and that what we had must be part of our past, delicious memories, which I shall treasure forever. But, oh Nicholas, I want there to be so much more…

Yours always,

Sloane

P.S. Today is my birthday – I think you know that. I wish for only one gift, Nicholas, and you alone know what that is.

Chapter 30

Nicholas

Boston, November 1, 1993

My dearest love,

I adore you. I thought I would burst with joy when I got your note. More than two long years and there you are, back in my life, slipping seamlessly in with just a few lines of ink, my lovely Sloane, incorrigibly popping up with a tenderness, a tenacity and your familiar flair. Not that you have truly been out of my life for one single second of the time we have spent apart.

Did I think it was all over? Could it ever be all over between you and me?

Of course I want to see you, to hear you, hold you, make love to you, slowly, gently, but with a joy that I can only express when I'm wrapped in your embrace.

I never imagined that I could love so completely: the very thought of sitting opposite you in a restaurant (and I must sit where I can read your eyes!), of talking endlessly about everything and nothing, of lying next to you (before or after) makes even the worst days bearable.

Why do I love you so very much? Perhaps because you're so beautiful, so tender with me, so patient with my Virgoan idiosyncrasies, because you take the steam out of my frustration, because you understand my physical and emotional needs; because I can be both ten years older and ten years younger than you; because in your loving care, I am safe. My darling, darling, Sloane, feel safe in my love too.

I love you. You know that I will always love you. How often have I examined that most central strand of my being? Nothing dims; nothing goes away. My only regret is the suffering I have caused and continue to cause you.

All my artificially controlled passion welled up in me as I read your beautiful letter. Need I say that you are always in my thoughts, your love forever locked in my heart?

I, too, very often focus on you – more often when I am alone – and cling to the moments we have shared. I know that they can never be damaged, devalued or destroyed by mundane existence. The void of real passion, real love that we both inhabit intensifies the memory of those most precious moments.

So often, sensory stimuli make me stop in my tracks and think of you, music, places, darkness, sadness. I focus on dates – the day we first met, that first precious time we made love, that awful day when we had to say goodbye, and a nascent, rudimentary awareness of the horoscope world. This meditative process gives me moments of happiness as I recall your sense of humour or my own wonderment at things you have said or the way you have said them.

I will be in New York for a book signing on December 6. I'll be done by four and I'll be in Houlihans Bar, base of the Empire State by about four thirty. Don't worry about Marcia, she won't be there – she's not real keen on this sort of event.

I know this is a long shot – how can I possibly expect you to be there? Although something tells me that in the same way I cannot resist responding to this, you will not be able to resist responding to me.

I want to see you, Sloane, more than anything – more than anything I have ever wanted in my life, but please, please, my darling, try not to put pressure on me. Marcia is still more fragile than you can imagine, still eaten up by what happened and feels it's all her fault she can't have kids. I've been useless, don't know how to help her, what to do, how to love her like I should.

In the meantime, remember that wherever you are, whenever, I shall be loving you then as now.

Yours alone,

Nicholas

Chapter 31

Sloane

So I am the one leading the dance; he is the one who will dance to my tune.

My God, I hate Heathrow, hate flying, in fact. This decision is based on very little knowledge, but if what I have experienced today is anything to go by, then I am not sure that this form of travel is for me. Which begs the question, why work for a travel company? Answer; so far they are the only people who recognise that I can write – but one day I will make all that change.

Getting away was easy. I used my travel vouchers. We get at least one free trip a year and I've been at High Travel longer than that now and I've never asked for any time off. All my journeys since Nicholas left have been in my mind. Maybe I can now begin to make them real.

As far as Stuart was concerned, it was just part of the job; a pre-Christmas trip to New York to prove what I can do – that I am worthy of promotion and mean to be a serious player in the firm. Did I feel guilty? No, Em, I wore deceit well. As he stowed my cases on the train, Stuart pecked me on the cheek and told me to have a good time. 'Don't worry about me,' he said. 'I'll be fine. And if I get lonely, I can always pop round to see Cathy and Pete. Maybe Pete'd like to go to the pub – I'll ask him later when I've done my marking. No peace for the wicked and all that…'

No, Stuart, no peace for the wicked.

The flight is early but JFK is packed and the queue for taxis winds in a snake. I stand impatiently in line, trundling my case behind me, sitting on it now and then when there's no sign of movement from up ahead. I know I have brought too much stuff. Always do and always will but there is one thing I took great care not to forget. As I lifted it from the crisp tissue in the box where it is stored, I shook out the Cacharel dress. More than two years have passed since Nicholas undid these tiny buttons, lifted it gently from my eager limbs. The fierce memory of our first moments of physical love is trapped within its folds, powerful persuasion lest doubt or guilt should tickle at Nicholas' mind. I also took care to pack an extra bundle of sturdy tights.

In front of me is a perfect family – cartoon-cute mop-haired children, one boy, one girl, maybe six years old at most. Mum, perfectly bobbed hair, soft-looking denim, expensive jeans and leather coat, dad, tall, dark and casually smart with ironed seams down his trousers and a green sweater with a logo that looks like something to do with golf. My stomach gives a little lurch. Stuart and I could be like this, I think. I try to bring Stuart into my own perfect picture frame but he refuses to come into focus. 'It's fine,' he says, when he brings up the idea of kids and I shy away, 'we're young, we've got time.' Except, Stuart, the perfect dad for my kids is not so young, he's far away and he's just not you.

I thrust my hand in my pocket, pull out a mint, put it in my mouth and make to move forward, but my shoe sticks on the grubby paving of the airport concourse and I bend to investigate the cause. 'Sod it,' I mumble under my breath and ferret in my tan, leather handbag for a wipe. The little boy peeps out from behind his mum. 'Gross,' he says, as I balance on one leg, leaning myself against my case. I smile and nod as I pull the gum from the heel of my boot. Gross.

'Where to, lady?' God, this guy sounds almost as aggressive as the immigration guys, talk about attitude. Suddenly I am nervous – this bloke could be anyone, take me anywhere. Maybe he has a gun?

I take a deep breath and shove the reservation under the cab driver's nose and he nods. 'You got it,' he says.

What would my parents make of all this, I wonder, or Auntie Jean? Me in a cab in New York; this big, gruff bloke at the wheel, the view across the Van Wyke Expressway of the lofty Empire State and the soaring towers of the World Trade Centre; God, it's impossible to think they tried to blow that up earlier this year.

They'd have seen New York on TV, my mum and dad, read about it in books, heard about the completion of the North Tower on the news, could never have dreamt in a million years of being here, and a lump comes to my throat. I wish they could see through my eyes, to feel the thrill of being somewhere else in the world. What would Mum and Dad make of where I am today – why I am here? They would have loved Stuart, I reflect. I sort of love him myself, like you would love a kind uncle or a favourite pet and for an instant I wish that this could be enough – that I could settle for second best and forget the one that got away. What would my parents have wanted for me?

I shake off my heavy thoughts and bury the nagging melancholy. I am here to meet my lover for the first time in more than two years. Why would my parents not be glad to know that their little girl is happy for a few precious days, a moment in contrast to the many days when she is not?

The driver is silent until we reach the Milford Plaza on 45th Street. 'Here you are, lady,' he says. I pay my fare and he dumps my bags on the pavement and I breathe in New York air, the smell of fresh brewed coffee from the diner, the tangy waft of Asian spice from the take-away and the exhaust fumes of a trillion cars pushing and shoving in the clamour of traffic.

'Watch out, lady, you gonna stand there all day?' says a guy in a loud, pinstriped suit as he steps through the hotel's chrome and glass doors and barges past me into the street, his briefcase swinging from his wrist. No, mister, I am not. I am going to go up to my room, make myself as beautiful as I know how and then I will walk to the foot of the Empire State Building, meet the man of my dreams, seduce him over a cocktail and make him regret every moment he has spent without me in the past two years. That is what I shall do.

I follow signs for reception, up the escalator to the first floor – or the second according to them. Why on earth is there no ground floor in the USA? The clerk behind the desk wears her hair drawn up in a bun. She has glasses most of the way down her aquiline nose and she taps repeatedly on the page with a chewed biro where she checks for my name.

'You have a reservation for a double room, is that right, ma'am?'

'Yes, a double.' I think she sees 'mistress' writ tall across my face and, blushing, I fiddle with my bag and hook out my passport, which she goes off to copy. I shove my hand in my pocket, grab another mint and suck on it hard. I can't wait to brush my teeth. There is still a nasty taste in my mouth.

I've always wondered why they supplied sick bags on planes. It's when the stewardesses sat down that my stomach really began to heave – not so much from the big dipper turbulence of the 747, more I think from fright. God, if the cabin crew have to sit down it must be bad, A white shaft of fear welled up in me resulting in a disgusting mess, which first time around only just made it into the bag, and then once the seat belt sign went off, made it several times more into the loo.

'Okay now, here's your passport and your key, Ma'am. The elevators are right ahead of you to your left and your room is on the tenth floor. Have a nice day now. Next please...'

I hurry across the road, cutting through the Avenue of the Americas on my way to Fifth Avenue. 'Walk,' 'Don't Walk,' says the sign at the traffic lights. I am going to keep walking; it's a matter of moments only until I see Nicholas for the first time in over two years. Despite the crisp sun, there is a chill breeze gusting up the road and I turn the collar of my red woollen coat up and wrap the cream cashmere scarf around my neck, tucking it to my chest. The Cacharel dress is no match for the season but it is what I wore then and what I have to wear now. My long, tan leather boots are not as comfortable as they could be and they chafe a little at the heel. I stop momentarily and adjust their fit and walk on satisfied with the small improvement I have made.

If I walked up this street in the normal way the glittering shops either side of the road would be beckoning me in. The window displays are ripe with Christmas pickings and decorated with stars, fir trees, angels, elves and Santas on sleighs, but my heart isn't beating to the tune of a shopping spree. My heart is beating to the rhythm of a love affair that I have kept wrapped up inside me all this time.

Tiffany's, Oh my God, Tiffany's. *Breakfast at Tiffany's* – Audrey Hepburn and all that. How can I be here at all?

I smile thinking of Meg Ryan in another film, engaged to the wrong man and picking items for her bottom drawer in the famous shop. A 'hope chest', I think they call it in America. I went to see the movie with Cathy one wet Saturday at a special showing in the Arts Centre not long ago. 'Why on earth would you want to go and see *Sleepless in Seattle*?' Cathy said. 'I just fancy something fun and light,' I replied. *It's because it also takes place in New York, Cathy, and that's where I shall be with Nicholas not one month from now.* Was there any hope in my chest when I married Stu? Only the hope that I would one day be back with Nicholas comes the honest answer from deep inside.

Oh my God, there's Macy's says a squeal in my head, and I dodge a thousand yellow cabs to cross the street and stare for a moment at the extraordinary mannequins and twirling, swirling figures in the window, depicting the fairy tale scenes of my childhood, Sleeping Beauty, Snow White, Cinderella and more.

I am only twenty-nine years old, in New York and about to meet my lover. Surely there is a fairy tale left for me?

I cross another street and look up into the sky. There is the Empire State Building and I think of how many times my Auntie Jean would watch another famous film – the one with Cary Grant and Deborah Kerr: Da, daaa, da-da, da da daaa, da da, da, daaa, da-da, da, da, daaa, da, da, the theme to *An Affair to Remember* purrs away in my head.

This is the city of movie moments and I want to have mine. I feel ten feet tall. My hair is freshly washed, it's grown a lot since last I saw Nicholas – I couldn't bear to think of his wife having longer hair than mine. I look good, my new leather boots, matching bag, and scarlet coat; *for a scarlet woman?* I push away the thought and surge forward with the crowd. The sky is turning violet orange as the sun goes down and I am nearly there. Another road to cross: carefully does it, Sloane, this is not the movie to get run over in. I want this not to be an affair to forget.

I have no idea where to find the entrance to the bar and I slow down, not wanting to seem clumsy or desperate. I want to stroll in with an air of insouciance – that same nonchalant scent that Nicholas gave off when I watched him from across the street that first time we met outside the bookstore in Paris. Here we are together in another of the world's great capitals of romance. I want romance again with a capital R.

I check my watch. It is just coming up to five o'clock. I am fashionably late. I had a horror of being here gauchely early. I search the faces of the commuters, the tourists, the hurly burly of people pushing and shoving their way to hotels, to theatres, restaurants, to their children, wives and mistresses, to bed.

'Excuse me, excuse me, please,' I say. I am relieved when the woman I have accosted does not spit in my face or swear at my presumption. She is much older than I am, the lines on her brow parading the legacy of her life. She wears a faded fur coat, mink, I think. Her hair is carefully coiffed, soft waves sprayed into place, not moving a jot in the icy wind. On her hands, gloves, but on one finger she wears a large gemstone ring over the deep brown leather.

'Do you know where the entrance to Houlihan's bar is, please?' I ask.

'Sure, it's just around the corner. You can't miss it — there's a guy on the door,' she replies.

'Thank you,' I say, and I turn to go but she reaches out. 'I recommend the Blue Lagoon,' she says, holding on to my arm. Then she looks me up and down, 'And better make sure he's worth it, honey,' she says and she reaches up and pats me twice on the cheek, 'you sure better make sure he's worth it.'

She walks off into the crowd and I touch the place she has touched, the cold of the leather still marking the spot on my face. I walk slowly around the corner, my hand still up to my cheek and I lean against the glass pane and try to catch my breath.

Oh God, I hate it when things like this happen. Unexplained things, things that set you on edge, nudge you off course. I try to shake off the feeling that this is one of those moments — a stupid little moment but the feeling that I should treat the weight of her words as something significant just won't go away. I feel in my pocket and draw out the pale green envelope, open it and slide out the sheets of matching paper. Maybe I just need to read Nicholas's letter once more, remind myself why I am here.

But then I hear my name; 'Sloane, Sloane. I'm here.' Nicholas is standing a few yards further on, holding open the door to the bar. I open my bag and stuff the letter quickly in, walk towards him and he takes me in his arms. I catch sight of the woman in the fur coat, waiting to cross the road and she looks back over her shoulder straight into my eyes. She smiles and shakes her head sadly as she turns away when the sign says 'Walk'.

Chapter 32

Nicholas

Did Marcia suspect anything? I don't know, but it was like she was watching my every move. When I was packing she was in and out of the bedroom, taking the odd thing from her closet, asking silly questions, 'What time did you say you were leaving, honey? Mom says would you like some of her brownies to take with you? You know how you love those cherry ones she bakes…'

It was all I could do not to lose patience, so when Sloane was late to the bar, I got real antsy. Thought for one moment she wasn't coming after all. I hadn't counted on it for definite, don't get me wrong. But after everything we'd said in our letters, after all this time not seeing her, wanting her like she said she wanted me, I just thought she would have no choice. She would have to be there just the same as there was no way it would be me that wouldn't show. And let's not forget it – she's the one who contacted me.

The book event went real well; pictures taken for the *New York Times* and all. I felt like I had really made it, this whole line of people just wanting to talk to me. For the first time this was something I'd done on my own, a big fat step towards independence from old man Harper. Live the kind of life Marcia wants us to live or at least her folks want us to live without having to take his damn hand-outs. Deep down, of course, I knew it was old man Harper who got the book in front of the right people in the first place – but how the hell else do you get published these days anyhow? *Not what you know it's who you know, son, that's the important thing.*

And my dad, well he seemed real proud. For the first time I reckon he thought he had something to be proud about and all his frat friends, well their wives at least, they all went straight out and bought my book and queued up at one of Mom's coffee mornings to have their copies signed. You could almost see the feathers of the old peacock fanning out – my dad was so proud.

Makes it all the more difficult, this thing with Sloane; disappointing them all over again now's just not an option. Far as they're concerned everything in the garden is rosy. Okay, there aren't any adorable little grandkids running about the garden but I guess we've all just learnt to live with that particular one.

But the big fat trouble is that living without Sloane's not an option either. I guess we both just knew that one of us would be in touch with the other in the end; just a question of time. But she was the brave one – the one that made what we both wanted a possible reality. I sure as hell needed her to turn up.

On the way over to the bar I picked up a bag of chestnuts from a street seller along the way. I was hungry, no time for lunch what with all the chatting and signing. It was the smell that got me; that sweet nutty smell. It was like I was back in Paris again, Sloane walking by my side, not real happy with me that first day but that electricity between us, that was unmistakable.

Jesus, I hope we both still feel that. It never occurred to me that the spark might have gone out.

She was half an hour late when I saw her. She was leaning against the window like she was out of breath or something and then she looked kind of panicked. She had my letter in her hand. That letter, Jeez, reckon I took longer to write that letter than my whole darn book. Didn't want her to be disappointed – wanted it to do justice to how I felt about what we shared. I wanted to write like one of her literary heroes. I guess it did the trick.

Looked like she was checking she was in the right place so I headed on out and called her in. When she turned to me I knew there was no danger of the spark having left. Holding her was like those two years were only a yesterday away, but then once we got settled at the bar it seemed to get kinda awkward.

'You look good. No, you look great.' She smiles and her eyes light up.

'You too, Nicholas.'

'Na, I'm looking older and I'm looking tired. You wouldn't believe the day I've had.'

'Maybe I would, Nicholas, why don't you tell me all about it?' So I tell her about my day at Barnes and Noble and how pleased the bookstore was with my sales. We're being polite with one another. She shifts a little in her seat and I see her looking at my wine. Jesus Christ, I've forgotten to offer her a drink. I dig in my pocket and bring out a wad of dollar bills.

'Jesus, I'm so sorry. Where are my manners? What can I get you to drink?' I wave at the bottles stacked on the shelves in front of us. The place is heaving with folk, grabbing a drink after work or before a show and the bartender is doing somersaults in his effort to keep up. 'There's quite a choice,' I say.

She answers in less than a heartbeat; 'A 'Blue Lagoon' please.'

I look at her sideways. How the hell does she know what to order in a random place in New York? She giggles. Jeez, that's a heavenly sound. I can't remember the last time I heard Marcia laugh. 'I had it recommended to me,' she says.

'Here you go,' says the bartender. 'That one'll blow your little lady's mind.'

She takes a sip through the straw and wrinkles her nose. 'Wow, she says, 'do you think it's called a Blue Lagoon because it makes you feel like you're drowning?'

It's so long since I heard her speak I had almost forgotten the charm of her very British clipped vowels, like Lady Di when we hear her on CNN. I think the news channels call her Diana, Princess of Wales, but to all of us here in the States, she'll always be Lady Di. Sloane here is my very own princess. No, don't laugh, I do know that sounds corny but I guess what I'm trying to say is that she's my princess because she makes me feel like a prince.

My Sauvignon Blanc is going warm so I order some ice to cool it down.

'So, how was the flight?'

'Don't ask,' she says.

Okay, I'll try something else.

'Did you have to stand in line long at Immigration?'

'Nope, not really – twenty minutes or so. They warned me at work how long it can take so it was quite a pleasant surprise. Rude though, I thought they were all pretty rude.'

'Something else pretty interesting came up today,' I say.

'Really? What's that, Nicholas?'

'I met this guy who's looking into doing some restoration work on the Château de l'Islette – it's this awesome castle in France where Rodin and Camille Claudel used to meet for, you know, hidden way, all romantic. Out in the Loire Valley. He did his famous bust of Balzac there and she did *La Petite Châtelaine* – the little girl who lived there. Claudel modelled this little girl time after time after she had, well, she had an abortion. I guess you won't have heard of it. I...'

'Of course I have,' she says. 'I've read your book, haven't I? And I can't believe you don't remember that we saw that sculpture of the little girl together in Paris. 'The Little Mistress', didn't you call it?

'And before you ask, I was a French teacher remember, before all this?' she waves her hand towards me and then back to herself, 'so I also know that Balzac is a famous French writer who lived in that part of France.'

Oh, God, I am getting this so wrong. That was damned crass and damned stupid. She's right. I should've remembered seeing that sculpture with her. I change the subject fast.

'And Cathy, how's she?'

'She's fine, Nicholas. Pete's fine, I'm fine, Stuart's fine, we're all fine. I didn't travel all this way for you to find out who's fine and who isn't did I? And why do you keep looking at your watch?'

I hadn't been aware that I was. Truth is I'd promised Marcia I'd phone early evening – it's what we always do when I'm staying away. I was going to do it before Sloane arrived but then got worried that Marcia would wonder why I wasn't calling at the usual time.

'For fuck's sake, Nicholas, this is stupid. Are you expecting someone here? What's going on? It feels like you're not really with me. I haven't seen you for more than two years and all you can do is check your watch. I might as well go now…'

'Whoa, Sloane, I'm sorry. I am sorry. It's just, I need to call Marcia, or she'll think there's something up. Just give me a minute. Two seconds and I'll be back.'

The barman directs me to the back of the room and I go to get up. 'I'll be real quick,' I say. 'The phone's just over there – you won't even notice I'm away.'

'Leave now, Nicholas,' says Sloane, 'and by the time you get back I'll be gone.'

Chapter 33

Sloane

It was a stupid thing to say, stupid, and ridiculously immature, but in that moment I just lost it. I just felt so damn jealous of Marcia, like he was never out of her clutches even for just one second. I felt cheap; I felt worthless. And he didn't even notice I wore the dress. Why not tell him how it made me feel instead of playing a silly childish her-or-me game? But life's not like that and hindsight is a wonderful thing.

He hesitates. His eyes dart first towards the telephone booth then back to me and finally back to the telephone booth again. *Oh my God, he's going to choose her.*

An instant before he moves, I move. It's less painful than watching him walk away. In a flurry, I unhook my bag from the bar stool, gather my coat and scarf and look into Nicholas's bewildered face. What am I going to say? There's so much to say but it's trapped inside my chest and if any of what is stored there spills out then surely there will be no stopping the flow. I can scarcely trust myself to speak. I will not cry. I have come all this way and all he can think of is his wife.

'Sloane, don't do this, Sloane…'

I pick up my Blue Lagoon and down it in one. 'Thanks for the drink, Nicholas, very kind. Have a nice life,' is all I can manage to say and I bang the glass down. The barman looks around. He thinks I need another cocktail and starts to head our way, but sensing the friction of the moment, he raises his hands in front of him, as if fending us off, and he turns his attention to someone else. 'Yeah, what's it to be, Sir?' I hear him say.

In a few short paces I am at the door and I swing it open, ignoring the 'have a great evening now, ma'am,' from the doorman as I stomp past. I have no idea which way to go and I blindly cross the only street where the sign says 'Walk,' bundling myself into my coat as I go.

'Sloane, Sloane. Don't go, Sloane.' I hear Nicholas behind me. He has followed me, this is good. My heart gives a little leap but my brain is still stuck on petulant so I do not slow down. Make him work for it now I'm this upset. But what if he gives up – is this how I want it to end?

I slow my pace almost imperceptibly but enough for him to catch up without knowing that it is what I have allowed. Nicholas puts his hand out, grabs me by the elbow and spins me around to face him. 'Sloane,' he says, and then he kisses me. It feels like coming home. He pushes me into a shop doorway and combs his fingers through my hair. He slips his hand under my coat and moves it up my body to my breasts. 'Sloane, Sloane,' he murmurs between his kisses, 'Sloane, my beautiful Sloane.'

My bag swings off my shoulder to the crook of my arm as I bring my hands up to his face and cup both his cheeks. 'Oh, Nicholas, I'm so sorry, so sorry. I've missed you so much. What an idiot… I just couldn't bear…'

'Hush, Sloane, hush. It doesn't matter. It's okay, baby, I get it, I understand. I've been so jealous of Stuart, you have no idea. I love you, I never stopped loving you, never will.'

He kisses my neck. His grey cashmere coat is awkward over his arm. He bends a little and lets his coat slide to the floor and as he does so, he buries his head in my chest. He stands back and holds my coat a little further open. 'Sloane, oh my God, Sloane, look what you're wearing. This dress, Sloane, you wore the dress... how could I not notice that you're wearing the dress?'

An elderly couple pass by the doorway where we are framed in the pink light from a neon sign. They have the tiniest dog on a lead – Chihuahua maybe – and it stops to do its business on the edge of the kerb. The man wears a tweedy, overlong greatcoat and a trilby hat. He stares straight at us then looks at his wife and nudges her. 'Must be cut price, eh Dolores, in the window of Daffy's,' he says, pointing up at the sign above the shop.

'Hush, Ed,' she says, 'they'll hear you.'

'Let's go, Sloane,' Nicholas says. Marcia can wait.'

Chapter 34

Nicholas

I know I should've called her. I always call her when I'm away, but with Sloane walking out on me like that I just had to follow after her. I meant to call Marcia later, but honestly, one thing just led to another and before you know it, the two of us are back at her hotel.

The desk clerk cocks her head to one side when Sloane goes to fetch her key. She hands her a note. 'Excuse me, Ma'am. You had a call while you were out – I typed out the message for you. Have a good night, Mrs Bone,' she says with a little bit of an uncalled-for emphasis on the missus to my mind.

Sloane leans her head on my shoulder as the elevator takes us up to level ten. She opens the envelope and unfolds the note and I read it at the same time as her. It's from Stuart:

Hope you had a great evening in the Big Apple.

All fine here but miss you. Enjoy your lunch with Gina – hope all goes well.

Love you, Stu.

'Oh my God,' says Sloane. I completely forgot about Gina. Good job that Stuart reminded me. I have to go to our office here tomorrow – part of the deal.'

So the great Stuart misses her. I would miss her too if she were mine. I wouldn't let this lady out of my sight for a single moment if she were mine.

She puts the key in the lock and pushes open the door. Instead of switching on the light she weaves past her bag on the floor, she walks around the bed and she goes and stands between the two windows. It's a corner room so you can look out over Manhattan both ways. She looks beautiful in the silver white light of the moon. Her hair is longer, it really suits her like that; it's lighter around her face, pretty. She is a masterpiece framed in the window. How can I ever let her go?

'Look, Nicholas,' she says. 'That *is* a cruise ship over there, isn't it? I saw it earlier. Don't you think it would be amazing to go on a cruise? To cruise into New York, like they do in the films? I have to write about it sometimes – for the High Travel brochures. Always wonder how on earth they get under the bridge? The Brooklyn isn't it?'

I look out the window to where she's pointing. 'Yeah, that's one of the places they dock. The Verrazano – that's the one they have to come under. I guess that bridge must be some 220 feet high – high enough anyways. They've always made it so far…'

'God, Nicholas, if we could just get on a ship and never come back.'

I grab a hold of her collar and slide her coat down her back. She shrugs it off and turns to face me. Some of her buttons are still undone from where I touched her breasts in the doorway. We were interrupted by some smart-arse elderly couple. It turns me on, the idea of her walking through New York with her buttons undone, her black lacy bra on show. I finish the job and open the dress wide. It falls off her shoulders and she steps out of it, pushing it to one side with the toe of her boot.

She's standing there in her stockings, French knickers and push-up bra, still wearing her knee-length boots and it's all I can do not to come there and then. She does a little wiggle and pulls the leg of her panties just a fraction to one side and strikes a little pose.

'They're Janet Reger – the bra and knickers. Do you like them? Same designer as Joan Collins wore in *The Stud*. I bought them just for you.'

Jesus, what's not to like? This woman is just so hot. Can I imagine Marcia going out and buying sexy lingerie just for me? Not a chance.

I take off my jacket and chuck it onto her bag. I reach for her but she pulls away. 'Sit there,' she says, pointing to a chair at the end of the bed.

There's a pile of something on the seat, and I can't sit down without moving whatever it is that's there. I take a hold of it. Jesus Christ, it's a whole bunch of pantyhose. I look up at her and she's laughing. There's a real nice glint in her eye.

Sloane lies on the bed and with her left hand she pulls the panties all the way over to one side and holds herself open. She licks a finger on the other hand and touches herself between her legs. It's like all the fantasies I've ever had all rolled into one. I watch for a while. Christ, she's sexy, and then I go to get up, but she rolls straight off the bed.

Sloane pushes me back into the chair and unbuttons my shirt. Her cool hands are on my skin and I am in Paris more than two years ago discovering what physical love is all about for the first time. She plants little kisses on my chest. She unzips me and pulls off my pants and my underwear. Still she tells me not to touch and I go along with it, enjoying her little game. She turns around and bends over, real deliberate, like she wants me to see, and she picks up the pile of pantyhose and drops them behind her on the bed.

She cocks her leg up and places her boot on my knee then lets her leg slide down the outside of my thigh so she sitting right astride one leg. She unhooks her bra and lets it fall to the floor. She leans in and kisses my neck. Her smell is deep, earthy, sensual, unmistakably Sloane.

She stands again and lets her breasts brush over my mouth. She lifts the other leg and lowers it past mine so that now she is sitting full on my lap and I'm sticking up in front of her like my dick belongs to her not me. What am I saying? It *does* belong to her; has done since that first time in Paris.

She leans right down to one side. Her hair is soft on my shoulders as it swings over in rhythm with her. She grabs my hand and bends it behind my back. Swiftly she ties it to the chair and then she fastens my other hand and both my feet. Finally she trusses me around each thigh. Paris, Christ, Paris in New York. Well, what do you know?

'Is this what you want, Nicholas?' she whispers in my ear.

'Jesus, Sloane, you know it's what I want.'

As she lowers herself onto me I can't budge an inch. But then why the hell would I want to? *Tie me up, Sloane, tie me up…*

Chapter 35

Sloane

'God, it's a beautiful day!'

'Not half as beautiful as you,' Nicholas replies, putting his arm around my shoulder as we cross Central Park.

'I've always wanted to come here — how amazing that it's with you.'

Nicholas turns me towards him and kisses me. His breath is warm in the chill air. The sun is shining in New York and I am the sort of happy I could never imagine being, happy with this man by my side.

We slept together last night – all night in the same bed and when each time I woke up, first at two o'clock then at four thirty, I had to pinch myself to make sure it wasn't all a dream.

Feeling his warm skin first thing this morning; watching the half-surprise, half-delight in his eyes when he opened them and saw me there, God, could I have ever imagined? He rolled over onto me and we made love gently, kindly, no tricks, no drama, just tenderness and love and it made me cry. 'Sloane, what is it? You okay?' How do you explain to someone that *that* kind of intimacy – it's like you are alive for the very first time. Maybe he sees it in my eyes, in my touch. I think maybe he reads me like I read him. I want it so much.

'Come on now, or we won't have time…'

Nicholas leads me down a pathway between the trees; woodland walkways in the heart of the city open into glades, lined with fragrant plants, rockeries and shrubs. This place is magical – I have to say it – magical – there is no other word. If elves and penguins and reindeer and mice dressed as footmen all landed here at once I wouldn't bat an eyelid. This is Central Park; it's what I expect.

The mosaic is just ahead in a clearing. On the floor the word IMAGINE is engraved in capital letters. I'm too young to have been a big Lennon fan but I know my Mum loved the Beatles so I hope she sees whatever I am seeing today – she would so have loved to be in this very spot with my dad by her side.

'So this is where he lived?' I ask Nicholas.

'Just over there in The Dakota on West 72nd,' he replies.

'And that's where he was killed? God, how sad! This mosaic is incredible – and so many flowers and candles.'

'It was sent from Naples, matter of fact. Yoko gave a ton of money but donations came in from all over the world. People have no idea.'

We stroll a little further and Nicholas points out an engraved brass plaque. 'See there – that's a list of all the nations that sent money for Strawberry Fields.'

There is a tap on my shoulder, 'Excuse me, Miss. Please? You take picture?' I take the camera from the Japanese girl who stuffs her red beret into her rucksack, pushes back her blue-black satin hair, removes her tartan jacket and poses by the plaque in a yellow sweater, denim skirt, stripy tights and trainers.

'Come on, come on, quick, quick,' she says, beckoning over a tall guy in a beige duffle coat. He has cropped blond hair and very blue eyes – definitely not from Japan. He puts his arm around her. The height difference is so great that it's hard to find the right focus in the viewfinder; I zoom in and his head's off the shot, I zoom out and the plaque and the girl seem minute. Finally I press the button and they are all thanks and praise.

'On holiday?' I ask.

The tall guy answers. 'Vee are on honeymoon,' he says, 'vee got married in Chermany, it is now one week, yes, and then we go after to Chapan.' The tiny girl puts her arms around his waist and beams up at him.

'Oh, how wonderful,' I clasp my hands together, 'have a lovely time.' They gather their belongings and stroll off hand in hand and my tears start to fall.

'Sloane, what is it, Sloane? Are you okay?'

'I'm fine, Nicholas. Fine,' I lie and I walk off down the path.

In silence we cross the road at the end of the park and stroll back up Fifth Avenue.

'Hey, you want to see something?' Nicholas asks. Without waiting for an answer he takes my hand, pulls me off to the right and leads me across the street.

Ahead of us is a concourse, flags flying and people are milling – a kaleidoscope of folk from all over the world. There is a buzz in the nip of the air.

'Look,' Nicholas says.

I peer over the railings, knowing already what it is I will see. This is the ice rink I've written about in *Christmas in New York*, a High Travel Holidays special, but I never dreamed I would ever be here to see it in real life. Bizarre, really, writing about all these places in the world, persuading all those lucky people to take this cruise, jump on this plane, visit this theme park, that monument and yet never going anywhere much yourself. Still, leafing through all the info from Operations is kind of like taking a holiday. I can forget myself in the brochures and the dazzling snaps sent in by the reps; forget that I still live in Stamford and that the person I love is an ocean away.

'Wow, what an amazing tree.'

'It's Rockefeller, what do you expect?' Nicholas puts his arm around me and we lean over, watching the skaters. The sun sends out spears of light as it catches their blades as they spin. Some of them are really good, showing off. I take a deep breath. I turn to face Nicholas and push my fingers back through the flop of hair on his forehead. I let my breath out and it is a white cloud in the cold.

'I am so in love with you, Nicholas Bride.' Nicholas grins, a cheesy, lop-sided grin.

'Here, there's something more.' Nicholas takes my hand again and leads me around the corner to a narrow avenue of trees, their boughs looped together with red satin ribbon supporting a host of dancing angels.

'It's all so beautiful, Nicholas. Magical.'

'Here's where the magic is…' Nicholas leads me into a shop. It's a Christmas shop – I have never in my life seen one of these.

'What happens here if it's not Christmas? I ask.

'It's always Christmas here,' he replies.

It's lovely mooching amongst all the sparking, glittering objects. Some are pretty tragic, for sure, naff doesn't even begin to describe it, but amongst the more tacky decorations are some real gems. I browse the tree ornaments and untangle one, setting it free and I dangle it from my index finger so that the crystals catch the light. I hurry to the counter and pay before

Nicholas cottons on and I pop my parcel into my bag. I look at my watch. It's almost time for my meeting and Nicholas has to go too.

'What time does the symposium end?' I ask Nicholas as we head down towards Macy's.

'It'll be over by four. Say, why don't you stop by for cocktails – we'll be having Champagne, smoked salmon, that kind of thing.'

I think myself into the role – guest of Nicholas Bride. Will they wonder at the mystery woman who sounds like a Brit? Will they ask? Will they maybe think I'm his wife?

Suddenly I feel like a fake. Role playing – that's what I am doing here, playing make-believe like some love-struck kid with a crush. I stop in my tracks. It takes Nicholas several paces to realise I am not keeping up and he turns back to me, then retraces his steps until he reaches the place where I stand.

'Nicholas, I don't know how to say this but I've just got to say it and whatever happens then happens.

'I can't handle it anymore. I know I promised and I said it was a promise I would keep, but seeing you again, being with you like this…' I feel his muscles tense. He sucks his lips in so that his mouth is a fine line. I've begun what I need to say. No point in not saying all the other words that will make these words make sense – the only sense as far as I'm concerned.

'Nicholas, I need you to leave Marcia. I know I promised, but I love you too much. I need you to leave Marcia and be with me.' There, I have made him have to choose.

Nicholas turns to face me and puts his hands on my shoulders. 'Sloane, Sloane,' he says with a sigh, 'did you not think I might see that one coming?'

The offices are on the corner of Sixth Avenue and 19th and easy to find since they are right next door to the massive Burlington Coat Factory, much fêted as the bargain store of choice by High Travel colleagues in New York. I swing through the glass doors bang on time and hover in reception, waiting for someone to appear.

Sometimes you have an idea of what a person's going to be like when you speak to them on the phone and it turns out to be completely wrong. Gina is the opposite of that. She is exactly the slightly dumpy, not-very-tall, bubbly creature I imagined her to be, and she definitely has plenty of people on *her* balcony – around about a 32E worth, I'd say.

'Aw, Gee, sorry ya had to wait – just had to visit the restrooms. Sure is nice ta meet ya, Sloane,' she says, unfolding her arms from beneath the ample bosom. 'I'm Gina, *Regina* originally – guess my folks had a sense of humour.' I feel myself blush and I cough. Why do we always do that? Like it's going to make it go away?

'Think nothing of it,' she says, 'everybody makes the rhyme in their head. It's why I get it over with straight off.' She cackles loudly, hugging me like I am an old friend.

'I got us some lunch here if that's okay wij you?' It sounds like she's sneezing – a sort of *wichoo*. I am dying to ask about her accent but think it might be rude.

'Here, have a try of this. It's pretty good stuff. The bahs brings it back from Seneca Falls – fabulous wineries around there.' *Ah, she means boss.*

'So, Sloane, I heard you got yerself all hitched up last year. Congratulations,' she says, chinking her glass with mine. 'How're you enjoying married life?'

'It's different,' I say.

'Lucky you hey, finding Mr Right.'

'Yes, lucky me,' I reply, 'yes, it does rather look like I have finally found my Mr Right.'

There is very little need for me to speak at all over lunch. Gina carries the conversation from sales through marketing to her family and friends and back again. It is exhausting just hearing her talk. I never do catch where she is from and I never do ask. My mind is too full of my conversation with Nicholas and I feel guilty that I am rewarding this nice lady's efforts with a miraculously timely 'wow' or a 'brilliant', having sometimes not heard a single word.

'Just give me a little time,' Nicholas had said when he left me that lunchtime, pain etched in the crinkles around his eyes. 'It's what I want too, God knows, it's what I want. I just need a little time to help Marcia to adjust to the idea. She's got her family and all but I just need to get the timing right.'

I am walking on air. Oh yes, Gina. I have finally got my Mr Right.

I freshen up in Macy's on the way. I 'borrow' a little blusher and lip gloss from the testers in the huge, brightly lit beauty hall, and I buy a clip shaped like a poinsettia en route to the loo. I comb my hair in the cloakroom and, gathering up my locks, plant the pretty, star-shaped hair clip on the side of my head, nodding in approval at how well it matches my coat.

I am feeling all Christmassy, I decide, and I smile at my reflection in the glass as I make my way back down the escalators and back into the street. It is only a step and a hop and I will be back with Nicholas once more.

I enter the building at dead on 4:00PM. I can't see Nicholas at first and I get a nervous fizz in my stomach. Look at all these college types, their cord jackets, well cut pants (*well, now aren't I the little Americophile*, I say to myself. Are trousers a thing of the past?). Jesus, they look pretty important – guess Nicholas is pretty important too. I move a little further into the room.

There he is, I spot him and give a little wave. He sees me and frowns. He shakes his head rapidly but with tiny, staccato movements. He raises his brows high and gives a half nod to the man standing to his left, urgent appeal in his eyes. I stand still, shrug my shoulders and mouth 'what?' and he tilts his head to the right, indicating the door marked 'restrooms', says a few words to the men he is with and strides off. I cross the room and head that way.

'Sloane, Sloane!' I think I hear my name behind me but decide it's not possible, a phantom noise in a crowded room but then I hear it again and turn.

And there she is – shiny, gently waving long, dark hair, cream lace sweater, black, hip-hugging knee-length skirt and on her feet, tiny black patent shoes. The heel is small but just enough to lift her slender frame, and across the front of each shoe is an emblem, Gucci, I believe. Around her swan neck is a string of pink grey pearls and her pearl-drop earrings are a perfect match. Of course.

'Sloane, oh my God, fancy seeing you here. Well what do you know? Dad, come over here a minute – look who's here. This is Sloane – we used to work together in Stamford. Sloane, meet Abe, my dad, Dad, this is Sloane.'

I am redder than my coat and I can't breathe. How can this be happening? Now?

'Well, hello, young lady, good to meet you.' Abe Harper grabs my hand, squeezes it between both of his and enthusiastically propels it up and down. 'Anyone who's worked in that venerated hall of academia must be someone special, eh Marcia? Sorry – what was your name again?'

'Sloane. Sloane Granger.'

'Ha – like Sloane Square eh? Used to take Mrs Harper to Peter Jones when we visited London in the seventies. Almost liked it as much as she liked Harrods, eh, Marcey? What was the name of that place we used to stay? Grosvenor – that was the place.' He pronounces it Gros-ven-nor, but now is not a moment to intervene on matters linguistic, and my panic mounts as I see Nicholas heading back this way.

'Wow, it's Sloane, isn't it?' He puts his hand flat on his heart. 'Nicholas. You remember,' he says. 'I did the Harper year at school. Don't tell me you came all the way to New York for a little after-school reunion?' He looks at Marcia and Abe and they all laugh. 'Although, I guess my poster's kind of hard to miss.' He nods towards the front of a building where a large hoarding proclaims him speaker of the day. I take my cue.

'Well no, I mean, I'm here on business – I work for a travel company now – High Travel.'

'Yeah, Cathy told me you were doing that,' Marcia says.

God, so those two are still in touch. Cathy's never said...

'Anyway, I just came from a meeting with Gina – she runs the office over here – and I saw your poster – thought that maybe Marcia was here – and here you are. In fact.' I laugh brightly, fix a smile on my face, hitch my bag higher on my shoulder and hold out my hand.

'Well, I can see you're all very busy so I'll... lovely meeting you, Mr Harper. Good to see you two again, I'll just...' Abe doesn't take my hand and I drop it back down to my side.

'Whoa, young lady! You don't get away from old Abe that easily. And you haven't met Marcia's mom. She's a big fan of the school – made me what I am today and my daddy before me. Trust me she'll be real mad if I let you get away.'

'But, I don't think…' I try not to look at Nicholas. I need another cue. I can't help but glance up but he is looking the other way. I am on my own.

'I hope they're putting you up somewhere real nice,' Abe continues.

'Actually it's not that… the Milford Plaza, off Times Square, it's fine. Location-wise, it's fine.'

'Feel sure that someone as charming as you deserves the Waldorf, hey Nicky?' He elbows his son-in-law in the ribs. 'Help me out here, Nicky. We can't let this little lady loose in New York, now can we? How about you join us for dinner? It'll give you kids a chance to catch up. Caesar'll pick you up from your hotel around six o'clock.'

I open my mouth, protestation on my tongue but Abe turns and walks off.

'Don't bother,' Nicholas says wryly. 'He always gets what he wants.'

'But I…'

'Nonsense,' says Marcia. 'You must join us. And in the meantime, Sloane, you and I need to have a talk.'

Chapter 36

Nicholas

Jesus Christ, Em, I knew I should have called her. When I got back to the apartment on 72nd there were nine messages, all from Marcia, wondering why I hadn't been in touch – why I wasn't there to take her call. I should have just called her from Sloane's hotel, from any-damn-where. Two minutes is all it would of needed just to make things okay.

So Marcia, she gets herself all in a stew. She decides she's worried enough to make it a whole damn family outing. She gets the goddamn chauffeur to drive them over four hours all the way to New York, a great big fucking 'surprise'.

Jeez, I can just picture the scene and hear the whole damn plot:

Marcia: 'I'm worried, Mom, it's not like Nicky not to call.'

Ma H: 'Don't you fret now, honey. He'll be just fine. He's likely just fallen straight to sleep after all that signing he's had to do.'

Marcia: 'But still, he's had a lot going on, Mom, what with me, the book and everything. Maybe we should give him a little more support. After all, it's not every day you get to address a convention in New York.'

Ma H: 'So what do you have in mind, honey?'

Marcia: 'Hey, Mom, wouldn't it be something if you, me and dad just went up and paid him a visit – surprised him over cocktails? Be there for him, I mean. It'd be fun to spend the day in New York – have dinner in the apartment.'

Nancy: 'Well now, Marcey, that's quite an idea – haven't been there in quite some time. Kind of miss seeing the old place, now you come to mention it. I could always call Bella – she'd go round and fix it up. Let's see if your dad'll come too. 'bout time we spent a day together...'

A nice little drama to cheer up their idle, stinking day; Let's just go find Nicky in case he gets too happy, happy without us around. Let's just go remind him who he is with our chauffeur-driven car, our fancy address, cook, housemaid, connections and stinking dollar bills.

Trust Abe Harper to come and take over the show.

When I left Sloane that lunchtime, I had thirty minutes to change and be back at the club. I heard the messages and called Marcia but hey the joke was on me, she was already in town, waiting to spring her big surprise with big Daddy H and Ma.

Got there and what do I see? Old Abe with his cronies, laughing, talking about this deal and that and no one even sees me arrive.

First I see Abe, then there goes Nancy and then, Christ, Marcia's waving across the room. Jesus fucking Christ, what do I do? I know I can't get in touch with Sloane and I'm sweating all through my all-important talk. Huh, who am I kidding? No one listened to a damn word anyway – all too wrapped up in what they were going to say next to impress Abe.

I'm like this interval act, all these publishing guys, media guys, every damn one of them – all they want to do is kiss his ass. Well, they can just go kiss mine.

Christ, Em, I know I was taking a chance, asking Sloane to come along for drinks. I guess I just got too damn cocky – let myself get swept up in the whole romance of New York. Truth is, I wanted her to be with me, wanted her to be the one by my side and it was so damn tempting, like acting the part would make it true.

These guys, in their world they're used to the odd broad hanging around – and Sloane was never going to give me away – I mean, I know she's hot, but she was never going to show me up.

But it was a mistake, Em. However you look at it, it was dumb. Dumb to invite her in the first place. Dumb to think I could get away with something as dumb as not giving Marcia a call.

Sloane was a real pro. Got to hand it to her she played it right down the line – got a hold of the situation real fast but boy, I was sweating. I was sweating but most of all I was angry. Damn angry that we'd been robbed of another night.

Chapter 37

Sloane

Well, Em, how stupid do you think I felt? Stupid, cheap and as ridiculous as you can get.

What the hell did I think I was doing there in the first place? And what about good old Nicky, hey? If he was so keen to leave his wife then why didn't he just turn around there and then and say, *by the way, Mr and Mrs rich-pickings-Harper, this is Sloane. She's my future wife, replacing your daughter, soon-to-be my ex-wife.*

Marcia, darling, you remember Sloane? Well, she's already taken your place in my heart and she's been practising in your place in the bed, and she's about to take over altogether. Everybody happy now? Why don't we have a drink? Or better still, let's all have dinner together like one big happy family.

But no, that's not how it played out.

'There's a bar upstairs, Sloane. Let's go have a drink. Fancy a martini?'

'Brilliant, thanks, that would be great.' Nicholas turns and walks the other way. Just perfect.

I follow the tap, tap of her shoes across the oak floor, my

lovely new boots a clump, clump compared with her princess feet. She presses the button for the lift. I turn and search the crowd for Nicholas. He's nowhere to be seen.

'Mom's gone off to Bloomingdale's,' Marcia says. 'You first,' she ushers me into the lift. 'You'll meet her later. She loves Christmas shopping in New York. Do you like Christmas, Sloane?'

Is this a trick question? Christmas? My mind leaps back to the twenty-four hours Nicholas and I have shared. Barely twenty-four hours. That was Christmas. I daren't look at her and I stare at my bag, fiddling with the clasp.

'Don't do very much really. Just Stuart and me last year, this year too – unless we see Pete and Cathy.'

What the hell is going on? Has Nicholas said something? Has Cathy? Is Marcia going to beg me not to steal him? *Jolene, Jolene...* get that stupid song out of my mind. Shit, is she going to make a scene?

The doors open onto a chrome and glass atrium. There must be twenty-odd floors above our heads. The bar is a bottle zoo – every variety of every species ever known to man. Imagine a *dégustation* like in a wine place in France. Just tasting each type of whisky would keep you drunk for a year.

'Do you miss the trips to France, Sloane?'

Christ, she's reading my mind.

'No, not really, like I say, I get to travel anyway now I'm with High Travel.' *Careful, Sloane, she's trying to trip you up.*

'And what about teaching, do you miss that?'

What is this – twenty questions? Why aren't I in more of a panic? Wow – I actually know the answer. I actually don't care. Actually. This is the woman who spent two years making my life miserable – bottom sets, crappy tasks, blaming me for anything and everything that went wrong, the wife of the guy I have been in love with for more than two years. And is she the one he loves? No, it's me. How do I know that? He said so this morning – and he said he was going to leave her. So there. Who cares if it happens a little sooner than he expects? What harm would it do? Wow, I'm feeling bold.

'I do miss the kids a bit,' *Sloane, you're lying. Why are you bothering to lie?* 'But it's fantastic writing for a living,' I add, 'it's probably what I've always wanted.'

'Yes, and Nicky,' she says.

Oh my God; is she saying she knows I want Nicky?

'He seems to like it even more than his art.'

Phew, maybe not so brave after all.

Marcia orders at the bar, waving me over to a table. I take off my coat, stow it on the chair next to me and then change my mind, pick my coat back up and drape it around my shoulders lest a quick exit be required.

Marcia tap-taps back across the floor towards me. 'They'll bring the drinks over,' she says and smiles at me — with her eyes. I have never seen Marcia smile with her eyes. This has to be a trick. I pull my coat around me and make ready to leave.

'Sorry, Sloane, are you in a draught? We can always move.' She looks around, hunting a free table away from the spectre of a draught that doesn't exist.

'No, I'm fine. Truly, it's fine. Someone just walked over my grave.'

She gives a little trill of a laugh. 'That's a funny thing to say,' she says.

'Sloane, there's something I need to say, something I've been wanting to say for some time – and now you're here, kind of a surprise, well, I guess it's like fate, so maybe it's a good moment to just get it off my chest.'

I hold my breath. Here it comes. The lift is over there, my bag is at my feet, my coat is across my shoulders and one foot is behind the other for an easy sit-to-stand move. God, Sloane, this is like some stupid soap opera. Just get a grip and keep it real.

'Sloane,' Marcia begins, and then stops again. The waiter has arrived with the drinks and plays about with fancy coasters, cocktail sticks, olives and nuts until the banquet is set and he finally stands up.

'Anything else I can get you, Ma'am?'

'No, that'll be all thank you,' Marcia replies. How easily it rolls off her tongue.

That'll be all. Will it be all? My Christmas in twenty-four hours?

'Sloane,' Marcia begins again, and I move forward in my chair. 'Sloane, I owe you an apology.'

Wait, this isn't right. What's the hell's happening here?

'I wasn't nice to you, was I, in school? I should have been more kind.'

'Weren't you?' I mumble. 'Didn't really notice…'

'Now it's you who's being kind and I don't deserve it. You worked so darn hard and I never even gave you a word of thanks. I've felt so guilty about it, Sloane, I'm just pleased to have the chance to set the record straight.' I open my mouth but she's not finished and I close it again.

'Thing is, I was jealous.'

What, this is mad! Or is it coming now…

'I was jealous of how young you were, how easily you got things done, how everyone seemed to like you – especially the kids. They loved you. I bet they miss you like hell.

'Thing is, I've felt so guilty – I thought that maybe it was because of me you left the job. I should never have blamed you

234

for those mistakes – my own mistakes most often – it was none of it your fault, and those crazy kids I gave you? Okay, some of them were pretty bright but I know they spelled trouble and I just dished them all onto you. I wasn't in a good place back then…

'You were real good, Sloane. Didn't matter what I threw at you, you did a darn good job. Don't let all that stuff put you off,' she says and she leans forward and pats my hand. Her touch is icy and inadvertently I draw my hand away. 'You should go back and carry on if it's really what you love because they all sure loved you.

'See, Sloane, I have this problem; I can't have kids – Cathy knows – I guess pretty much most folks know,' she sighs and twists her wedding band around and around. 'You were so young, so pretty, you had everything I wanted and me, I just saw myself getting older, I was just plain jealous and I'm sorry. I am truly sorry and I hope you will forgive my meanness and that we can start over and become friends. There – I've said it. Phew, I'm so glad I got the chance. Cheers, Sloane,' she says, and raises her glass.

'I raise my glass to meet hers and swallow hard. 'Cheers, Marcia,' I say.

'Looky here, Nicholas. You're in the *Times*,' Marcia says, holding a copy of the *New York Times* open on her lap.

'Listen up.' She reads from the paper, 'Respected Harvard scholar, Nicholas Bride has surpassed himself this time. Bride visited Barnes and Noble on Fifth Avenue, New York yesterday to sign copies of his bestselling novel, *In the Hands of the Mistress*, a study of Rodin's relationship with sculptress, Camille Claudel.

'Indications are that Bride has once again surpassed himself with another fine work to add to his many artistic triumphs.

'In a refreshing twist away from the studies so far published in this regard, Bride treats the subject from Auguste Rodin's point of view. Reviews have been outstanding. Critic, Guy Sullivan from Write Art, proclaimed the work 'a masterpiece' and stated, 'it was as if Bride had been transported back in time and talked to the master sculptor himself.

'Wowee, Nicky. So you *are* a genius after all. Time to eat, everybody,' Marcia says without pause.

So what's all this stuff about artistic triumph? From what I understand, Nicholas's artwork has never really taken off. I look at Nicholas. His face is blazing and I understand. This is Harper speak – Abe Harper has even the journalists in the palm of his hand.

'So Caesar picked you up okay?' Nicholas says.

'Clearly,' I say. *Who has a chauffeur called Caesar?*

'So what's on your agenda for tomorrow, young lady?' Abe asks as he slides a chair out for me.

I slip into the space he has made and I steady myself on the table. He hits the back of my legs with the chair, pushes it right under me, unbalancing me and I sit with a thud.

'Doing a little sight-seeing around this lovely city?' Abe goes to take his place opposite me at the circular walnut table, its surface a mirror from years of polish and expert care.

The housekeeper is fussing behind me at a sideboard of matching wood, upon which sit two magnificent porcelain candlesticks. I'm guessing *Meissen* from all the pink and blue cherubs and the fancy work.

Music is playing in the background and I take a second to tune in. James Taylor is singing. *Winter, spring, summer...* ah, that'll be about Marcia then, my new best friend. You've got a friend, Sloane. Lucky you, you've got a friend.

'You should come see us in Boston sometime – now that's a wonderful place.' Abe says as he lowers himself into his chair.

'Actually, I'm leaving tomorrow. My flight is at six – in the evening,' I add, hoping that Nicholas has taken note.

'I did quite a lot of sightseeing this morning,' I say, picking up from his earlier question. 'I wasn't very far from here, in fact, at Strawberry Fields, such a romantic place, don't you think?' Nicholas starts picking at the skin around his thumb. 'In fact, I asked someone where John Lennon had lived. Isn't life strange? And now here I am in the very same apartment block.'

'We call it an apartment *house*, dear,' Nancy Harper says as she enters the room, her skirts swishing like some movie star on the brink of a dance routine.

'It's not just John Lennon who lived here – Rosemary Clooney, Judy Garland, Lauren Bacall, Rudolf Nureyev – so many greats. It's not easy to get a place here, you know. Everyone has to agree – the residents and all. But Abe sorted it all out, didn't you, darling? He's so generous with his donations, aren't you, dear?' Nancy swoops past her husband and brushes his shoulders as she takes her place around the table, shakes her napkin out and puts it on her lap.

'He's buried at Sainte-Geneviève-des-Bois, you know, Rudolf Nureyev, near Savigny – where the kids go for the exchange. There's a Russian Orthodox cemetery there – that's why he's all the way out there and not somewhere lovely like Père Lachaise.' Marcia is sitting to my right and Nicholas to my left and I look from one to the other. Her mention of the cemetery takes me back to Paris with a jolt. I look back at Nicholas and he is looking down at his hands.

'No, I didn't know,' I reply.

'I hope you don't mind that we are in the morning room, dear. It's just easier not to use the formal dining hall when we're just popping up for the night. So much silver – and Bella hates it if she doesn't have it just perfect when we dine in there, don't you Bella?'

The housekeeper turns to Nancy at the sound of her name and with a tiny curtsey-like motion she says, 'Yes, Ma'am,' in a very small voice and then continues her tasks.

What must it be like to live this woman's life? Does she have any other life besides? Forty-ish, her skin is deep black and her hair pulled back under a white cap that matches the apron which covers a grey cotton dress. Little frizzes of hair escape here and there where they will not be tamed. What is it like to be on stand-by for this family of expectation, exigencies and excess, a cog in the wheel of their dazzling social whirl? And how can this *not* be the formal room?

'You know, Nicky – we should have asked Patricia-May and Elliott – what a pity we didn't think of that.'

'No, Mom, they couldn't have come. Elliott's flying off to Palm Springs today – remember. He's got that golf tournament of his,' Marcia says.

'Okay kids, let's say grace.' Nancy gives a little nod to the housekeeper who bustles off and stills the music. Abe opens his arms and spreads his hands and the rest of the family follow suit. There is no option but to join in. We have to stretch across the table to link up and I close my eyes as the warmth and tingle of Nicholas's hand on the one side contrasts sharply with the sudden chill of Marcia's on the other. Oh my God, this is unreal.

'Dear Lord, we thank you for the blessings of this day and for the opportunity to share our table with our welcome friend.

We give thanks for your mercies and we ask you to bring comfort to the families whose relatives were involved in the terrible tragedy in this fair city not two hours ago, and to bring peace to the souls of those who died. Amen.'

I reclaim my hands but not before I register the insistent pressure and the sensual wave it sends spiralling through my body. Nicholas takes a split second more time before he lets go of my hand. He has noted what I said about my flight, I feel sure that is what he wants to say.

I open my eyes and look up. 'Gosh, I haven't heard anything. What happened, Abe?' I ask

Nicholas answers, 'Police just released a statement; guy just shot six people dead. Random killing, injured a ton more.'

'God, where was this?'

'Long Island Rail Road, packed with commuters on the way home, poor souls,' says Abe.

'Doesn't bear thinking of, does it, honey? But don't let it spoil our nice evening. It's all well and good to pray for them, Abe, but Sloane doesn't want to know the horrid detail...'

'Oh no, Nancy, I mean, it's right to pray for this kind of thing – God, what makes someone do something like that?' I ask.

Marcia joins in; 'Police are saying he was a bad lot, kind of weird, got all het up and paranoid about racism – saw insult where there was nothing to see, that kind of thing. Been arrested a couple of times already. Folks were big players in Jamaica until his daddy died.'

'Poor old Giuliani won't know what's hit him – talk about a baptism of fire. Poor bastard, 'scuse my language, doesn't even become mayor until January and he's already got to deal with all this. Clinton'll have to sit up and be counted too, some places it's so damn easy to get yourself a gun,' says Abe.

'Beats me how they get all the information so quick.'

'You'd be surprised, Nancy,' replies Abe, 'people love to talk when something like this goes down – neighbours, colleagues, everyone likes to have their say, their fifteen minutes o' fame.'

'How old was he? When his father died?' I ask.

'What did they say now, Mom? Twenty, I think. His dad crashed his car, big in the government, he was, and his mom died too – cancer, not long after.'

'That's right, Marcey; top of the class with a lovely home and happy family one minute, parents dead and fortune gone the next. Just shows you how we need to count our blessings, kids,' says Nancy. 'Amazing what grief does to a person. Fancy that. Twenty years old and your parents all gone and dead – now, that must be tough. Let's hope that you and Nicky can steer some poor kid back from the edge, hey kids?'

My head involuntarily shoots up and I look straight at Nancy. Is there devilment in her eye? I switch my gaze to Marcia, 'What kid is this?' I say.

'Aw, I guess that you haven't heard, Sloane, but then why would you have? Nicky and Marcia, they're going to adopt,' says Nancy with a smile.

I look into my lap. How about thirteen years old with your parents 'all gone and dead'? Maybe I too am capable of dark deeds?

Chapter 38

Nicholas

It was nearly midday before I could get away. I leapt straight in a cab and went to Sloane's hotel. The woman at reception was curt so I slipped her a ten dollar bill, which she pocketed before she leant over toward me, 'She left – about twenty minutes ago, just ahead of check-out time.' She comes in closer and beckons me near. 'But I did see her in line over there,' She points with the chewed end of a pen towards a door across the foyer, 'I guess she left her bags here for a while,' she adds, tapping the pen on the desk. 'Sure hope she enjoyed her stay,' she raises her eyebrows before she turns away.

I should have been in a meeting downtown near Battery Park but I just knew I had to see Sloane before she left.

Christ, what a farce, Em, that whole damned evening. I couldn't even tell her 'goodbye'. Abe just escorted her down to the car like she was some precious piece of gold, fawning around her, making a complete fool of himself in front of Nancy who seemed none too pleased in the end. Kept asking Sloane about the goddamned school, like she knew more than Marcia or me, obsessing about this kid he knew, how big he is in banking, some other kid who's made it in the diamond trade.

Jesus, who you know not what you know, that's the name of the game!

I was so damn mad about the piece in the *Times*. How dare Abe get them to big me up like that? Who does he think he is? Almost walked out of there, there and then – but I wasn't gonna leave Sloane. She did real good – again. I owe her – she could have made the situation a whole lot worse. When she started on about John Lennon I thought she was going to spill and then I cottoned on that she was teasing me – just having her own little game.

God, she looked gorgeous, demure but sexy hot, and I couldn't help imagining what she was wearing under that pretty blue dress. I needed to get to her but there was absolutely no way. Nancy, Marcia and Abe, well they were watching like hawks – seemed that way, at least. They had me trapped fair and square and there wasn't a damn thing I could do.

I had to see her before she left New York, so I had no choice but to wait it out and I grabbed a seat in the diner from where I could see the comings and goings through the hotel swing door.

I down the dregs of the coffee, cold now in the bottom of the cup, and look up to see her coming through the door. She walks in briskly and heads straight across the foyer. Leaving a bunch of dollar bills and coins on the table I get up and walk across the hall and pace up and down outside the restroom door. Five minutes later she is out, adjusting the strap on her shoulder and then she turns and sees me waiting. I expect her to be pleased.

'What the hell do you think you're doing here?'

'I…'

'What right have you coming back here and stirring things up again? So I can fall back in with your plans, play the cute little English girl for your father-in-law, some sort of mascot of times gone by?'

Whoa, didn't see all that coming, for sure...

'And when were you going to tell me about the adoption, hey? Christ, what do you expect me to say? That's it, Nicholas, I've had enough of cloud cuckoo land. It's clear you're never leaving her otherwise you wouldn't be shopping for some kid.'

'Sloane, just give me a chance...'

'To do what? Fuck me again a few more times before you break the news?'

'Sloane, hush, keep your voice down. Be reasonable. There are kids...'

'Oh, suddenly you're all concerned about the poor little kids...'

'Sloane, just stop it will you, stop it. I have no intention of staying with Marcia and I have no intention of having a kid, let alone some damaged fucked-up kid from Mexico or any other place. Yeah, we talked about that kinda stuff but it was never my idea – just Nancy and Marcia cooking up some crazy solution to paper over the goddamned cracks.'

Finally she stops and she starts to cry.

'Sloane, I'm so sorry. I had no idea they were coming to New York. They only came because Marcia persuaded them. She was worried when she didn't get a call...'

'Oh, so it's my fault now, is it, that we lost a whole night and day together? That we got stuck in that unbearable place with those unbearable people instead of being together, having fun in New York, making love and...' she starts crying harder.

I pull my handkerchief from my pocket and I pass it to her. She blows her nose loudly and gives it back to me. 'Here,' she says, 'that's all you deserve.'

Her mouth breaks into a smile and I sigh with relief. I love this woman. The thought of not ever having her again scares me. This woman has unlocked me, unchained me from everything I thought I was and hated to be. How can I ever let that go?

I put my arms around her and hold her close. I smell the scent of our passion – she's sensational, adorable, oh God help me I have to be with her, no matter what the cost.

'I love you, Sloane. We'll sort it out, you and me. Properly – no jumping in at the deep end. If we're going to be together, we have to do it right – Stuart, Marcia, my job, your job, where we're gonna live. We just have to be patient, baby, we'll get there.' Sloane puts her head on my shoulder and I stroke her hair. The aching is unbearable, like someone's got me in a vice. Sloane pulls away.

'I got you something, Nicholas, yesterday, in that Christmas shop. I want to give it to you now,' she says. Sloane opens her purse, unzips a compartment and brings out a little package wrapped in green tissue, 'Green, like your notepaper, Nicholas, your beautiful letter.'

I go red. That notepaper – it wasn't even mine and she thinks I've chosen it specially. I just took a couple of sheets from the back of Marcia's drawer.

'It's okay, Nicholas, you don't need to be embarrassed,' she says, 'I didn't expect anything from you – it's just a little surprise, that's all.'

I tear at the paper and it falls on the floor. Sloane bends and picks it up. I look down at the object in my hands – a Christmas charm, a decoration for the tree.

'See, Nicholas, see what it says.' She takes it from me and dangles the two wooden doves of peace joined by a sign. 'Look, see what it says: 'Our First Christmas Together'. Bring it back to me, Nicholas, when all this is over. I want to hang it on our first tree.'

Chapter 39

Sloane

'Are you absolutely certain?'

I nod at Cathy, tears rolling slowly down my cheek.

'Three tests and a doctor's visit worth of certain,' I reply as she shoves the box of tissues my way.

'For God's sake, Sloane. I thought you were on the pill?'

'I was… I am, but I kept being sick on the flight over – just never gave it a second thought, that's what Dr Day thinks did it – apart from the obvious, that is.'

Cathy smiles weakly at my feeble joke. I pick up my mug of coffee and take a sip. 'Ouch, that's hot,' I say, 'Got any sugar?'

'You never take sugar.' Cathy stands and walks to the dresser, plucks a white china bowl from the top shelf, rattles in a drawer, plonks spoon and pot on the table in front of me and leans against the sink as she dries a stack of pink flowery cups.

'How was the meeting?' I ask.

'Fine,' Cathy says. 'We sorted the stuff for Easter and the exam timetable's all done….

'For God's sake, Sloane, you didn't come here to discuss my sorry little departmental tea party — what the hell are you going to do? How do you know for sure it's not Stuart's? God, Sloane, you told me it was all over, you and Nicholas. What the hell were you playing at, stirring it all up again?

'Don't think it never occurred to me – when you went over to New York, but I just thought, no, Sloane's learnt her lesson, she's married, she's mature, so just shove it out of your mind. Poor Stuart... he really missed you while you were away – and what about Marcia? Does *she* know?'

'Oh,' I say, 'I forgot she and you were best buddies.'

Cathy folds the tea towel neatly, hangs it over the sink and folds her arms. 'That's not fair,' she says. 'She was there for me through all that business with Pete – and I felt sorry for her. Still do...'

'Oh excuse me. Pardon me if I'm in danger of upsetting your friend...'

'Sloane, don't be silly,' Cathy says and walks over, strokes her hand down the back of my head and slips her arm around my shoulder. 'I'm *your* friend, too. You know I am.'

'It can't be Stuart's because Stuart and I stopped doing it about this time last year. I had a bit of an infection... down there,' I drop my head and place my hand on my belly. It doesn't feel any different from normal. How can there be some new human inside? 'We didn't do anything for a bit and then we just didn't seem to bother. And Stuart wasn't Nicholas so...'

Cathy gives a little pat on my head, places her hands in the small of her back and eases her shoulders back as she stands. 'God, Sloane, what a mess.'

I drag my fingers through my hair. It's all tangling, a mess. I didn't even comb it before leaving home. It's a mess, I'm a mess. Oh my God, it's a mess. In my mind I rewind the action, consciously vomit my way to New York, think clearly, think smart and buy condoms and Nicholas slips them on each time we make love. Ha – what use is rewind in your head?

'So what next?'

'Oh Cathy, you don't understand, I don't have a choice.' My eyes sting and I rub furiously at one and then the other, wipe my damp hand on my skirt and then rest it back on the place where I imagine my baby lies growing.

'Don't be silly, Sloane, of course you have a choice. You just have to decide what's best for you, the baby,' she nods at the place where my hand remains. I go to move it, shame sweeping over me in a surprise assault but then leave it there, scant protection for a few tiny cells, 'and everyone else…' her voice trails. 'Oh Sloane, this is so sad. I know this is a dreadful thing to say, but could you not pass it off as Stuart's? I mean, he has no idea about Nicholas so why not let sleeping dogs lie?'

Cathy pulls out a chair. It scrapes loudly on the grey flint tiles as she flumps into the seat opposite mine. I look at my friend. She's much fatter than she was, her clothes unflattering, swamping her podgy frame. I look at her face, oatmeal beige etched with lines and little red veins and her frizzy hair, all rooty with pepper-salt strands. God, she looks old. When did Cathy get so old?

Sleeping dogs lie? No, it is sleeping people who lie – sleeping people who should not be sleeping in other people's beds.

'I can't, Cathy, even if I wanted to, because Stuart and I won't be together.' I take a deep breath.

'But if he doesn't know…'

'No, Cathy, you don't understand. Nicholas and I… we have a plan.'

'What do you mean a plan? You're not thinking of…?'

Oh hell, I hadn't meant to tell her but I just feel so... I don't know, sort of numb, like my brain is paralysed with the enormity of what's going on, frozen rigid in adrenalin mode so my thought processes go haywire in a sea of stress the moment I try to create a pattern and make some sense.

I feel numb but at the same time there's this ache. Part of me just wants to breathe out, to give Stuart a hug and ask him to make everything alright.

Stuart is kind, considerate, even and good. Could I tell him the stupid, ugly truth, beg him to forgive me and be a good Mrs Bone? Withdraw from the battle and no one gets hurt? Except Stuart, of course, he would get hurt and me, well pain is part of my future. I have to surrender something whatever I do next.

But part of me wants to breathe in and to hold on to the possibilities of a universe where only two people exist, and to hell with the rest of the world. I want those stolen moments with Nicholas to climax in a stolen lifetime. To be with Nicholas, in his arms, feel his fingers running through my hair, over my body... God, how can I think of that in a situation like this?

I am going to tell her, I know I am. Who else is there to I tell? I just can't do this on my own. All I am doing is delaying the moment of the telling. She says she is my friend – she has been my friend and I need a friend right now. To hell with it, I need a friend.

I open my handbag and draw out a green envelope, slot my finger in the tear along the top and tease out the letter inside. I unfold its two pages and smooth them out slowly on the table as if my caress of their content might invoke a solution to the message they bring.

'Here, read it. Then you'll understand.' I swivel the sheets around to face my friend.

'Oh God, Sloane – it's the same notepaper; that letter that came to my house. Oh God, to think that I... you should never have got me involved. Sloane, I don't think... are you sure you want me to read this? It's not really any of my business... I...'

'Just read it, Cathy,' I say, and she purses her lips, shrugs her shoulders, bows her head and begins to read aloud.

Boston, February 4 1994

Sloane,

I love you. No question. I think I have loved you from the first moments we shared on our way to France when you mesmerized me, bewitched me with your star sign voodoo, your haunting eyes and your glorious, glorious body. I ache for you, Sloane. I want you. I miss you. Never doubt that I need you too.

Your phone call caught me off guard and I'm sorry if I was a little short with you.

Sloane, you'll have to forgive me, baby, I was pretty shocked. I get what you said about being sick – I didn't mean to accuse you of anything, I just didn't know what to think. A baby was never part of the deal and I reacted badly, I know.

'Oh God, Sloane... you told him on the phone?' Cathy interrupts her reading and looks up at me, 'Christ, Sloane, I ...'

'Just read on,' I say.

She looks back down, clears her throat and quietly reads the rest.

I know I said we would deal with it, build it into the plan, but Sloane, I am sorry, my darling, that's never going to happen –

it's romantic, for sure, but we have to be practical, it's just not right for us.

Think about it, Sloane – think how it would change what we have. We are two souls, bonded forever and nothing will dim, nothing will change that love, but this extra element – factoring in a baby, I just don't see that will work. I have never made a secret of the fact that I have no burning desire for a child. You are who I want, Sloane, selfishly, greedily, I want the whole of you without distraction, without the demands of responsibilities that are outside of our control.

And think about it, Sloane. It's bad enough telling Marcia I am leaving, let alone for her to find out that you are having my child. Think what it would do to her – her not being able to have kids. Think about it, baby. That just wouldn't be fair.

Sloane, I am asking you, begging you to consider what it would mean. The apartment is terrific but it's no place for a child – you'll see what I mean when you get here. You'll love it – all high ceilings and with a balcony on three sides. And just think, Sloane, we are weeks away only from those moments – those moments when nothing will stop up from being with one another where we want, when we want, making love, going to the theatre, eating in restaurants, lazing in bed – all the things that we have ever dreamed of doing we can do – together, just you and me, enjoying one another wherever we want, whenever.

By the time you read this letter I'll be gearing up for the spring book tour. Marcia will be staying with her folks while I'm away so I'm going to tell her that I am leaving before I go – that way she'll have plenty of support and that way I can go straight to the apartment (*our* apartment!) from Houston when I fly back into Boston. Some of my things are already there. I am not going to tell Mom and Dad – they'll find out from Mr and Mrs H soon enough.

Sloane, I love you and can't wait to be with you. This baby, it's all wrong – bad timing, just not right for us. It's not like I am asking you to choose or anything, but honestly Sloane, I really don't think I could cope with a baby as well as everything else.

Sloane, I know you'll do the right thing. I love you. I miss you like crazy, always.

Remember what I said? Remember that wherever you are, whenever, I shall be loving you then as now,

Nicholas

Cathy looks up from the letter. 'Oh Christ,' she says. 'Follow me.'

Cathy takes my hand and leads me along a little pathway. The uneven paving stones take us through an archway to a kind of secret space at the back of her garden where there is a wooden bench beneath a drooping tree. In the far corner is a vase with fresh flowers before a small wooden cross. On the floor is a stone slab. So this is where it is.

'Look,' Cathy indicates the makeshift grave.

She reads the epitaph engraved in the cold marble:

'Il vivait, il jouait, riante créature. Que te sert d'avoir pris cet enfant, ô nature?'

I translate the words in my head as she speaks: *He lived, he played, a laughing creature, what good has it done you, oh nature, to have taken this child?*

'Victor Hugo?'

Cathy nods and dabs at her eyes, 'My favourite poet,' she says.

'Oh Cathy,' I hug her hard. 'I'm so sorry. How awful of me to…' This is so confusing, so exhausting. I feel like my head will explode and my blood will drain out.

'I couldn't bear it when I lost our baby,' Cathy says. 'I felt so alone, so empty. There was no body, nothing to show. One minute she was inside me and the next she was gone.' I note that Cathy says *she* and wonder if she knows for certain it was a girl. I do not ask the question.

'It was like there was nothing left – I was so sad, bereft, but there was nowhere to go, nowhere to find some peace.

'This was Pete's idea.' She looks down and then she looks back up and hooks a wild greyish lock behind her ear. 'You know when we were in Paris and I thought he'd gone off to meet *her*?' Cathy cocks her head to one side. 'Well, I was wrong. I never got the chance to tell you with all the Nicholas and Marcia stuff going on. Oh, Sorry, Sloane – I didn't mean to…'

'It's okay,' I say and link my arm through hers. 'Go on… tell me.'

'Turns out that Pete had gone up to the stonemason's opposite Père Lachaise – long way to go and a crazy idea but it meant so much to me that he'd done it when I found out.

'He somehow knew that if he'd just gone up the road – Peterborough, somewhere ordinary – it would never have been special enough – not had the same effect. He took so much trouble, so much care, going all the way up to the cemetery – twice – once to order it and again to pick it up; creating somewhere to honour our baby's memory, show he really cared too. Make up for, you know…*her*. I felt so bad. I almost accused him of…that would've been awful.' Cathy wipes her hand across her eyes.

'I saw him there,' I almost whisper.

'Where?' Cathy says, 'What – Pete?'

'That day, when Marcia turned up in Paris – when I found out that she was his wife – Christ, I didn't even know Nicholas was married. After you rescued me and Elodie disappeared off, I just walked for hours in the rain. God, I was in a state.' I laugh at my own stupid statement.

'That's an irony – as if I'm not in a state now. Oh my God, that's getting on for three years ago, Cathy. How can this have gone on for so long? God, Elodie – I can't remember the last time I wrote. I've just been so…'

'You were telling me about seeing Pete,' Cathy prompts.

'Yes, sorry. He was there – coming out of the memorial shop with this package under his arm. I didn't know exactly what it was but I guessed it was something like this.' I nod towards the stone. 'I meant to tell you about it, but like you say…'

'The thing is, Sloane, you have to be really sure. Losing the baby, all this sadness, it makes you realise that you can never take anything for granted. Look at me and Pete. We've been trying for a baby ever since but it's just not happening. I've got to accept now that it might never happen – I might never have a baby…' Cathy takes a tissue from up her sleeve and wipes her eyes.

'Oh God, Cathy, I'm so sorry. I didn't mean to upset you like this. Sorry – look I'll go. I've messed up enough of your half term.'

'Sloane, you're not listening.'

I am listening, Cathy. I just don't want to hear.

'So when are you telling Stu that you're leaving?' Cathy asks.

'As soon as I've dealt with all this,' I look down at my belly, 'I just need to sort it all out – stick to the plan.'

'Look, Sloane, I know you're younger and you've still got time, but think about what it'll mean – if you do leave Stuart for Nicholas. There's nothing to suggest he'll ever want kids. Is that what you want for yourself – no kids and a bloke ten years older? Who'll most likely die before you do?'

'But Pete's older than you, not so much but…'

'Exactly. Don't you think I've thought about that? No kids, no Pete, no sisters, no brothers and a lovely lonely old age to look forward to. Think about it, Sloane. I feel sure that Stuart… Stuart's a really lovely guy – he'd never in a million years be unfaithful. You should count yourself lucky.'

God, I wish I could, I so wish I could, but this aching will not go away. Nicholas is in my skin, between the beats of my heart, winding his way in and out of the neurons in my brain, causing havoc and joy, chaos and delight. He is me and I am him, and inside me is a union of both; which he does not want.

'You can still change your mind. Are you sure you've really thought this through?' Cathy pulls on the handbrake and turns towards me, her brows knitted together in concern.

'Cathy, I know you mean well but I have to do this, I don't have a choice. I'm just glad they could fit me in quickly – get it over and done with so Nicholas and I can move on.'

'Sloane, you do have a choice, you could…'

'We've been through all this. Now if you don't want to come in with me then fine, but if you really are my friend you'll just support me in this. I've made up my mind. If Nicholas doesn't want the baby then nor do I. It was kind of you to drive me but I can always get a taxi home.'

Truth is I do want the baby. I just want Nicholas more. I am not going to risk losing the one man who makes me feel alive. How sad that I have to kill my child to feel alive.

I get out of the car, throw my red winter coat over my arm and slam the door behind me. I head towards the clinic, resisting the urge to look back. There is a pause but then I am relieved to hear another slam and the bleep-bleep as Cathy sets the alarm. Her feet crunch on the gravel behind me.

'Don't be daft, Sloane,' Cathy says, catching me up. She grabs me by the arm and marches me in through the door.

This is not what you imagine a clinic should be. It is a Victorian house in a back street in Nottingham, as anonymous as all the rest. I can't help wondering if the neighbours mind an abortion place next door, sullying their leafy residential community with the bloodstains of innocent babies hooked or sucked prematurely to their deaths from their mothers' wombs.

'Have you got your consent forms? Two doctors have signed?' I hand the slips over and nod.

'Thank you, Mrs er...' The nurse looks at the sheet I have filled in, 'Bone, Mrs Bone. Just take a seat over there. Will you be stopping?' She looks at Cathy. Cathy nods too. 'There's coffee on the table in the waiting room and the loos are over there.' Cathy nods again.

Cathy shrugs off her coat and we sit side by side on the orange plastic chairs. She looks at me and begins to raise her brows. 'Don't,' I snap. 'Please just don't.' She leans forward and scoops a magazine from the table in the centre of the room and flicks through the pages. 'Sorry,' I say.

Cathy puts her hand on mine and starts to hum quietly. It's familiar – where have I heard that recently, what the hell? And then it comes to me, the memory of the wretched evening with Marcia's family in New York, the night after Nicholas and I made our baby. I form the words of the song in my head; *La-la laa laa laa la-la la, you've got a friend...*

'Mrs Bone?'

They're calling me. This is it. I open my mouth and nothing comes out. I clear my throat. 'Me, that's me.'

'This way please.' The nurse turns and walks away and I gather my bag and coat.

'I'll hang on to your coat if you like,' Cathy says, grabbing it from me and hanging it over the chair. She stands and she hugs me tightly. She eases the pressure around me but before I can move away she hugs me closely in again.

'Now you take care,' she says, and I see there are tears in her eyes. I bite my bottom lip hard and fight the prickling sensation behind my eyes. My nose tingles with the effort of holding back the tears. I turn to follow the nurse. 'Sloane, Sloane,' Cathy says. I walk away filtering out the sound of her voice in my head.

I am amazed to be lying on a couch in the equivalent of someone's front room. This is a bona fide clinic and yet there is a bay window with net curtains like any other net curtains in the street. I can see people passing by – people in their everyday clothes doing everyday tasks – bringing home the shopping, coming home from work, picking up the kids. I turn to face the nurse. 'Don't worry, they can't see in. I know it's a bit weird,' she says.

Above me is a bright light shining directly down and I wonder if my baby will see that. Like the bright light they say we go towards when we go up to heaven.

'Just a little prick in your hand,' the doctor says. 'You won't feel a thing.'

Chapter 40

Nicholas

Look, Em, I know that looks bad but I never told her outright she couldn't have the kid. Never spelled it out – if that's what she wanted to understand from my letter then that's her interpretation, right? Doesn't mean I wouldn't have stood by her. It was her decision in the end – you have to believe me on that. I'm going a little crazy here so I may not get all this down as correctly as I should but I know I need to be honest so that's my objective, Em – honesty at all costs.

Everything was taken out of my hands when Marcia found out. Damn it, I should have made that phone call. That was all Sloane's fault. I wanted to call her and she stopped me making that call.

If I'd made that phone call Marcia wouldn't have come haring to New York and she never would have seen me and Sloane together – never would have picked up the vibes. Nancy, she's got a nose for that sort of thing like some kind of ferret, always poking around in other people's business. She put it into Marcia's head and I guess it kind of clicked. Female intuition, she called it. But if it hadn't been for that other interfering bitch it would never have gone as far as it did.

When I told Marcia I was leaving, she put two and two together and asked me straight out if it was Sloane I was leaving her for. I just didn't know what to say, Em. Of course, I denied it and just said it was better if the two of us just got some space from one another, maybe just a time-out break – time to reassess a little where things were going between us two.

She just broke right down and she begged me to stay – begged me. It was pitiful, Em, I felt so sorry for her. She started going through all the stuff with Jake and how sorry she was and about not having kids and everything.

Truth is, Marcia and me, we went back a long way, and the affair with Jake, well that wasn't the reason I was leaving. And I wasn't leaving because I wasn't fond of my wife. If I hadn't met Sloane I'd probably have just gone the whole way without even thinking about life without Marcia, I'd been with her for so long. Truth is, it wasn't that I couldn't live with Marcia. I just couldn't see a way to live without Sloane. So I left despite the begging and the pleading. It wasn't until I reached the hotel in Houston that I got the call.

It's Nancy on the phone and she's sobbing and talking so fast that I can't make head or tail of what she's trying to say. Tell her to slow down and finally Mr H, he comes on the phone.

Turns out that Marcia's tried to kill herself, Jesus Christ, kill herself. She goes into one of the garages, shuts the door, gets into one of old Harper's fancy cars and turns on the ignition and just sits there waiting to end it all. If it hadn't have been for Caesar doing his evening rounds, she would have died there and then but he got her out, got her to hospital and it's thanks to him she's alive. And it would have been thanks to me if she'd died.

Well, you can imagine her folks and my folks when the story all comes out; turns out that Marcia's got on the phone to

Cathy to ask her all about Sloane. It's the middle of the night and it's Pete who answers and he's all confused, thinking it's a wrong number and all.

Cathy, she tells Marcia everything – about Sloane, about me, about New York and then she can't stop at that – she goes and tells her about the baby. Marcia, she decides that there's nothing left for her to live for – Sloane can give me everything I need. That stuck up bitch, Cathy. She spills every last bean and what for? If you ask me she was jealous of what me and Sloane had.

It's mind-blowing, Em, the idea of Marcia being dead – of killing herself because of me. No one should have that kinda hold on another person's life, now should they?

Chapter 41

Sloane

I undo the package. It bears USA stamps. I know it is from him. Inside there is an envelope and a smaller package, wrapped tightly in red tissue. I place the parcel on my desk, rip the letter open and read.

Boston, February 21 1994

Sloane,

I hate to do this to you, to us – to have to write this all down instead of telling you face to face. I know you will be in your office when you read this and I am sorry for that – there is no other way, my darling. I am sorry.

There is no easy way of saying this so I will just say it straight out.

Sloane, my darling Sloane, I can't leave Marcia. Not now since she tried to kill herself. She's too fragile, too vulnerable. How can I be so selfish as to risk her life again?

I've promised the folks that I will take care of her and make everything right. Please, Sloane, try to find it in your heart to forgive me. What choice do I have? She needs me, Sloane. I just can't leave her, not like this.

Please believe me when I say that this is the last thing I want. I miss you, Sloane, your beauty, your exquisite touch, your glorious body, your laugh and your smile. When I close my eyes I can still feel you breathing in the bed next to me in New York; that moment of waking up with you by my side. I will hold that moment in my heart forever.

Sloane, my Sloane, know that wherever you are, whenever, I shall be loving you then as now.

Yours always,

Nicholas

I put the letter on my desk. I pick up the package and tear at the wrapping. I already know what it is. I pull the tissue away from the two doves of peace and dangle the ornament from my fingertip. *Our First Christmas Together*, it reads.

I snatch up the letter and screw the green notepaper into a tight ball and I throw it as hard as I can against my office door. It bounces back and rolls to rest at my feet. I bend down and pick it up and the tears start to fall all over again. So what now, Nicholas? What now?

Chapter 42

Nicholas

You're going to think badly of me, Em, for not telling her straight – for sending her that letter and not at least giving her a call, but that's not exactly how it happened. Now, I'm no coward, so I don't want you thinking that. Like I said, I'm not thinking too clearly and I'm kinda running out of steam so I need to set the record straight.

I said that when Marcia called her, that bitch Cathy damn spilled every last bean. Well now, that's not strictly true – she saved the last bean for me to deliver in person.

So I fly back. The spring tour's shot to pieces but what the heck? Marcia, she's crying and sobbing and saying sorry for what she's done and I tell her not to worry, that I'm not going to leave, reassure her that I love her, that kind of thing, and then she looks up at me, her big baby eyes full of tears.

'Nicky,' she says, 'I've got an idea. We could adopt it – the baby. Call her, Nicky. Call Sloane. See what you can do. We could give it a good home, love it, bring it up in a good home and give it everything it needs. After all it *is* your baby too. What has Sloane got to offer a child? Speak to her – I'm sure you can make her see sense. Offer her some money, Nicky, make it worth her while.'

I don't want to do this, you understand, but Marcia, she's got it all sewn up, designing nurseries in her head.

So I call Sloane. Take a chance and call her at work. She tells me straight out that I can relax about the kid — that everything's fine. Says she's excited, can't wait to see our home, to see me. So it turns out there is no baby anymore.

Now me, to be honest, I'm kinda relieved about the child what with all this happening with Marcia so I just fill Sloane in a little, make out it's all under control because Sloane, reading in between the lines, she sounds kind of fragile so I think maybe it's best not to say it as it is but to write it all down instead.

But Marcia, well, she's beside herself when I tell her that the baby's gone — Marcia being Catholic and all. Thought maybe I'd say that Sloane had miscarried, but then I remembered that stupid bitch, Cathy. She'd be bound to blab at some stage so I decided I may just as well come clean.

Jesus Christ, Marcia, she's so upset that I think she's going to try to kill herself all over again. *Christ*, I'm thinking, *what am I doing trapped here in this mess when I should be making a brand new life with Sloane?*

Chapter 43

Sloane

You'd have thought, Em, that I would have had enough. Enough of Nicholas, affairs of the heart, and I tried, Em, I tried but I couldn't keep away, such was my addiction to this man.

I had a chance – a chance to make a real go of it with Stuart but did I take it? Why am I asking you? You know damn well I didn't or our story would not have an end.

I told you this was your story – our story, Em; the terrible consequences of our wanton lust. It was our pivotal moment and it pivoted the wrong way. Whoever is to blame must pay.

You might think that I, with my enviable education and all the brain cells endowed me by two intelligent parents and an aunt who never let me stray – you might think that I would know when to say enough is enough. Stop the pain, stop the roundabout, let me get off and find some peace from this maniacal mess of a love affair that won't go away.

Did I even want to get off? Honestly? Even the pain in my belly was not enough to persuade me of the toxicity of my pairing with this man.

Did I know what Cathy did? Of course I did – how could I not know when it was Pete who answered the phone – Pete who listened in to the conversation and sopped up every rancid word that spouted from her bitter mouth; Pete who thought it his duty as a friend to tell Stuart the tales of the whore that was his wife.

We almost didn't make it, Stuart and me. Not because he didn't want to, but because all I wanted was to run to Nicholas and beg him to take me back. How could I even look Stuart in the face when, after all the hurt, the betrayal, the lies, the cheating, the shameless, abandoned, mouth-watering, heart-wrenching discovery of another man's body, the only name on my breath at night, first thing in the morning, when I dream of love, physical love, passion, the in-out, in-out of flesh upon flesh, the only name on my lips is *Nicholas*.

But after a while it gets easy to carry on with lies; open my legs for Stuart with Nicholas in my heart. If Stuart wanted me then I thought I might as well stick with it. I was beyond caring. Nicholas was my one true love – my only lover in my head, the only one I ever wanted in my bed. Nicholas's hands were wrapped so tightly around my heart that there was nothing else to feel.

Would I have wanted a baby that was part him and part me? Oh, there was some romantic notion swirling in my head that if I couldn't have Nicholas at least I'd have had his child but we are here for the purpose of honesty and we must adopt a forensic approach if we are to uncover the truth.

Em, the agony of the reality that I would after all not be with Nicholas consumed me, used every pulse of pain I had. So keenly did I mourn my loss of Nicholas that there was no space in my head to grieve the loss of his child. That grief came only with time.

I still believed that Nicholas and I had a chance. I had done what he wanted, there was no child to get in the way and he had told me he would love me forever. What else was I going to believe?

You may laugh, but the woman on death row does not give up hope, the terminally ill pray for a cure, the terminally lovesick think their prince one day will come.

Stamford, 15 March 1994

Dearest Nicholas,

I love you, I love you, I love you.

When I got your letter I was angry. Not with you, my darling. I could never be angry with you.

How selfish of Marcia to put pressure on you like that. Of course you have no choice but to stay, for now at least. Things need to calm down, I do understand, but Nicholas, you cannot stay with a person because of a suicide threat.

That sort of pressure is unfair – not right. If she kills herself, it's her choice and not your fault. You have to believe that my darling because we have to be together one day. Being apart is not an option, but darling, I will wait. Our love is worth waiting for.

Nicholas, I ache for you with every fibre of my body, in my mind, in my heart, in those places that the two of us have explored and enjoyed.

Like your love, my love too is steadfast. I dream of you at night, your hands on my body, your voice in my head. Life without you is bleak and dark. Promise me that you haven't given up our dream; promise me there is hope. I will wait for you, my darling, I will wait.

Let me know where you are and when you will be there. We must meet soon, my darling, or I shall die of wanting, needing. I ache for you, Nicholas, with all that I am, I ache for you.

Remember, Nicholas, what you said and again I say it back; wherever you are, whenever, I shall be loving you then as now.

Yours forever and always,

Sloane

Work can be a sanctuary when the heart is in turmoil and when each second spent with the wrong hands on your body generates a shameful flinch.

Promotion hailed opportunity; travelling was part of the job – crystal lakes and towering mountains abounded in my written word. It was carte blanche for a ticket to anywhere that Nicholas and I could meet. Anywhere we could satisfy our appetite for the dish we couldn't get at home.

Shall I list the cities, Em, in which he and I betrayed those with whom we lived? Shall I catalogue every detail of where and when I had my legs wrapped around his waist; when he had his face between my thighs; when I held him firmly in my mouth; when I tied him tightly to the bed? But however tightly he was tied it was never as tight as the noose that he had tied around my heart.

Marcia and Stuart, I don't believe they did not suspect our treason. They said nothing but saying nothing does not mean a person doesn't know. How many of us are locked into silence because the power of speech will bring consequences we cannot bear? And sometimes it is easier to stay than it is to leave.

When Libby was born, the lies became harder to tell. Lying in hospital, her heartbeat tick-tocking the hours to her birth, charting each contraction that tore up my insides, took breath from my lungs, my head flitting in and out of consciousness, it was Nicholas whose face was before me, the throbbing sadness that this child was not his, ever present as my labour progressed.

I held this child in my arms and felt the soft in and out of her breath, inhaled the fragrance of her innocence and I knew I was in love. Her face was perfect as it was tiny; her eyes were blue and her hair just wisps of curly blond.

When I returned to work just six weeks after her birth, it was Stuart who played the good parent; picking her up from the nursery, preparing bottles, providing tea and stories and tucking her in at night. His school hours worked perfectly to mould her life into ours but the truth is I was far more absent than dictated by my work.

Stuart was the brilliant father I always knew he would be and I was glad to give him the child he so badly wanted, cementing the illusion of our love. But in my mind she had been born of the love I had for Nicholas. This child would be with me always but I was meant to be with Nicholas and one day, the three of us would share a life.

Chapter 44

Boston, April 12 1998

My darling,

Congratulations – I can't wait to meet the little mite.

I hope you like the yellow roses – a surprise for your first day back at work to remind me of the sunshine that is our love.

Look forward to seeing you in Rome.

Wherever, whenever, N

Chapter 45

Stamford, 3 March 2000

Dearest love,

I'm off to Munich in May. Any chance you could make it there?

I feel sure the students at the university must have a keen interest in your books. I hear the latest is already a *New York Times* Bestseller – clever you!

Whenever, wherever, S

Chapter 46

Boston, August 4 2001

Darling S,

Any chance you could get to London on 10th of next month? I'm giving a talk at the Festival Hall.

Can you stay over? The thought of you in my arms again is turning me on. Don't let me down now. Last week was amazing. I can't wait to come back for more.

Wherever, whenever, N

Chapter 47

20 August 2001

Dearest N,

All sorted. S will have L and I can stay overnight.

No problem with work – just need to pop to London office on one of those days.

Whenever, wherever, S

Chapter 48

Sloane

It is early morning and I sit at my dressing table with Libby on my lap. I look in the mirror and there we are – mother and daughter. I trace the lines of my face in my reflection and compare them with hers. Does she look like me, this angel child? I am thirty-six years old. What will Libby's life be when she becomes me? My stomach lurches and I hear a prayer in my head, *Dear Lord, protect my child from married men...*

'Here, let Mummy do it,' I take the hairbrush and send it softly through her pale yellow locks, the colour of seaside sunshine, of early spring light on a fresh dewy day.

When I leave for work today I won't see my daughter until tomorrow and I am the only one to blame because I cannot say no.

I hug her tightly and plant a wet kiss on her cheek. 'Ugh,' she says, and wipes it off, scrambling from my lap and running to her bedroom next door. She scuttles back in with her pink teddy in her arms and holds him out for me to take, 'Fizzy's turn,' she says. I smile and sit the toy on my lap and pretend to comb its fur.

It was Stuart who called the bear Fizzy, 'After you,' he said, pointing to me. 'It's a gift from you so it should be called after you – and Felicity's too hard to say.'

'More, Mummy, more,' Libby pleads.

'Mummy has to go to work now, Libby-Lou,' I say and she grabs me around my legs and squeezes as tight as her little fists allow, 'You'll be okay,' I add, detaching my limpet and swinging her up into my arms. 'You can do me a nice drawing at nursery and then Daddy will be here with you tonight. Have a think of what you can draw. I'd love a nice picture for my office wall.'

I bury my nose in her hair. She still has that baby smell that I love. She looks at me through her long lashes, 'Mummy stay,' she says.

'I'm sorry, darling, Mummy has to go. Let's go and find Daddy, shall we?' She clings to my neck as we go down the stairs. 'Careful, Libby,' I say as I unhook her fingers from my collar. 'You'll mess up my blouse.'

Stuart is in the kitchen putting milk in the fridge. 'I'm off now,' I say, passing Libby from my arms to his. She won't let go and starts to squeal. 'Come on now, Libby, don't be naughty, Mummy can't *not* go.' The edge of guilt slices through me as I lie to my child. I turn my face from Stuart and he kisses my cheek.

'Got your mobile okay?'

'Yes,' I say, patting my pocket.

'I'll call you later so we can all say 'goodnight'. Shall we do that, Libby-Lou? Shall we call Mummy?' My daughter nods. I kiss her head and run my fingers through her hair.

'Safe journey,' Stuart says.

It is midday by the time the train pulls into Kings Cross. I snap my compact mirror shut, satisfied that the reflection I see is worthy of the man I will meet.

Buffeted by anonymous bodies, criss-crossing the concourse, I make my way to the taxi rank, justifying in my mind the unnecessary expense. It is a day of sunshine but a light breeze skims the air and my hair must look perfect for my date.

'Where to, Miss?' *Ah, 'Miss' – I must look young today...*

'Stratton Street, please, Langan's. Off Piccadilly?'

'Yep, one Langan's Brasserie coming up!' The driver indicates and we pull away from the kerb and he negotiates the roaring jungle of London traffic at lunchtime.

He is there when I arrive and has made sure we are downstairs. We always stay downstairs – so much friendlier, Nicholas says – more chance of spotting a star. *I am not interested in star-spotting, Nicholas. I am only interested in you. The clichéd stars are in my eyes.*

We always have fish and chips. 'So British – I love British,' Nicholas says, trailing his finger up and down the palm of my hand. He licks his lips, a flash of raw sex on his tongue.

'Why must we always eat British?' I say eyes innocent and wide. 'I'm quite partial to a hot dog now and then.'

This is the stuff of our meetings. Seductive comments tossed this way and that, an enticing trifle flicked across to me, an inviting glance flipped back to him. Our banal intercourse is an appetiser, prelude to the main course; a tennis match of flirtation, coaxing and building the throb of heat between our loins.

Marcia is a moot point. So is our child. Our child, Em, take note, might have never existed for all the attention paid, a story petered out into nothing, a mere blip in the quotidian.

The hotel is around the corner off Berkeley Square. Nicholas always books *The Chesterfield* in his name and the receptionist addresses me politely as Mrs Bride. I do not correct her. It's who I want to be.

The intimate surroundings are the perfect foil to our twilight lives. We hide in the plush drapes of the piano bar; we lose ourselves in the soft sheets on the bed and beneath the soothing waters when we bathe. We drink from the forbidden cup and dismiss the shards of guilt that graze our minds. Guilt is not in our brief.

We stroll to Shepherd's Market once our hunger for one another has been for a brief moment slaked, eschewing a fancy French meal for a mad medley of Polish and Mexican in 'our' restaurant. The waitress in *L'autre* knows us well and leads us to our table in the corner out of sight. We are the invisible whispering couple, ghosting through London on white wings, touching no one save one another, owning no life save the one we create in our minds.

'I love you, my Sloane,' Nicholas says. It is not the first time this evening he has said it. It bled from his mouth as he climaxed beneath me, his hands tethered behind him, his ankles bound to the bed.

'You are my witch,' he says, as I open my mouth to receive a forkful of chocolate mousse and I smooth my tongue across my lips as he draws it back.

'I need you, Nicholas. More than you know,' I offer in reply. 'This being apart, it…'

'Sloane, Sloane, I know. Don't you think I know? Every moment without you is agony; I feel it right here.' He places his hand between his stomach and his heart. I imagine the muscles, taut beneath his shirt, his heart beating fast when he cries my name. I know the place where he means – the place where it hurts, and I put my hand there too, feeling the silk of my cream blouse, soft to my touch.

'Where are you supposed to be?' I ask.

'Relax, baby, it's all sorted. I'm 'with the publisher' this evening,' he holds up his hands and makes little quotation marks with his fingers in the air, 'and Marcia never calls when I'm away. I always make sure I call her.' Nicholas shakes his head knowingly and I look away.

'Maybe we shouldn't do this anymore.' I stick my chin up, defiant. I know this is a game. I cannot be defiant to this man to whom all parts of me belong.

Nicholas reaches below the table and I feel a pressure on my knee. He shifts in his seat and slides his hand deftly up my skirt and I feel myself contract.

'Do you really think that we can stop?' he says as he touches me between my legs. He knows the answer before I slowly shake my head. His control is absolute, my arguments null and void.

'Early night?' he says and raises his hand to get the bill. I don't offer anymore; he never accepts so what's the point? Nicholas picks up the tab for everything we do that isn't paid for by my firm. I have a meal ticket to anywhere in the world, courtesy of Harper Enterprises and the irony is never lost. 'You owe me, Marcia', I think as I drain my glass of mellow, oaky wine.

He is on top of me as my telephone rings. 'Damn,' I say. I should get that – it'll be Stu.'

Nicholas does not let me go. My hands are above my head, pinned firmly in his grasp and he pushes into me hard. My thoughts blur. The phone rings again and then again.

In a minute, I'll call in a minute, I promise myself, tearing my mind from the excruciating pleasure of Nicholas as he fills and empties my body in turn. But the promise evaporates into the air as I come and I slip from light into dark.

'I love you, Sloane,' is the last thing I hear.

We have no time for breakfast or lunch, feeding on love until past the moment when we should be left for work – Nicholas to a bookstore and me not far away where High Travel is based.

London is quiet as I cross Berkeley Square, strangely quiet, like it's a Bank Holiday that somehow I have missed. The Rolls Royce showroom, usually buzzy with the overly-rich is deserted and there is not even a queue as I stop at Lloyds to get some cash from the bank.

I pull a bar of Galaxy from my pocket, hitch my bag higher on my shoulder and pick at the foil wrapper. I break off a piece of chocolate and stuff it in my mouth, working it around my tongue and then chewing hungrily as I march up the street towards the familiar and colourful red, white and blue High Travel sign that swings from the Victorian brick building.

I heave open the heavy, wooden door, walk into the office and stop as if some eerie force field bars my way. Despite the ringing of phones there is a tangible silence that feels like death. My London colleagues are gathered around a screen, their hands to their faces as if what they see is other-worldly; like they fear what they do not understand.

I hesitate to break the spell that holds them bound. With effort, I take a step forward, wanting to know and yet not wanting to know what it is they see.

Julia looks up. I gasp. Her eyes are red, tears streaming down her cheeks and her mousey, wavy hair is hanging limp and wet in front of her face. Julia is the only colleague who's moved from my office into London – level-headed, ambitious, focussed – all the things I am not. If she's upset there has to be something seriously wrong.

She moves towards me and gives me a hug. 'Oh my God, Sloane,' she says, 'Oh my God,' and she pulls me across the room to where the crowd of High Travel staff huddle, and I see the North Tower collapse.

'The South Tower has already gone,' Julia says between sobs. 'Oh my God, Sloane, oh my God...'

My breath catches in my throat and I feel a claw inside my chest.

Do I think, Em, of all those who have died? Is there a prayer on my lips for those poor souls, for their families, for their friends? I have one thought, one thought alone: thank God that my lover is safe.

'Look, guys, I know this is tough, but please will you get in here and give us a hand?' a voice shouts from the office next door, 'The phones are going mad and I cannot do this alone.'

The women melt away from the screen and I draw closer and watch. People are screaming and running to escape from the smoke and debris, the carnage that was The World Trade Centre in New York.

'Give us a hand will you, Sloane? Gaynor Summer is Head of Operations worldwide. I am not going to say no. Her face is dark with the enormity of events, a frozen frown stark contrast to her usually animated features.

She nods her pretty blond bob towards the bank of phones. 'We've got hundreds of people stuck all over the place,' she says, 'so there's no way our meeting's happening today.

They've grounded all the flights, and diverted anything in the air – our clients are everywhere – Canada, military bases – every-bloody-where, it's chaos and the phones are going crazy. Everyone's ringing up about relatives – and we just don't have any info.'

In reply I dump my bag, take off my coat and sit at the nearest empty chair and start taking calls, logging for my colleagues what is happening where and trying to reach Tour Managers all over the world. Still, I have a kind of distance from events, as if my colleagues have been touched by some fever that I have failed to contract.

'Oh shit, Sloane,' Julia says between calls. 'I meant to tell you and completely forgot. I'm sorry. Stuart's been ringing all morning. He thought we were going out last night. I said I hadn't seen you. He wants you to call home. Sounded pretty urgent – I'm so sorry I didn't say, only with all this going on…'

'It's okay, Julia,' I reassure, but I feel an icy chill.

I never called him back. Fuck, I never called him back. Stuart knows. Stuart must know. I filter through the possibilities in my head and stop the dial on Marcia and Cathy. What do they know – what do they suspect? What tasty morsel of half-truth has Pete passed on to Stuart now, and how do I explain my whereabouts last night? Fuck, I should just have answered the phone.

'I'll ring him later. Better get on with this now.'

'Anyone want coffee?' Julia asks.

'I'll make it,' I say, glad of a task to free me from the anguished voices of relatives, the stressed, barked requests of the Tour Guides who should have been leaving from Gatwick, Heathrow, Birmingham, you name it, dumped with an aircraft worth of clients, fed-up, upset and scared all at the same time.

I put the kettle on and wash a pile of dirty mugs while I wait. I often think it would be fun to work here in London, the fizz of the place compared with our sleepy market town. But there's no Production team here – we are all kept out in the sticks. And anyway, Stuart wouldn't think much of me being down here. Stuart. Fuck.

I grab the jar from the cupboard and drop a heaped spoon of coffee into each mug, thinking the extra caffeine might help. This lot are in for a long day. I look at my watch. Time I made tracks. I want to be home in time to tuck Libby in.

'It's for you, Sloane,' Julia pokes her head around the kitchen door and mouths 'Stuart'. I nod and sigh and follow her to my borrowed desk. 'Coffee's in the kitchen,' I tell Julia as I raise the receiver to my ear.

'Hi, Stuart, terrible news about…'

'Where the fuck have you been? How dare you switch off your fucking phone?' Stuart's voice is distorted with rage.

'But I…' I swivel round and fish the phone from my pocket and look down. My battery is flat. 'My battery…'

'Yeah, right… your battery…'

'I'm just here trying to help – it's so dreadful…'

Stuart's voice drops a pitch. 'Yes, Sloane, It is dreadful news. Look, the phone doesn't matter now. Just come home. You have to come home, Sloane,' he says more gently. 'It's Libby… you have to come home.'

'Are you sure you'll be okay on your own? Julia asks, handing me my bag. She thrusts a company mobile into my hand and I bury it in my pocket. 'Just in case,' she says. I step up into the train and nod.

'Let me know as soon as you know, okay?' I nod again.

'Stuart said she was in a pretty bad way; that nobody seemed to know what had happened for sure. He thinks some sort of accident…'

'Yes, Sloane, you said. Look, give us a ring when you know what's happening. I'll let them know at the office in Stamford – you won't need to bother ringing in.' Julia gives me a hug and strokes her hand across my head. 'Good luck,' she says, 'hope she's okay.'

I push my way down the train and take a seat opposite an older lady. Her hair is tired blond with darker roots. Her glasses, brown tortoiseshell, are on the table in front of her with a novel, splayed open face down, *The Pilot's Wife*.

I shift in my seat and pull out the office phone, picking tiny sods of damp Kleenex from the keys, and I send a text to Nicholas. I need him to know what has happened.

The woman looks up and I see she has been crying too. 'Such awful news,' she says, 'My daughter's boyfriend is out there at the moment. We can't get through,' she nods at my phone, 'so awful, she feels so helpless…' She holds a soggy, crumpled tissue. She tries to open it out to stem fresh tears but it comes apart in her hand.

Ah, helpless – that's a good word. Where was I when my daughter needed me? Ah yes, I was being helpless beneath my lover's body, not giving her a second's thought.

Reaching into my bag, I draw out a packet of tissues and offer them.

'Oh, that's so kind of you, thank you.' She smiles weakly. 'You don't expect to need more than one packet in a day, do you? It's just so awful.'

I want to comfort her, to tell her things will be okay but I don't believe they will. I don't believe that things will ever be okay again.

My phone is in my lap; still no text. Why has he not texted me back?

I look around the carriage. The electricity of shock and silence hangs in the air and is drawn on the faces of the few people who travel with me towards home.

'Do you know someone over there, dear?' the lady asks. Her eyes are circles of blue-grey where she has rubbed shadow and mascara into swollen, crinkled sockets.

'I think my daughter is dead,' I say.

Chapter 49

Nicholas

Well what was I supposed to do, Em? Drop everything and run back over there when I have customers waiting in line? And there's the agent and the photographer — all wanting their piece of me. What was I supposed to do?

Soon as I got the text, I wanted to go, offer some comfort, help her out, but I had commitments – what was I supposed to do with all those folk who had turned up just to see me?

Truth is everyone disappeared pretty damn quickly in the end. Guess everyone's nerves were jangled by what happened in New York. The agent, he dangles a contract in front of me and then he goes off to his wife and kids. No one wants to be away from home, like being home could keep your family safe.

Then it hits me – I'm stuck here in London with stuff in Boston that needs my attention. What the hell am I going to do? How the hell am *I* going to get home?

The whole thing was a mess, Em, but I had no real idea what had happened – anymore than she did at the time. And I had no idea either what was happening back home. No idea at all.

Chapter 50

Sloane

The nurse hands me a hairbrush. 'Would you like to do it?' she asks softly and draws back so that I can lean in and brush my daughter's pale blond hair.

I am doing this and yet I am not. It is some other person standing here, hairbrush in hand, dead daughter chilling on a slab, her hair framing her face, a golden halo against ashen skin.

I bend and kiss her. She is there and she is not there. I think I feel her and yet I do not. Is there any essence of Libby bound in this body before me or has all that is Libby vanished with the stopping of her heart?

Her icy cheek feels firm beneath my lips. What is it they have stuffed in her cheeks to make them firm? Or maybe that is just how it is when you're dead.

All that I am is trapped in the back of my throat, frozen like her little body, wanting to spring to life, to find the vital signs and begin again pulsing blood through veins, breath through lungs. She looks asleep. I want to sleep. Here. With her. Always.

'Sloane, I am so sorry.' I look up and it is Cathy by my side. 'The service was beautiful. I just don't know how you...'

'You,' I say.

'Sloane, I'm so sorry – for everything. It's not the moment now but you need to know that I *am* sorry. When Marcia rang me that time, it was the middle of the night. It sounded like she knew everything anyway. I didn't know what to do. I've really missed you, Sloane.'

'Go away, Cathy,' I say. 'I don't want you here.'

'Please, Sloane, I...'

Pete comes and he takes Cathy gently by the arm and leads her away.

'They're ready,' says Stuart, 'this way.'

What do you do with your daughter's dead body? Do you bury it in the ground in some decaying old churchyard? Stick it in a grave in the local cemetery where thugs congregate at night, drugs and condoms strewn on holy ground? Imagine it rotting day by day. When does the last strand of yellow blond hair fall from around her face? How long does it take for maggots to eat her skin? Is the teddy she was buried with still there – six months later – a year? Or has that too lost its stuffing, a hollowed out form that once brought so much joy? And what use a piece of polished marble with etched out words? A place to come when all other places are alien, hostile, unforgiving?

Or do you kiss her corpse goodbye and then send it to be burnt? Send it up a chimney to be belched into the air, tiny particles of dust settling finally in some stranger's back garden, to be crapped on by a pet cat or dog. Take your little pot of ashes and scatter them where? Off a cold, lonely cliff to wash far out to sea? In some playground where you have pushed a swing or some stinking shopping arcade where you bought her first shoes?

Where is the blueprint for what must be done? When was it they said that you would not see her grow up and wear your high heels, play with your make-up, get married and have a child of her own, grandchildren lost in the wake of her death – futures snuffed out between the beats of her heart?

The little wicker basket is lowered. I cannot stop myself – I have to touch it one last time and I sink to my knees in the soft earth and grasp at the coffin as it disappears from view, my hand grazing the prick of its straw. I have no reason to move from here. I am iced up in the misery of what has happened, petrified, as stony as a tomb.

In the air hangs the smell of fresh mown grass and on my skin I feel the warmth of the sun; so different from that rainy day when they buried my mum and my dad. I watch a robin as it hops along the side of the open grave and I think that this is a better place than many to bury a child.

'They think it was long QT syndrome, according to the Post Mortem, although we'll never know for sure,' I hear Stuart say. 'One minute she's bending over to pick up her toy, the next minute... She didn't stand a chance – some problem with the beats of the heart – arrhythmia they call it; much more common than you think.

'No, I didn't tell her until she got home....she was away... London,' I walk away, through the patio doors and into the garden.

I don't want these people here. My colleagues, Stuart's colleagues, neighbours, what do they know about anything? Celebrate her life rather than mourning her death, the vicar said. But her death is my death so how can I do that?

'Sloane,' I turn around and all my grief is anger.

'No, Cathy. No. Just go away will you? Just get out of my garden, out of my house and out of my life.' I push her hard on her shoulders, propelling her away and she stumbles backwards into the garden bench, hitting her elbow crack on the arm of the seat.

She grabs her elbow and holds it into her chest. She is crying. Stuart comes out through the patio doors, in his hand a bottle of wine.

'Cathy, are you okay?' he says.

'What's it got to do with you if she is okay or not?' I say. 'She shouldn't be here anyway. This is my daughter's funeral and she is not welcome in my house.'

'It's my house too, Sloane, and my daughter's funeral.'

'Cathy has done nothing but be a good friend to me – and to you for that matter, trying to protect you when all this crap with Nicholas is going on. Years we've put up with it now. Did you think we were all blind? Years of your lying and your cheating and your sneaking and the three of us, well we just pretend it's all not happening, expecting you anytime soon to come to your senses and be a proper mother and wife.

'Thought you loved me deep down and that it would all work out – especially having Libby but no. How stupid could I get?

'I know you were with him. Don't bother denying it, we all know you were. I'm not sure I even care. You have done this, Sloane. You, Nicholas, your selfish, selfish, fucking selfish behaviour, so don't you go blaming Cathy. You've only got yourself to blame.'

'You okay, old girl?' Pete strides across the garden towards Cathy. Cathy nods and then flicks her eyes towards Stuart and Pete takes his cue.

'Stuart,' Pete says, placing a hand on Stuart's shoulder, 'Come on old chap. Not the best time for this, eh? Come back inside, have another drink.'

Stuart slams the wine down on the edge of the garden table. It remains suspended, for a split second could go either way, but then it topples over, crashing into the concrete paving and shattering at our feet. Stuart glares down at the red stain spread up his trouser leg and looks straight at me, his soft, kind eyes hard and cruel. He turns away, years of cool passivity ignited finally into fury by the torch of my affair, welcome anger to staunch briefly the flow of pain.

Cathy is still clutching her elbow. 'Let me,' I say, and I sit beside her and rub the spot where a pink patch is starting to swell.

'Cathy, oh Cathy,' I say. She shifts in her seat and puts her arm around me and I rest my head on her shoulder. 'All these years, all this wasted time. He's right. I am to blame. All the stuff – the affair, the abortion, Marcia, and now Libby... I am being punished – it's all my fault, Cathy.' A pitiful mewl comes from deep inside me, it twists around, pulls at the knots, works them loose and sets free another wave of pain.

'It's okay, Sloane, just let it out. You need to cry...'

'It's just – the doctor, she gave me some stuff, to help me sleep, get through the funeral – it's just, I don't know where I am. I can't feel, it's all in here,' I push my hand into my stomach, contracting my muscles like I have been punched in the gut, 'And I just can't let it out. It's like I am floating on top of all this, can't feel, can't breathe. Oh my God, I can't believe she's dead, Cathy, can't believe she won't just come running through the door...'

Cathy holds me tightly. I can feel she is crying too.

'Oh, I'm sorry, Cathy. So sorry – I should never have got you involved, never have asked…'

'It's okay, Sloane, it's okay. I'm sorry too. It's just all been a mess. We just have to calm things down now, Sloane, have to take stock.'

I nod. Take stock of what, I think. What is there left?

'I brought something for you, couple of things, actually,' Cathy says when finally my sobs fade to exhausted little sharp intakes of breath. She stands and makes a sling of her hand to hold her elbow. 'Just a second – I need to go to the car.'

The house is empty. It's only now that I realise the guests have disappeared, gone home to gossip about the slanging match at the wake, fodder for their smug dinner parties from now until next year.

'Here,' Cathy says, sitting back on the bench. She opens her large canvas bag and hands me a green envelope.

'I wasn't going to give it to you here, like this, but it doesn't really seem to matter now. Not against all this…' Cathy looks around, taking in the empty swing in the garden, the broken glass on the floor.

I tear it open, draw out a single sheet of paper and read out loud:

'Dear Stuart and Sloane,' I begin. I look up at Cathy. She shrugs and wrinkles her brow. I tilt the note towards her so she can read it too.

Dear Stuart and Sloane,

We have heard your sad news and wish to express our sincere condolences at the loss of dear Libby.

You are both in our thoughts and prayers.

May the good Lord be with you and your families and comfort you at this difficult time.

God bless you both,

The Harpers and the Brides

So that's it then – the only communication from Nicholas since Libby died. If indeed it is from him. So that's how much he cares.

I let the letter drop onto my lap.

'There's something else,' Cathy says, drawing a flat package from her bag, 'I want you to have this.'

'Oh my God, no, Cathy… you can't – not this, it's yours.'

'No, it's yours now, Sloane. Open it. Please,' Cathy says. I tear open the pale pink paper and read the engraving on the stone memorial.

Il vivait, il jouait, riante créature. Que te sert d'avoir pris cet enfant, ô nature?

'*She lived, she played, a laughing creature, what good has it done you, oh nature, to have taken this child?*' Cathy says, 'You should have it now, Sloane. It's a poem for a child – not a baby that has never even been born. Maybe it was always meant for you.'

Cathy is gone and I sit in the silence. The house is so quiet where once it was full of a lively child's giggle and bubble, a soft creature who would snug to my skin and be happy for just a kiss and a hug. I could have done that more – hugged her, held her. Now that she is gone I think how often I could have been holding my child instead of someone else's man.

I stand and put one foot in front of the other, walking trance-like along the hallway and I shoulder open the door to Libby's playroom. Stuart is at the window, staring out. He turns to face me.

'Drink?' says Stuart.

'Why not?' I say. Maybe the wine will free me from this hollow thump in my chest, this feeling that I should be finding Libby somewhere, calling her name in the still of the cemetery, searching for her in the park. I hug myself as if doing so will make me feel her hugging me.

Stuart takes care not to brush against me as he passes, as if to touch me would somehow infect him.

Libby's playroom is still as she left it, pencils strewn on the carpet, the pink plastic dolls' house wide open, its occupants banished to the floor awaiting Libby's latest recreation of their home. I sit and place the beds inside, a pink sofa, dining table and chairs and finally I reinstate the family, mother, father, brother, sister and dog, and I close the dolls' house door.

Libby's red striped fleece is over the arm of the chair. I pluck it up and hold it to my face, breathing in the scent of my child who is gone.

Stuart reappears in the doorway, 'I forgot to give you this,' he says, handing me a white piece of card. I turn it over and there we are – Daddy and Libby in the house, Mummy outside.

'Libby drew this for you the night you stayed away,' he says, and I look up at him through the mists in my eyes.

'You are outside because you are always away, she said.' Stuart hands me a glass of red wine and rolls his eyes with a sneer.

'Some mother you turned out to be. Have you checked your phone?' he says as he walks away.

My mobile is charging in the study and I wrench it from its socket and turn it on, impatient to bring it to life. The little bleep signals there is a message and I press the keys to find out what it is.

I hear Stuart's voice in the background. There is a giggle and then another and then a gap. 'Go on,' Stuart says, 'you have to say something.'

There is a pause as he hands her back the phone and then my daughter speaks to me for the very last time.

'I love you, Mummy,' she says, 'Night, night.'

Chapter 51

Nicholas

Now that's not fair, Em. You can't blame me for that note – it was right to include us all. What else could I have done? I had to think of Stuart. And maybe I just didn't have it in me to write what I know Sloane would have wanted to read. Truth is, I had other things on my mind.

To start with I had no idea the child had died. Just thought she'd had some kind of accident and that Sloane, you know, she was just getting all het up like mothers do. I only found out about Libby because Cathy called to speak to Marcia and because Marcia wasn't there, I took the call.

I didn't let on to Cathy that there was trouble this end – why would I? It's not like she could have done anything about it and she had enough on her plate with what was going on with Sloane.

Thing is, Em, I didn't know I cared quite so much – about Marcia, that is. Yeah – there's an irony for you.

It took me forever to get home. I finally managed to get in touch with the folks and Harper got me on a flight first class. When I got there it was Caesar who met me from the airport. Boston was crazy – it's never like that in the afternoon. Rush hour doesn't start proper until four at the earliest but this was like a zoo.

Took so long to get out to the house and Caesar, he was weird, like he didn't want to talk to me. I kept asking how things were panning out – you know, after the twin towers and all and he just kept saying stuff like, 'Oh you know how these things are, Mr Bride,' or 'I guess we just have to cope with what God sends.' Caesar, now he usually likes to chat, tells me about who's been doing what while I've been away but not this time. He's just not giving anything away.

'Oh thank God you're home, Nicky,' Mom says when I get out of the car. She's wearing an apron over her dress –I guess she's been doing some baking.

'Hey, Mom, how're you doing? Baked some brownies for me?' Caesar closes the door behind me and then disappears off behind the house.

'Listen, Nicky, forget the brownies. I need to talk to you before…'

'You don't need to talk to him about nothing, Patricia-May,' Dad appears from nowhere. He's practically running up the drive.

'Where the hell have you been, boy?' he says and he grabs me by the scruff of my neck like I'm some kid. I forget myself for a second and I go to fight him off but my mom's screaming to my dad to let me go and to me not to hurt him. It's like the world's gone mad. My dad lets go real sudden and I lose my balance and fall back against the car.

'You've been with that English whore,' he says. 'Well, haven't you? You've been with that goddamned whore when you should have been here taking care of what's yours.'

'Elliott, please, Nicholas has no idea what you're talking about, have you Nicholas? Tell him, darling. Tell him what's happened. You're not being fair.'

'Well, you better not have been, son. Because if they find out you've been screwing that bitch while all this has been happening and the rest of us have been worrying ourselves sick, well it's all over, Nicholas; all over for you, all over for us and sure as hell all over for the business. No one's going to want any of us once the Harpers have chewed us up and spat us out.'

He spits on the floor at my feet and storms off into the house. I look at Mom.

'No one told you, did they, Nicky?' she says and she starts crying.

'No one told me what?'

'Let's just go in and I'll fix us a drink,' she says, wiping her face on her apron.

'Wait, Mom – I just need to go see Marcia. Her phone's been turned off since… you know… and she was out when I got a hold of Abe.'

'Abe – there you are, I was just coming over…' Abe strides towards me straight across the lawn. He's swinging his arms like he's trying to win some walking race.

'So you're here, eh?' he says. 'Well, why don't you just come along with me, Nicky? You and me, we've got us some talking to do.'

'Abe, don't,' says Mom. 'He doesn't know any more than we do.'

'We'll see about that,' he says. 'Reckon this is all to do with that English girl who came over that one time. At least, that's what Nancy says – and I figure from the look on your face, she got that one darn right.'

'It's not what you think, Abe. Sloane and me, we go back a long way – whatever Marcia's said, I don't want you to think. I love Marcia, you know I do, I'd never do anything to upset you all – not like that.

'Mom, I don't understand. What's going on – why are you crying like that?'

'Tell, him, Abe – just tell him. Abe, I know what you're doing, you and Nancy – you're hoping against hope that Nicky can explain what's happened, but we all know he won't be able to – we all know the truth. It's just that none of us wants to face it. Being angry with Nicky won't fix anything. That won't do us all any good.'

'Will someone just tell me what the hell is going on? Where's Marcia? She'll tell me. Have you all lost your senses or what?'

'Nicky, Nicky, that's what I'm trying to tell you. You can't ask Marcia because Marcia is missing. Marcia has disappeared.'

Chapter 52

Sloane

Em, oh Em, is this where your story has led us? To this point where my child is dead and a wife is missing? I know now, you see, I know that this story only ends because of you – and that the madness started because of you. You should have been a beginning and we made you an end. Don't you see that this is how it happened? Don't you think that I would undo it if I could? But you cannot bring people back from the dead.

Stamford, 23rd July 2011

Dear Nicholas,

I thought I heard Libby last night. No, that's wrong. I know I heard Libby. I was in the kitchen, writing the novel – the one I told you about it in my last email – when I heard her calling softly from upstairs. I went up but I couldn't find her. I so wish you had been here. Maybe with your help I could have found her.

I miss you so much, Nicholas. It's so long since I felt your arms around me, your fingers through my hair. I know you need me like I need you so can we not at last be together? Marcia has been gone such a long time now. What is there to stop us being a couple? Being a proper couple – like we have always dreamed we would. I love writing for a living but it does get so lonely, especially with Cathy gone.

The blog was a terrific idea. Who would have thought it would go this far? That was so clever of you, Nicholas. How clever of you to know exactly what it is I need. But then you have always cared about my needs, haven't you, Nicholas? As I have always taken care of yours. I need at least to hold your hand. Please, Nicholas, please. Please get back to me soon. I know you are busy, but it makes it even worse when you don't write.

Remember, Nicholas, that wherever you are, whenever, I shall be loving you then as now.

Yours forever and always,

Sloane

'Good morning everyone and welcome to *Women Today* with Suzanne Radisson, the radio programme that focuses on you.

'I am delighted to introduce our special guest today – Sloane Granger, author of the book that's been storming the charts, *Everything You Ever Wanted to Know about Loss and Always Hoped You'd Never Have to Ask.*

'That's a pretty long title, Sloane.'

'Good morning, Suzanne. Thank you so much for inviting me. Yes – it is a long title but it needed to say exactly what it is on the can. There are lots of sentimental books out there about bereavement and loss, giving heart-wrenching examples of people's own specific battles but I wanted to write something that took that element completely away and focused on how to deal with loss in a more practical sense. Just straight talk, dealing with it almost as if it's your job, I suppose, without breaking your heart all over again reading a load of other people's sad tales.'

'Now you're pretty qualified to talk about this, aren't you Sloane?'

'Yes, you could certainly say that. My parents both died in a car crash when I was pretty young – thirteen – and although I was brought up by a very loving aunt, there was always the sense that part of me was missing.

'When my daughter died suddenly in 2001 aged just three and a half, I didn't just mourn her, I found myself mourning all the losses that I have ever had in my life. Not just the death of people I loved but also separation from people, disappointments, betrayal, that kind of thing. You can't help revisiting all the bad things that have ever happened.

'It also made me realise that everybody's worst is exactly that. People used to say to me that this must be the worst thing for anybody and I don't disagree – but not everybody, thank God, has to go through the loss of a child. That doesn't mean though that they don't hurt every bit as much when they go through the loss of their first love or a divorce or even the death of a pet.'

'Isn't that taking the theory a bit far?'

'No, I don't think it is. Anybody, anything or any situation – when it changes in a way that's out of your control, it sets off a cycle of feelings – you think that maybe you could have done something differently, you feel angry, guilty, helpless, alone – because grief in whatever form is very isolating.

'Even with my husband, we reacted in completely different ways. He shut down, wouldn't talk about Libby, which pushed me further and further away – so it doesn't necessarily help to have the proverbial problem shared.'

'In fact, you and your husband split up after Libby died, didn't you?'

'There were several factors involved but it was certainly partly because of the intensity of the situation. We didn't communicate and we blamed one another too – I blamed Stuart because he was unable to save her, he blamed me because I wasn't there. Blame and guilt have no place where loss is concerned because they do not unite, they simply drive a wedge.'

'You used to work for High Travel, is that right?'

'That's right, Suzanne. I worked for them for a number of years – I was at their offices in London when Libby died. I went back to work for a while but I just found it too difficult to focus on what is essentially a luxury in life when my whole baseline for happiness had disappeared.'

'Now you told us, Sloane, that there was a certain irony to you being in those offices that day. Would you care to share your story with our listeners?'

'Well, as we all know, we are approaching the 10-year anniversary of 9/11 and it was that very day in 2001 that Libby died. I was in the High Travel offices while Libby was dying at home. I feel like I should have somehow known that she was dying without me...'

'You said that your child passing away on 9/11 made life even more difficult for you. How come?'

'Can I just say – like I say in my book – euphemisms don't help anyone move forward. Libby died – she didn't just pass away, like she fainted for a bit. She died and she's not coming back.

'Thing is, Suzanne, everyone mourns what happened at the Twin Towers on that day. I was just one mother whose child had died – compare that with all the heartache that went on – still goes on in New York, all the people who lost loved ones, people who are still missing. I found, especially in the early years after her death, that it seemed somehow selfish even to mention Libby.

'After it happened, everyone was talking about New York, Washington, the planes, the horror. People would cross the street rather than talk to me – because there was nothing for them to talk about except 9/11 if they weren't going to talk about Libby – and they couldn't talk to me about 9/11 without acknowledging my own personal 9/11, if you see what I mean. So neighbours, colleagues, everyone just avoided talking to me.

'It's going to be ten years since Libby died this year – but it's also ten years since 9/11. Who's going to be interested in what I went through compared with that? It's like history has taken away my right to grieve.

'The thing is, Suzanne, you never get over the death of a child – vocabulary like 'coming to terms with', 'getting over', those kinds of phrases, I just chuck them straight out. What you can do is to adjust and incorporate those people you have lost into your life in a different way. Learn that life does become normal again, but it's a different sort of normal. Learn how to honour their memory and celebrate their lives through living your own life as fully as you can – in a way that you think would make them proud.

'And I'm not proud of a lot of what I have done in my life, Suzanne – and I think that many of us would say the same.

When something like this happens it changes perspectives – you have to re-learn what life is and it can be an opportunity for change. I know this is a crazy thing to say but I firmly believe that this has made me a better person. You can be bitter and give up or you can accept what has happened and move forward. There is a choice.'

'Your book has been very well received – why particularly do you think this is?'

'I think maybe because I have been completely frank and honest and it comes from the heart. It also comes in the hope that if just one person reads it and manages to take back their life after a major loss, then it has done its job and for me that's a blessing for sure.'

'I understand that sales of your novels have been going extremely well too. I suppose the next thing will be film rights on your life story – something akin to *Eat, Pray, Love*?'

'Well, that seems a bit far-fetched right now but you know, never say 'never' and all that…'

The flight is on time and the *tgv* from Paris to Tours swings us swiftly through the miles from the capital of France to the capital of the Loire Valley. When I complain about the breakneck speed of the train, its lurches and curves, Elodie simply shrugs with another of her little *bof* sounds.

'What do you expect from a high speed train?' she says, '*Train à Grande Vitesse* – that's what *tgv* means.' I know that, of course, but allow her a moment of linguistic glory. It is the least she deserves after coming with me to the studios and organising this end of our trip. Our return journey is not to be by train – high speed or not. We are to be chauffeur driven in her lover's Mercedes Benz.

'Thanks for coming with me, Elodie. I hate this sort of thing – just makes me nervous – and it's all such a load of rubbish. Makes me feel dirty somehow – making money out of misery, out of Libby.' I run my fingers through my hair and shake my head, as if I can somehow shake away the stain of using my daughter's death to sell books.

'You know is not true,' Elodie says, 'the people who are miserable – you 'elp them with your book – you 'elp me.'

I laugh. 'How do I help you, Elodie?' I emphasise the *h* for good measure.

'Your *courage*,' she says, pronouncing it coo-rarge.

'You mean courage, Elodie,' I say, correcting her, 'And I'm not brave at all. I just put on a good show.'

'*Bof*,' she says, shrugging her shoulders, 'You are a good person. Why you cannot see this?'

Em, when Cathy died, it felt like there was no one left in my world. I have forever since been grateful of the small space that Elodie has always occupied, a kind of half-world existence in my life, pulling my on-off love affair with France close every now and then.

But it was not Elodie, it was Cathy who had been there for me day after day once Stuart moved out. It was Cathy who had called the doctor when she found me in the bath pulling nails from my fingers and hair from my head, slipping slowly beneath the tepid water, wanting to slip into oblivion. Only cowardice prevented an end to the in-and-out of my breath.

The strands of hair came easily away, the physical pain welcome, concentrating the mind away from the stabbing hollow and fearful chasm that Libby's death had cleaved through the core of me. So easily they came away, the locks from my head, like the wet tails of sodden rats, dirty parts of vermin torn from a soiled and repulsive woman who had let her child die while she lay wantonly in the wrong man's bed.

What use is hair when your child is dead? When all you want is to be that child so you are dead that she might live. Or to be dead too, so that the two of you can be together – so that she is not lonely and alone wherever it is that she hovers in the ether; your lonely child who died without you, when your guard was down and she was taken from you. She died without you when you cared more about being somewhere else than about protecting this precious being who clung to you, telling you not to go. Holding you close like she knew in her little heart that those were the last moments you would spend together and that her hopeful hug was the last you would ever feel from her warm, living arms.

'I have to go,' I had lied, when all the time it was she who had to go, and her going was forever where my going was for nothing, like everything else I have done since her death.

I would have died myself were it not for two things. One, Cathy refused to leave my side thus removing all possibility of suicide and two, the strange fact that my urge to live somehow remained despite the pain.

Cathy told me when she was dying, when the cancer had eaten almost everything but her brain, which remained quick and real until the end; she told me that looking after me gave her a kind of purpose and allowed her to make up in some way for her interference in my life. When I made to protest she raised her shrunken hand to my mouth.

'No, Sloane,' she said, 'I was wrong. I was like Marcia – I was jealous. Secretly, I called you 'Golden Girl' – not so secretly in fact. Pete knows, Marcia knew. Other people too. It was unforgiveable.

'I know that you didn't mean for everything to happen like it did and I did believe you about Nicholas and Marcia – that you didn't know that she was his wife. It was just – well, everyone seemed to want you – Nicholas, Stuart, the kids at school loved you, never took the piss like they did out of me, then you had Libby – and the swanky job. I couldn't even manage to hang on to Pete, was never really able to trust him after – well, *her*.

'I wanted you to have a hard time but what happened to you, Sloane. God, what happened to you, I...'

Ha, makes me laugh, Em, people being jealous of me. What do I have except a long line of mostly dead people I have loved and who have left me?

I'll tell you what I have – I have this damned, annoying upbeat personality that keeps me going and going even when I should know better – when I should lie down and give in and show others my pain. The pain does not stop, the missing and hurting and missing and hurting – the relentless thud, thud, thud of the great gap in my heart where Libby should be; the realisation morning after morning that she is not, after all, coming back; the endless rewind of the moment when I could have chosen to stay; the daydream where I do not after all leave her side and where I am the one who saves her.

If I had been there would I have saved her, Em? The crucifying fact is that I shall never ever know if my absence was the difference between my daughter's life and death.

I didn't go to Cathy's funeral because I knew that Stuart would be there for Pete. I won't see Stuart. I can't. I haven't seen him for nearly ten years.

The bereavement counsellor Cathy carted me off to reckoned I should see him – that we could offer each other some support despite our separation, but Stuart accuses me without even opening his mouth. I cannot ever again see that look on his face. I will not. I am terrific at self-flagellation. I do not need him to do it for me. Besides, Stuart has moved on; new wife, new child. He has a new life. He does not need reminding of what he doesn't have.

And what of this book? This joke of a self-help book? Well, that was Nicholas's idea.

Oh yes, Em, there's a shocker. Nicholas is still in my life. This man who is the very reason that I did not spend my daughter's last moments with her in my arms, the reason I made no frantic attempts to resuscitate her and bring her back to her life that she might go to school, take exams, have a boyfriend, lose her virginity, get married, have children – my grandchildren, to have a life, to live, love and breathe. This man who is the reason for all that is still in my life – and I am on my way to meet him today.

When I close my eyes I can see the look on his face – the ecstasy-stroke-agony look when his eyes shine with longing and he whispers the words in my ear; 'tie me up, Sloane, tie me up'. I cannot resist him and he cannot resist me. It is simply how it is.

We see little of one another since he took over at Harper. He feels he owes it to them all, to keep that whole empire going, especially after what happened to Marcia. I like that he feels he has a duty to fulfil but I hate that it keeps us apart.

Em, I do not believe one word of the book I have spewed from my soul. Perhaps I thought I did but not now. The garbage that spills its stench from the pages is equal only to the pain that is buried in the cesspit of my mind. How can I still want to fuck this man when this man has fucked up my life? How can I pretend to people that there is a way forward from the death of your child? This whole rubbish about time healing; it's not true. Just not true.

I liken bereavement to labour pains only in the reverse; when you are giving birth the pains get closer together and stronger and stronger; when your child dies the pains get further and further apart and less powerful over time. But then just when you think you have made progress, bang you are thrust back into the same stark reality, anger and clean, pure pain as if it were only yesterday you buried your child. To tell people differently is to tell lies. And Em, we are here to tell the truth.

Truth? Well, that's a joke too. My appearance alone is a lie; this together kind of person, shiny hair, neatly groomed, impeccably cut designer jeans, tailored jacket from a fancy New York boutique, branded luggage, elegant with a price tag to match; it's like I have fitted into another person's life and I have no idea who this other person is.

At least I know that this person is attractive and that she can still turn heads. That I can turn Nicholas's head is crucial to how our story will end.

When Nicholas was asked to give a speech at the opening of the newly renovated Château de l'Islette, he insisted that I should be there, that I have been part of his whole success with the Rodin and Camille Claudel book and many since. 'Remember, that's where the lovers worked and secretly met,' he said, 'you should be here, Sloane, by my side.'

Bring Elodie, he'd suggested, and I thought it a good idea – to meet up with her in that glorious part of France. Elodie decided she would bring her man too and after all these years, we were to meet this elusive but very important boss of hers from the Palais du Luxembourg, the Upper Chamber of the government in France. I was intrigued to say the least.

Nicholas had seemed different, lighter somehow, less reticent; he had this child-like buzz to him when we spoke of our plans, and it was infectious. He said he had a surprise for me – a surprise for me, Em.

I expected him to refuse when I suggested stopping off for a couple of weeks in Paris after the *soirée*, but he readily agreed to extend our time together beyond that one evening in the Loire. He seemed delighted even, when I told him we could have Elodie's *appartement de standing*, her upmarket, kept-woman's penthouse all to ourselves. She and her man were heading off down to Cannes. 'A little business trip,' she had said, the tone of conspiracy in her voice conveying a wink of the eye.

For the first time since I could remember, I was looking forward to something. I had made a decision, Em, and this visit would be the perfect chance to carry out my plan. Nicholas had a surprise for me, and as it happened, I had one for him.

When I asked Elodie to come to England first, she didn't hesitate for a second. 'Of course, *ma chère amie*, it is a small thing which you ask. And it is easy of course for me to take a day or two from work. Who is going to miss me?' she said.

Elodie recognises who I am and she knows exactly who she is, which is why I needed her to be with me in those radio studios that day. In the years since Libby died, we have met, this side of the Channel or that, and I find her quiet acceptance that things are simply as they are reassuring somehow. Like black and white is not necessary and that the shades of life are acceptable, normal even, to her.

As they placed the headphones on my ears, gave me water to drink in case my mouth got dry, briefed me on what areas we would cover and tested my voice in the huge microphone that hung down in front of my face, it was Elodie who gave me the thumbs up and mouthed *courage* as we went on air.

It is courage that I shall need now, Em, to complete the story that is yours and mine.

Chapter 53

Nicholas

Marcia missing? I just couldn't believe my own ears. And you want to know the worst of it, Em? Everyone's acting like it's my fault. Everyone except Mom, that is. Thank God I could prove that I was in London way after Marcia was seen for the last time or else old man Harper, he'd have had me arrested on the spot – as if I am the kind of guy who'd stash his wife away somewhere or commit murder!

Kind of weird in the end that proving I was in the same place as Sloane made me innocent of a worse crime, but in their eyes I was guilty alright. If I hadn't been away then Marcia would never have gone to New York.

She needed a little distraction, Caesar told us. She had a darn good idea of what I was up to so she got him to take her all the way to New York, to her favourite store to buy designer clothes at knock-down prices. Right beneath the World Trade Centre on the day the planes took it down. Jesus – all for a bargain.

The store was still standing so, you know, we all had some hope – that maybe she had lost her way or lost her mind with everything that went on. Day after day we went down there to the place they now call Ground Zero, posting her picture, writing her notes, hoping that she would be seen somewhere by someone and that she would one day come home.

I think that Nancy and Abe hoped against hope that I really had got Marcia hidden away somewhere. That I'd kidnapped my own wife for some crazy reason – at least that would have meant that she'd be safe. But as time went on we all knew that it was hopeless to hope; that Marcia had been there, caught up for no good reason in the Trade Centre disaster and I grew to believe it really was my fault. I should have been around to stop my wife frivolously going off for the day to some store in New York for some bargain she didn't need because I was not there.

It was Caesar who saw her for the last time; Caesar who dropped her off, who saw her last smile and her last wave as she took her last elegant steps into that store. He was supposed to go back but couldn't even get close – just came home crying and saying she was gone, that he hadn't been able to fetch her and had no idea where she was. The family, they were all just hoping and praying that I knew something they didn't, hoping against hope there was an explanation other than what they refused to accept.

How could I think about Sloane, Em, with all that going on? The legal stuff was endless. I was the one in her will – the one to inherit everything if she should die and the one to take over Harper if there were no kids in line for the job. And we all know what happened there.

I didn't want it, Em, I swear I didn't want it and my dad, well he was so mad with me for not fighting for what was legally mine. He told me I was no son of his – that I had ruined everything he'd given me on a plate and that as far as he was concerned I had killed Marcia with my philandering so I was dead to him too.

I know you won't believe it, but I didn't even have to fight hard for that whole Harper empire in the end. It just landed straight in my lap. Abe and Nancy, they were so cut up about losing Marcia that they just about gave up, and it wasn't long after Abe's heart attack that Nancy had a stroke. I visited her in hospital a few times. Had to make sure my mom and dad weren't there – by this time my dad had forbidden my mom even to talk with me – and then Nancy died too. I reckon her heart just broke in two.

When Mom died, three years later, Dad didn't want me at the funeral. I went just to spite him, and he spat right down in front of me and in front of my mother's grave as they lowered her into the earth.

'That's what you are son,' he said, 'spit on the ground. You're not worthy to tread the same earth as your mother lived on, God rest her soul.'

When he died the following year, I didn't bother to go. Just a few of his golf and business buddies showed up, and some woman in a black car, according to Caesar that is. He went. Said he needed to pay his respects to Elliott as part of his duty to the family that remained – meaning me, I guess.

Oh, Em, that's not to say I didn't still love Sloane or want Sloane. We did still meet, here and there from time to time, but she was so sad, so absent. I guess losing Libby really hit her hard.

Plus there was this one big problem: Marcia's will.

There was this whole condition to me taking over her share in Harper, and then Abe's share when he died. Like I say, I really wasn't so bothered whether I didn't or I did, but there was this one clause, a codicil they called it, which said that if I married anytime within ten years of Marcia's death, then the Harper fortune would be withdrawn, go to some charity of her choosing. So I found myself not wanting to get too close to Sloane. Not just to her, but to any woman, if you get my drift. Plus I had to show that I was maximising profits. There was this huge damned pressure to stay on top.

Sloane got real keen at one point; 'Oh Nicholas, Marcia's gone and we can be together,' she would say and it was hard to disagree – but then it seemed kinda insulting to tell her that I was hanging on to my fortune and that having got used to it all, it would be pretty hard to let go.

She said she had no one to talk to – about her daughter, that is – so I suggested she have a go at writing a blog. Seemed everybody was at it and I thought it would give her focus – I knew her writing just wasn't taking off. Well, she just got right into that one and before long she has hundreds of followers and bingo, the blog becomes a book. Well, she had me sweating for a moment there. Thought she might have spilled the beans about us and that would have been very bad for business, but I should have known I could rely on her to be discreet.

The two of us, we met in London a couple of times a year, New York for old times' sake, never Boston, never Paris, it just didn't feel right. I always paid for Sloane, mind you, so she was never out of pocket.

But the honest truth is that it wasn't just the clause in the will that stood in our way. If I'm honest, Em, as I know I must be, there was this ghost of Marcia that was with me night and day. Even when I was making love to Sloane.

Don't get me wrong – Sloane, she was great in the sack — and she still had this thing she did tying me up with her pantyhose, just like in Paris. Now that could get me every time. But Marcia, it was like she was standing there at the foot of the bed, tapping her foot, reminding me of what I had driven her to, reminding me that she would still be alive if I hadn't played away.

But it was coming up for the ten years when I got the invite and that seemed significant in a strange sort of way.

There I was, being asked to the opening of the very castle where Rodin and Camille Claudel lived and worked; where they hid from society, from the folks who didn't approve of their affair. True, it was also where Camille had come to recover from an abortion. But I liked to dwell more on the positive, especially where Sloane was concerned. Sloane didn't need reminding that it was a little girl that Camille had sculpted over and again in the Château de l'Islette.

I thought this is it; this is the moment when Sloane and I can move forward – like it was kind of meant to be. I know that's a little corny but I wanted to get back some of that romance and make it up to her a bit – me not being there as maybe I should have.

Plus, if I'm being honest, her last few messages had me pretty spooked. She sounded out of it, a little unhinged even. Kept telling me she could hear her dead daughter around the house. She had been alone way too much – what with Cathy dying and all. I thought it would be nice for her to bring her French friend along – seemed like she was pretty much the only real friend Sloane had left; That made me feel bad, like it was maybe my fault. So I emailed Elodie – got her address from one of those crazy pass-this-on-to-ten-friends circulars that Sloane sent every now and then – invited her along – and asked her if maybe she could keep an eye out for Sloane on the trip. Elodie was totally up for it; even suggested staying on at her place while she went away with her guy. We decided to keep it between ourselves, let Sloane be the one to ask Elodie to come. I didn't want her thinking I was going behind her back. Sloane was delighted – real happy that Elodie was coming too. Perfect, I thought. It was all working out.

So this moment was significant, Em. And I was lonely, I wasn't getting any younger and I was tired of running in circles to keep all the business balls in the air. The ten years written into Marcia's will were nearly up and it felt like I was on the brink of freedom from the ghosts of the past. Sloane and I were finally going back to Paris, where the two of us began. I thought, Em, that this was the moment I could finally ask Sloane to marry me.

Chapter 54

Sloane

My evening dress is deep blue with crystals in zigzagging lines down the sleeves and at the hem. It fits me perfectly, hugging close around my breasts and waist and then flaring out, skimming my hips and floating behind me as I walk, the softest silk chiffon fashioned into a suspicion of a train at the back.

My hair tumbles in contrived tresses from a clasp high on my head and my earrings are a cascade of tiny, shimmering diamonds. A diamond locket, which contains a curl of Libby's hair, hangs low around my neck, just nudging into my cleavage, which has happily not been flawed with age.

Finally, I have sold the house in London. It is to his credit that Stuart wanted none of it from the divorce. 'That's between you and your parents,' he said. 'You will never have to sell it because of me. I have no need to take what's not mine in life, Sloane, *unlike you.*' I heard him add beneath his breath.

It is time to move on; the diamonds are my symbol, not of wealth, but of clarity, although the little trip to Garrards once the house sale was complete was fun; I would be lying if I did not admit to that.

At last, Em, I am seeing things for what they are and I am seeing your role in all that has happened – and I know now that it is up to me to get Nicholas to see that too.

Elodie looks astonishing, so Parisian, so utterly chic. Her hair, still short, is woven with blond highlights, which catch the glow of the chandelier as she walks by my side. Her gown is black shot with gold, a deep plunge at the neck and a long slit at the thigh. Her towering black patent shoes flash a tell-tale red sole and tucked under her arm is a black leather clutch bag adorned with a jewel-encrusted skull.

I stand back in admiration; 'Oh my God, Elodie, you look amazing. You just never ever seem to age. Is it a French thing or what?'

'No, *chérie*,' she purrs, 'it is a Botox thing. You should try – is good,' she says, playfully pulling up the corners of her eyes with slender fingers and then pinching the roses of her cheeks, 'the filler too. Is terrific,' she says. 'It is important for, you know.' She cocks her head to one side and shrugs her shoulders, pushing a blond wisp off her face.

We go to the window and take in the view, our men still not back from their pre-prandial stroll of the castle grounds. I have hardly seen Nicholas but then I hardly need to. To know he is there is enough.

The drive sweeps away from the house with all the grace of our hosts by whose generosity the spirits of this château live again. Looking out, it is possible to imagine two sculptors, seduced by the quiet calm of this place, finding solace in one another and in their work, allowing the romance of the lake, the boats moving gently in the moonlight and the trees swaying in the September breeze to cast away the shackles of society's expectation and disdain. Might it have been possible for Camille Claudel to forget for just a moment that Rodin, the love of her life, did not choose her; that she aborted the child she carried for him because he did not choose her?

I close my eyes and see myself with Nicholas on that lake, the lazy trees dipping their branches into the water and reflecting in the mirror of its tranquil surface. I think of how it might have been had we not met in times when the surface of our lives was already divided into the pieces that others would want – if it had been calm and whole with only the two of us inhabiting that space.

Tomorrow Libby will have been dead for ten years and I will not be able to visit her grave. No matter, Em. What I shall do instead is far more significant and pertinent to her death. She will forgive me my absence, I am sure.

'She never got over it, you know.'

'What's that, *chérie*?' asks Elodie.

'The abortion; when Rodin wouldn't give up Rose, Camille had an abortion, got rid of his child. She went mad in the end.'

Elodie shrugs her shoulders but just before she turns away I catch the slight quiver in her mouth. 'Sometimes these things, they are necessary,' she says.

'Remember that time, Elodie, in the Jardin du Luxembourg, when you told me it was the mistress who had the power?'

She nods and turns to me, 'So?' she says.

'So does she really, Elodie? Does she really have the power? Do *you* have the power?'

'*Bof,*' Elodie raises her shoulders and makes that French shrugging sound, 'He looks after me. What can I say? The apartment, my job – still he has influence, always promotions, more money – it is not such a bad life.'

'What about children? Did you never want to have children? You've been with Olivier for, what is it now – twenty-odd years? Did you never want to marry? Have a family of your own? Do you think he will ever leave? Her, I mean. Surely, Elodie, if he won't leave her, it is the wife who has the power, *non*?' If I am skating on thin ice, I ignore its fragility. I have never dared question this, my sophisticated, chic friend, 'And how come we get to meet him now – after all these years?'

'This evening, it is good for him to be here – his work, now is in culture, this is culture, is good for the, how you say, the profile. And children? As for children, sometimes they die. At least I can never feel that pain.

'Come, let us go and meet them,' Elodie nods to the staircase and loops her arm through mine. The question of her lover's wife is closed.

'A great speech, Nicholas,' says Olivier, offering his hand for Nicholas to shake.

Elodie's man is tall and slender with longish greying hair; long enough to be distinguished, short enough not to be try-too-hard. He is good looking as you would expect him to be and the deep grey suit he wears has money and taste written all over its soft, cashmere weave. I see that despite their formality one with the other, it is apparent to anyone caring to notice, that they are a couple. They would be a perfect couple if one were not married to another.

I am not so sure whether Nicholas's speech was so great. What does he ever contribute that was not known about this story before? A different point of view, he would say, but I can't help thinking that some relative of the Claudel family would have been a more suitable choice for this private view.

I know, of course, that Harper money is involved. It is always Harper money – it seems to make the world go around.

It is hard to believe that this evening we have trod where those sculptors trod. We have eaten in the room that was their studio, looking at the walls that surrounded them as they created some of their most important work. On the bureau sits a stone copy of *La Petite Châtelaine*, her hair drawn back down her shoulders in a thick, loose plait. I run my hand over the petrified cheeks of the little girl and I see Camille Claudel, the desperate woman creating again and again this child that she had lost from her womb. The life she terminated. It makes me want to cry.

We are standing on the terrace, enjoying the carefree moments of exquisite food and too much wine and Olivier's phone rings. He mutters a *'pardon'*, raises his eyebrows and walks away from us into the shadows cast by the chopped-off turrets of the towers; excised by previous owners when funds for repairs were scarce.

I breathe in the crystal cool air and sip at my brandy, listening to Elodie and Nicholas as they debate the morality of *foie gras*. I do not want to hear how geese are fattened. The pâté was delicious. That is good enough for me. If I were planning a last supper, this evening's menu would be an ideal choice.

There is a squeal of delight and I turn to see an attractive girl in a deep green velvet ballerina-style dress. Four puppies are bundled together, squirming in her arms, her long, honey blond hair tangling around their ears. 'Ooo, let me hold one! How cute! *Ils sont adorables,*' the cries fly into the quiet calm of the starry night air.

'How old are they?' I ask.

'Seven weeks only. They are, 'ow you say, fox'ounds. 'alf French and 'alf English. The French, they 'owl and tell us where is the *proie* – the prey – and the English, they are better 'unters, so we do the cross and *voilà*, is a perfect 'ound.'

'Gee, they're cute. What are their names?' asks a short, dumpy brunette, her hair scragged into a bun, escaping now wildly around her eyes. Her scarlet dress is far too tight and far too short and she keeps pulling it down as it wriggles its way back up her lumpy, perma-tanned thighs. She did not need to speak for me to know that she was not French. Her dress sense screams 'Texas'.

'Guillaume, Geneviève, Gretel et Gustave,' the pretty blonde nods down at each dog in turn.

'Why all starting with G? Doesn't it make it hard to remember all the names?' I ask.

'*Mais, non,*' she replies. 'It is 'ow we do it in France. Each year we 'ave a letter of the alphabet for zee names of dogs. Last year it was F, so our puppies, they were Françoise and Fanny, next year it will be H, so maybe Henri and Heidi – who knows?'

'*Brigitte – où es-tu? Où sont-ils, les toutous?*'

'Oh – *Maman*, she is calling me. She seeks the dogs. I go.' She giggles and runs back into the house, clutching the soft, warm creatures to her chest.

'Gee, you learn something every day,' says the American.

I wonder what it is that I will learn, Em.

I turn and see Nicholas staring out into the garden, leaning on the cold stone walls and I wonder why he is not still talking to Elodie. Then I see her, deep in conversation with Olivier. Every now and then an angry exchange bursts towards us. Nicholas and I look at one another. The party is breaking up.

Just as I decide I have to interrupt, Elodie turns and, despite the elegance of her gown and the height of her shoes, stomps towards us, the hint of a frown on what I now understand to be her non-surgically-made-youthful and therefore frozen face.

'It is the wife. 'e 'as to go.' Her English falters under the strain of the moment and I see tears sparkling in her eyes, incongruous as they are in contrast to her style and panache. I see that she hurts; that being a mistress is not all good.

'Is no problem,' she says, 'The driver, he will take us to Paris and then I go on to Cannes. 'e come when she let him. She do this often. Is no problem,' she repeats.

It does slightly upset my plan but no matter. It is fitting, Em, that we should begin not today but instead ten years to the day from when my Libby died. It is fitting too that what began in Paris should end there.

Chapter 55

Nicholas

Jeez, Em, I thought Sloane was going to freak out when it turned out that Elodie had to come back to Paris. She seemed really jazzed. Boy, she was on fire, like she couldn't wait to get me alone.

To be honest, I felt the self-same way. It was an incredible feeling – to be ten years down the line, to have this damn clause out of the way. Say to hell with the business and get on with my life. I already had it planned. Sell the whole damn Harper shebang. Get rid, get married, move on and enjoy all that money I had worked so damned hard to get. All those years kissing Harper's ass, all these years watching my back, years I have wasted since Marcia died.

Sloane, she looked hot. Got to hand it to her, she's really kept herself well. Those breasts, well they were just screaming out to be held and this time I wasn't going to hold back. I wanted this woman – hell, I had wanted her for over twenty years. It was time – time finally to come home.

As it happened, Elodie never came back to the flat. She stayed in some place where she worked – a courtesy apartment she called it, but I guess it was just a place for lovers to fuck, somewhere she hoped that Olivier could sneak off to. Jeez, that seems such a lonely life.

So there I am, Sloane is with me, the world is our oyster – and then I go to unpack. Right there at the top of my suitcase is the letter. I remember now, it was Caesar who handed it to me just as we left for the airport. 'This came for you, Mr Nicholas,' he said, as he gave me the green envelope and I shoved it into my bag. It looked kind of familiar but the address was typed on a label so I thought nothing more of it – until I unzipped that bag. And it's only then that I realise that there's no postmark, no date, and that it's been delivered by hand. I remember that paper – that green notepaper and those envelopes. They were always in Marcia's drawer so how the hell...

Sloane is in the bathroom so I rip the letter open fast and scan the pages. I can't believe what is written right in front of my eyes. Jesus Christ, how the hell do I deal with this?

Chapter 56

Sloane

It is not hard to seduce Nicholas Bride. I have done it many times so I know that today it will be an easy task. I have felt the hardness of him as he has pressed himself to me and I have smelt his breath on my cheek. I know he wants me. He has no wife to fetch him home and we have time in Paris alone. Today the two of us will make love here in Paris, where we are meant to be.

I stand over him, a glass of wine in my hand, a fruity Vouvray, straight from the V*al De Loire.* Although it is only midday and we have just woken from the excess of yesterday's 'triumph' as Nicholas says, I know he will accept the wine and I know he will want to make love.

He is still sleepy and it is easy to slip the powder I have crushed into the chilled glass. As if the pills my doctor prescribes could really help me sleep. I cannot sleep as my Libby is dead and she is dead, Em, because of you. This drug is far better used as I use it now – to calm my Nicholas, to lull him into completing the task I must set him – the task I must set him because of you.

We killed you, Em, Nicholas and I, and we must set the record straight. Where is the control and where is the blame? Who had that power? Who is it that set this in motion? This murder, for that is what it is. And it is this murder, Em, for which we have paid – Nicholas and I.

I believe you knew that it would happen because this started long ago. First you took my parents and then you took my Auntie Jean. But I couldn't have known then, Em, couldn't have known that this was your warning and that what we did to you should never have been.

Then you took my Libby and you took Marcia too. And the rest of them, they weren't far behind. Stuart left, then Cathy died – and everyone else. Everyone went because of you.

You would be what? Seventeen years old? I am sorry, Em, they never told me whether you were a boy or a girl but I have felt all these years that you were a girl; I felt the presence of your woman-ness. I reached inside when Libby was born and drew out of my heart the idea that she was somehow your reincarnation and that you had come back to me, Em, and that all would be well.

But I was wrong, wasn't I, Em? Libby was just on borrowed time. You let me have her just long enough to make the pain as bad as anyone could bear and then you took her too. You took her as my punishment for killing you. But I never wanted to kill you, Em. I wanted you so much – wanted you, me and Nicholas to be a family just like he promised, just like he said we would.

You are still a child, somewhere there in heaven with my Libby and I am hoping, Em, that between us we can reach the end; the end to all this suffering that started when we killed you. I am going to make him see that this is what we must do and then Em, I want you to be at peace.

Enough, Em, enough! It's time we did what we came for – added it all up, the blame, the guilt and the shame. In Islamic faith they say there are angels who sit on your shoulders, right and left, counting good deeds and bad, monitoring the accounts of your life for the day of reckoning to determine where, in the afterlife, you will go. This is what we must now do.

We must take apart our every step, discover the blame and apportion it justly so that you can judge us; so that we can move on or not. This all depends on you and what it is we find.

Chapter 57

Nicholas

When Sloane came back from the bathroom I hid the letter. Didn't know what to say or do – needed time just to think it out.

It was the middle of the night – damn long journey and if you ask me it would have been polite to let us stay. But then I guess as guests go we were down the end of the line with all the Honourable-this-person and Count-that-person who were no doubt way ahead of us as far as rooms for the night were concerned.

We slept. I didn't think I would be able to but with all the booze and the jetlag, before I knew where I was it was late in the morning and there she was, standing over me, a glass of wine in her hand.

This was one swell apartment that Elodie had going on – sewn this little one up pretty well with her sugar daddy, I guess. Top floor, left bank, private elevator, doesn't get better than that – plus one very comfortable four-poster bed, no prizes for guessing what she and Monsieur Smooth got up to around here. What a pity things weren't going to work out just like I'd planned. That letter, it changed all that, and somehow I had to find a way to tell Sloane.

'Woah, this is a little bitter. What did you say it was, a Vouvray? Guess it wasn't a real good year.'

This isn't exactly what I had in mind for breakfast but it seems to be what Sloane wants and I'm gonna go with the flow. I'm guessing it'll take us real quick to where we both want to be. I push myself further up on my pillows and go to place the glass of wine Sloane has given me on the table by the bed but Sloane is having none of it.

She sits beside me and lifts her glass. Leaning over, she snakes her arm into mine, her hair spilling sexily across her eyes. I can smell the scent of her, 'To us, Nicholas,' she says, and we drain our glasses, kind of twined together by the wrist.

She nuzzles into my chest and slides across me, her breasts just peeping out from her satin nightgown – so I can just see her dark nipples and her smooth skin. Age has been kinder to her than it has to me, I guess.

If I'm honest, too much good living has made for tight trousers and a pretty wrinkled face – I am lucky to have Sloane, to have had her wait for me like this.

She sits astride me and reaches down, taking me in both hands. I am as ready for her as she is for me.

Jesus – the letter! I remember the letter. I should tell her what's happening – let her know that things are going to change, but Christ, this feels good. It's been so long. Maybe it wouldn't hurt just to go along a little further before...

Sloane sits up and shrugs her gown from her shoulders and it shimmies down over her breasts and pools around the curve of her belly. There's this beam of light coming through the muslin drapes at the windows and it bathes her in a kind of glow, so the wispy bits of her hair are like they're on fire.

She smiles, that kind of secret smile, the one she uses when she's going to take control. Her eyes get this mischievous glint.

It's like she is twenty-six all over again. I should stop this. Tell her. Take back the control but, Jesus, I can't.

She leans forward and brushes her breasts across my chest. I push myself up. I need to feel her swollen nipples in my mouth but she pulls away and smiles.

I'm feeling kinda woozy. I guess I had more booze last night than I thought – and the wine this morning hasn't helped. It's left a bad taste in my mouth. Sloane hasn't kissed me so I guess she can taste it too. The image of a green envelope slips in and out of my head.

Sloane leans down and pulls something out from beneath the bed. I close my eyes, knowing what it is that's coming next.

She takes a hold of my wrists. I allow her to raise my arms and she clamps my hands down above my head.

'What do you want, Nicholas?' she murmurs in my ear, 'What is it you want me to do?'

The green envelope is far away, drifting in my head, not wanting me to take a hold of it but it is there just the same, just out of reach.

'Tie me up, Sloane, tie me up,' I hear myself say.

Chapter 58

Sloane

Nice to know it really does take so little to seduce him even after all these years. He's looking a little paunchy if I am honest and honesty is what we are all about.

He was asleep by the time I tied him up. Proper ropes this time; there is too much stretch in pairs of tights. Not that he saw what I had in my hands. He was too far gone by then — drifting off courtesy of the sleeping draught, so I had plenty of time to sort him out.

But now he's waking up and we are at the point our story has brought us to, Em; the point where it all starts so that it can all come to an end.

'Jesus, what the fuck?'

I am looking out of the window onto all of Paris. It seems quiet down there, and then I remember that it is the ten-year anniversary of 9/11. I think there is some special event. Maybe Paris is in peaceful, collective thought, gathered somewhere in this beautiful city, or pressed up to their TV screens, re-living the memory of that day.

The light is pale; thin ribbons of sunbeams weaving through silver grey clouds. It is like I am seeing it for the first time when I hear his voice behind me, and I turn to Nicholas who, still naked, is tied tightly to the bed. I have left him naked since when I am around naked is generally how Nicholas likes to be.

'Sloane, what the fuck is going on here? Get me out of here, will you, this hurts.'

'I'm sorry, Nicholas but I can't. Not until you agree to what I need you to do — what I need you and me both do.'

I can see him looking around, a little wildly, as usually captives do — trying to work out whether there is any way he can loosen the ropes around his ankles, his thighs and his wrists; any way he can escape from the four-poster bed of a prison I have created for my lover, my one and only true love.

'What the fuck? What the hell do you mean — and how the hell did I get like this?'

I see his eyes settle on the wine glass and almost imperceptibly I nod my head. He knows he has been drugged. He knows that this is for real and I am not messing about.

'We killed a child, Nicholas. That's what this is about. Between us we killed a child and that's why my Libby died. It's why Marcia died; it's why everyone has died. Don't you see Nicky, it's our punishment. We have to make amends and there is only one way. Between us we have to work it out — where the guilt lies, what we did, when we did it and how we came to kill a child.'

'What child? What are you talking about? For fuck's sake just let me go. We can discuss all this, Sloane, but you don't need to keep me tied up.'

'But I thought that's what you liked, Nicholas, being tied up.'

346

'Come on now, Sloane, be reasonable, there's no need for all this. What the hell's all this about? I love you, you know I do. There's no need for all this. We can work something out, whatever it is that's eating you.'

'But you didn't love me enough, did you Nicholas? Not enough to choose me? Not enough to choose to be with me when I was carrying your child and not enough to be with me once I'd flushed it away – just like you wanted me to. No, you chose Marcia, even though she'd had an affair – no, don't bother to deny it. I know all about it. You chose Marcia and we killed our child. That's why all these bad things have happened. We killed a child and then my child was taken, ten years ago today. A life for a life, Nicholas, a life for a life.'

'Now Sloane, don't you say that. You know what happened. What was I supposed to do when my wife tried to kill herself? Ignore her and leave anyway?'

I do not answer him. He will have time to work this out. I watch his eyes dart this way and that, an animal caught in a trap of his own making.

'And the kid? That's nonsense. Libby's death wasn't because of the kid – and anyway, it wasn't down to me that you got rid of it. It was just an abortion for God's sake. People have them every day.'

'Just an abortion? Just an abortion? Did you have the abortion then, Nicholas? Did you have to live with the consequences of an aching, empty womb?

'Oh, don't worry, I know I am guilty too – don't think I am trying to load this all onto you. But I never thought it through, Nicholas, because all I could think of was you.

'And don't you pretend that you don't know about the consequences of an abortion. You, who have practically plagiarised an entire story to make it your own, all because you knew the right people, had the right sort of connections and the right sort of money. And where have we just been? Oh yes, to the Château de l'Islette – the very place that your precious heroine went after she had her abortion.

'What was it in that letter Camille Claudel's poet brother wrote after she went mad? Let me see if I can quote it correctly now: "It is horrible to kill a child, to kill an immortal soul! It's dreadful! How can you live and breathe with such a crime weighing on your conscience?"'

'That's about it, isn't it, Nicholas? I don't have your book on hand but I think I got it pretty much right. What would you say? Maybe you never bothered to read what you've written in your precious book – because with you, I guess it's all about the money. Where would you have been without all your precious Harpers, hey, Nicholas? Not superstar famous and rolling in riches, that's for sure.'

For a second I feel triumphant to have scored this point. Paul Claudel's words encompass so precisely what I feel, and Nicholas cannot deny that he himself has made use of this quote. I see him slump back, for a moment defeated. I notice as his head sags to his chest that he is going a little bald and I marvel at how close a neighbour love is to hate.

But this is a small triumph; a small point scored from a small part of the tale, and I feel a little cheap to have been side-tracked this way. The real triumph will be in the telling of the whole.

Chapter 59

Nicholas

I'm still there, hurting like crazy, feeling sick, exposed, with these knots just cutting into my skin and I'm hoping that she's just, you know, kidding me. Like it's some kind of sick joke or a kind of off-the-wall role play that she's got planned and then it hits me, boom. This lady is not kidding me one bit. She's dead straight and I am going to need to think fast.

'We killed Em, you and me, Nicholas,' she repeats, and now we are going to work it out.'

I'm stalling for time and I ask her why she's called you Em — why she'd have a name for a baby that didn't exist.

'Em is short for Embryo, Nicholas. I thought you'd be smart enough to work that one out.'

I have never claimed to be smart. Does she really think I am fool enough not to know that I cashed in on someone else's story – got beaten to the post but then got published anyway? Doesn't she know that I know darn well that the only reason I got this far is the damned Harper name? Jesus, I know I'm just a nobody who lucked out by marrying the right girl.

Lucked out? Huh, that's a joke all by itself. What am I really, hey, Em? A has-been college dude who could barely keep his head above water once he got to swim with the sharks; a preppy little bastard despised by his own dad, and who would have drowned long ago if it hadn't been for the big fat Harper nets.

You have to understand, now, Em, that at this stage I don't know what it is she's after. I think she's maybe going to stab me, starve me, Christ knows but hell, what do I really care? Things have got so bad, what with the letter and all that. I'm pretty much beyond caring because whatever it is she's going to do can't be that much worse than the stuff that'll happen anyway.

And let's face it, Em, this is Sloane; this is my Sloane who despite everything that's happened and everything I've done, I have truly always loved. There is nothing in it for me to lie now. Why should I bother with a lie? Surely if I am honest then she will see.

'What is it Sloane? What is it you want us to do? Tell me and I will do it. We'll do it together if it means that much to you. I love you, Sloane. Nothing else in my life has really made any sense. You were the one, Sloane. You were the one who made me believe in myself, when you saw me for who I was. Remember, Sloane, you saw right into me with your star sign witchcraft. Remember how we sat in Monoprix right here in Paris and you ticked off all the signs, month by month, until you came to Virgo and I knew then, Sloane, that anyone who can see me, really see me like that, I mean, they have to be someone special.

'I knew I loved you, Sloane, from that moment on. You made me what I am today, you and your witchcraft, and I knew then that I would never want to let you go.'

Then Sloane, she gets this strange look on her face, a kind of twisted smile, like she's suddenly realised some big secret and then she starts to laugh out loud. She comes over to me and I'll be honest, Em, she had me pretty scared. She leans down and she's still laughing and then she laughs right in my face.

'So that's it, hey, Nicholas? All comes down to me understanding what the poor little boy was all about? Christ, Nicholas, you are even more of a fool than I thought.

'Fool,' she spits again, 'You thought that I could wave some magic little wand and pluck your star sign out of nowhere? Somehow see into your soul?' She cups her palms together as if in prayer and rolls her eyes up to the ceiling in a grotesque beatific pose, like she's straining up to see the halo on her head.

'Ha! What an idiot! So it was my fault. That's what you're saying. All of this was my fault,' Sloane says.

She's pacing up and down the room now, wringing her hands. Then she stops, pulls her hair back from her face and lets it flop again. I notice she's wearing the same dress she was wearing when we first made love. It's that flowery dress, some French make – Cacharel, whatever. She bought it especially that first day – the very day we're talking about, when she stole my heart in Paris. Because Em, she did steal my heart and even though this is not a Sloane I recognise, she must be in there somewhere. How do I get her back?

'No, Sloane, that's not what I am saying. I am saying that it was you who saved me – you who made me see that someone out there could understand me, love me for who I am. You gave me confidence, helped me be a man. I'm not blaming you for anything. Why would I want to blame you, Sloane?'

I try to reason with her but quickly see we are beyond that and what she says next crushes me completely.

'No, Nicholas, you don't understand. I never saw into you,' she makes quotation marks with her fingers in the air, 'I never divined,' the quotation marks again, 'your date of birth by witchcraft or any other means.

'I tricked you, Nicholas. I wanted you to want me, wantec to score a few points and then sending you crashing down. I guess the joke now, Nicholas, is rather on me.'

Chapter 60

Sloane

I am sorry if the name Em offends. I called you that because an em-bryo is what you were, and it's a name for either boy or girl. Whatever you were, Em, you were a child. That's what you wanted me to realise, wasn't it, Em, a child and not a random bunch of cells?

Now I see more clearly than ever that it is only by going back that we go forward.

What if it really was my fault? Did I with that one trick set in motion everything that has happened since; the affair, Marcia – first her suicide attempt and then her death, your murder, Libby's death? Was that simple trick all it took?

And what if I am right about you? What if your soul somewhere in heaven saw all this coming in some a priori way, and so disposed of my parents when I was just thirteen, knowing that in my life to come I would behave so badly as to merit that terrible karma in preparation for the rest of my life?

When Nicholas made fun of me reading horoscopes I wanted to teach him a lesson. No, I wanted to teach him a lesson way before then – when I thought that this puffed-up arrogant American had stolen my chance to run the trip and to shine. Oh my God, how sad and ridiculous does that sound now? I didn't know he was married to Marcia; wouldn't have gone near him if I had. In fact, I would probably have hated him just for being her husband. I just thought that here was some guy who thought he knew it all and I would show him that he didn't.

Nicholas is shocked. He looks so sad lying there, trussed on the bed, like some pale, hairy chicken waiting to be stuffed.

'Yes, Nicholas, I played a stupid trick on you. Remember Cathy?' Of course he does.

'Well Cathy and I, we used to do the timetables together but we were also in charge of the Common Room – all the social stuff for the staff – you probably don't remember all that, away in your ivory tower as you were.

'Remember how when it was someone's birthday, there were always buns at break? Well, they didn't just get there by magic. Cathy used to order them a term in advance from the bakers down the road and I used to make sure the bill was paid from staffroom funds. Are you following me so far, Nicholas?' He nods.

'Thing is, Nicholas, the only time we didn't manage to play catch-up with birthday buns was if someone's birthday was in the summer. The holidays were just too long – we never used to bother and no one ever complained – all just grateful to have eight weeks off.

'So it was easy, you see, Nicholas. You were never on the list for birthday buns. Oh, I might not have known who you were, but I would definitely have recognised your name. We'd just done the orders for the summer term. I'd paid all the bills from spring and autumn and your name was never on the list – so I knew that you hadn't had a birthday yet that year.

'Okay, I did have to guess between two star signs. You could have had a birthday in July, which means that you could have been a Leo. But, honestly, Nicholas, with all your messing around with the papers on that trip – meticulous or what? The way you sat picking away at your nails, the nervous, fussiness of you, I knew you had to be a Virgo. That much was real – but that much only. All the rest was a trick.'

I look over to Nicholas, my chin up in defiance of what I think he might hurl at me next but the anger I expect is not there; in its place I see only sadness. Then I see that he is crying. Tears are rolling down his cheeks and he cannot brush them away. His hands are locked still above his head and deep grooves are showing around his wrists where he has struggled against the bonds.

My breath catches sharply in my throat. Look what I have done. Look what I have done to this man I have loved for more than twenty years.

Chapter 61

Nicholas

So, Em, it was all based on a lie. There really was no one in the world who understood where I was coming from – what made me tick. Jesus, all along I thought it was Sloane but hell, maybe it was Marcia after all. She was the one who I grew up with; she was the one who saw how things were – with school, with my dad. And I just hurt her, didn't I Em? I hurt her like she's hurting me.

I look up at Sloane and I see pity in her face. It is the face of my father, the pity I saw there when I missed the ball, failed to reach first base, failed to touch down. Yeah, I feel sorry for myself. I can see just how spectacularly I have screwed up. It's like nothing matters now so I may as well just say what I need to say and let it happen, whatever it is that she wants.

I am dead beat, exhausted, thirsty and I am beginning not to care at all. Yeah, I could trick her into untying me and then plan for my escape, but what would be the point, hey? What is there out there for me now? What is there in here for that matter, if Sloane has been a lie?

Sloane walks slowly over and takes the hem of her soft cotton dress and uses it to wipe my eyes.

'God, Nicholas, I'm sorry. I am so sorry. It's Libby, everything, it's got me so confused. I hurt so much. I have no idea what I'm doing.'

'It's true though, isn't it? What you just told me, it's true.' She nods and I see that she's crying too.

'What is it you want, Sloane? What is it you want us to do?'

'We have to write it all down, Nicholas. We have to be honest and tell the story as it was. Find out who was to blame for what and when. It's the only way we might be forgiven – the only way we can either of us find peace.'

'Jesus, Sloane, that'll take forever.'

'No it won't, Nicholas. We have two weeks – here in Paris. If we work at it hard we can do it in two weeks and then it will be done. Please, Nicholas. I need us to do this. I need to know how everything happened to be at peace with Libby's death.'

I go to say something but she furiously shakes her head.

'Please don't argue. We have to do it, don't ask me how but I know this is the only way. Will you do this with me Nicholas, please – please, if you have ever loved me...'

'Don't say it, Sloane, you know I have – do,' I say, and I find that still after all this I do mean it. I do love Sloane. Maybe this *is* the only way. Maybe we both have to tell the honest truth.

'Here, let me untie you, Nicholas. God, I'm so sorry – look you're hurting. Let me help you.'

'Stop,' I say. Jesus, Nicholas, I say to myself, she's about to set you free – what the hell are you doing here?

But I know I can't hide anything now. What point in trying

to hide? This is all so fucked up that a little fuel on the flames is like a match in a blazing fire.

'In the suitcase – right on top; the envelope – open the letter. Get it out and read it, Sloane. If we're going to tell the truth then we might just as well start with that.'

Chapter 62

Sloane

I want to untie him but he tells me I have to read something first. My fingers tremble as I lift the lid of the case and when I see the green envelope I feel dizzy; I feel like I'm going to faint.

In my head, I conjure the green envelopes I have opened thus far. I see, Em, that the letters chart our tale; the first from Nicholas, which drew me to New York, where you, Em, were conceived; the second where I learnt that to be with him, I must be rid of you. In the third, he chose Marcia over me even though, Em, you were gone, and the fourth came when Libby died, perfunctory, emotionless lines from a family I scarcely knew. Here, Em, is number five.

I take a deep breath, pluck it up and smooth my hand over the space it has left on Nicholas's pale pink sweater and I walk slowly back to the bed.

'Sit,' says Nicholas. 'Trust me, it can get worse than this,' he nods at his bound hands and feet. I think I see a faint smile on his face, like he is sharing some private joke with himself.

'Now there is one thing you mentioned that you can't pin on what happened with our child, call it Em if you like – a little flaw in that whole theory of yours.

'Read it out loud, will ya, Sloane? I don't think I quite took it all in first time around.'

I unfold the pages and I begin.

New Hampshire, September 8 2011

Dear Nicky,

I know that this letter will be a shock to you and I apologise for that – and for all the years during which you have thought me dead. I decided that a letter would be less of a shock than me just arriving home one day soon.

I hope you will believe me, Nicky, when I say that I did not take my decision to 'disappear' lightly.

The pressure on us both was intolerable – from both sets of parents as well as from our own need to try to be the wife and husband that other people expected us to be.

I was careful not to be found, so please do not think that your and Mom and Dad's efforts to find me were somehow lacking. I knew that you would check out my phone, my credit cards, all the stuff you see in films – all the stuff that was reported after the attack on the towers.

I know it was wrong to use that tragedy to end our own – but truly, Nicky, it was a tragedy that we were both living a lie. I had wanted so many times to escape and it was like I was being presented with an opportunity I had to take.

know that I have now been declared dead – it's strange reading all about your own death in the papers and it pulled me up fast, made me see that it's time to face up to what I did by making you all believe I was gone; that, and the fact that things with me are changing.

I know you didn't see me at the family funerals. I was there each and every time. I know too that you had a hard time with your Dad towards the end – I'm sorry about all that. It was bad of him not to leave his money to you and I know he will have done that out of spite. He always blamed you for messing up our marriage when you messed around with Sloane.

The years I have spent with Jake since 9/11 have been worth all the deceit, Nicky. It hurt like hell to walk out of Mom and Dad's lives but every day I spent without Jake hurt me more.

Time was when I thought that being without Jake was worth it for everyone's sake, and I wanted to be a good wife, truly I did. But then when you were unfaithful, Nicky, it felt like it had all been in vain. Jake was gone, you were gone; it felt like I had nothing.

I am still sorry about Jake and the 'miscarriage' (let's stop pretending, shall we – we both know I had an abortion) – but Nicky, I am sorry because I should have had Jake's child – not because the result was that I couldn't have a child for you.

We never planned what happened on 9/11. How could we have? I had no idea where Jake was in the world so I called him up as soon as the first plane went down, just to check he was okay. It was Jake who thought up our plan. He'd wanted

so many times to leave Patsy but being so famous, having his
kids, it was all so hard to contemplate.

There was no time to think. I was so unhappy, Nicky. I just did
what Jake said but Nicky, I have no regrets. I believe it was
meant to be. Nobody was home so I left taking nothing save
what I would have taken for a day trip to New York. Caesar drove
me north from Boston and then told you all he had dropped me
to buy some designer dress at Century 21, that shop where
Mom and I would always go just opposite the Twin Towers.

So it was Caesar who saved my life for the second time –
Caesar who has lied for me all these years.

Jake and I met up in New Hampshire – a little inn at Weirs
Beach, where I cut my hair and dyed it to be as different from
my photos as I could be. Jake and I have spent as much time
as we could together between his spending time with Patsy
and the kids. If she has known about me she has never said –
not that it was me, I mean – because she knew I was presumed
dead on 9/11 – but she's never suggested she has known that
Jake has had someone in his life besides her. I have lived
simply and Jake has taken care of all my needs. It has been
the life I always wanted to lead.

You don't need to know the detail, Nicky, but I just need to tell
you that I am sorry for whatever this all did to you, just as I am
sorry if it has had an impact on Patsy's life. There is a cost to
everything as I am sure you well know.

I said things were changing. If you have not already read it
in the news, you'll soon know that Jake has cancer and will

shortly be dead. Ironic really, his death will bring me back to life. But at least, Nicky, we can now live life honestly.

I will take whatever the press and authorities throw at me but you need to know that it is my intention, of course, to take back Harper and everything that should be mine. No doubt your books will be sufficient income for you, but if you do need a little more I am sure we can work something out.

I think you will find that there is a clause in Daddy's will that makes provision for my re-birth, so to speak. I know that Caesar dropped the idea into Daddy's ear – to include that clause in case for example I had suffered memory loss and then reappeared.

In fact, Nicky, memory loss is probably a good way forward. I feel sure we can come to a little agreement based on that after all we have both been through. Don't be too hard on Caesar, Nicky. He's always had this protective thing going as far as I am concerned and after he rescued me from the car I guess he decided it was his job to rescue me from whatever, whenever. It was Caesar's idea too, to provide the clause withdrawing the Harper fortune should you remarry within ten years or should you not make every effort to maximise profits. I have been following the markets, Nicky. My, for a Fine Arts Major, you have done well.

It would have been inconvenient had I been gone longer, had you got as far as marrying Sloane for example, but nothing my lawyers couldn't fix. As it happens, fate has wrapped everything neatly up in those ten years. Life has a funny way of working out, Nicky, don't you think?

I'll be in touch soon, Nicky. Enjoy the Château de l'Islette. Caesar told me you have been invited – how very exciting for you and for your career. Daddy was such a kind man to help you on in the way he did. I have been doing a little writing myself while I have been away – a kind of memoir I guess, now that my memory's returned. I feel sure some publisher will want to snap that one up, don't you think?

Have a wonderful time, Nicky. I hear the Loire Valley is lovely this time of year.

Yours,

Marcia

It is late.

I am surrounded by sheets of paper, a scrawl of history floats around me as I lie down and rest my head on the soft, white pillows. In the grate, embers burn amber, pockmarked with tiny curls of green, just a trace still of Marcia's words hang in the air.

So tired, I am so tired but I can hear Libby's voice out there, calling to me, urging me on. I reach out for her but she moves further away until she is almost out of sight.

'Mummy,' I hear her call, 'don't go'.

'I'm not going anywhere, Libby, darling. I never did. Mummy never left you. I will be there always for you, Libby. Don't be scared, my darling, Mummy's nearly there.'

Somewhere far away I hear knocking, knocking and banging, knocking and banging. Don't disturb me – not now.

I am done and Libby is waiting. Please go away – we are at the end.

Across the sea drifts a voice, melancholy, keening and moaning. Is it Libby?

'Hang on, Libby, Mummy's nearly there.'

The voice is not Libby's. Elodie; Elodie is at the door. I can hear her, she is sobbing and she is calling out my name.

'Sloane, Sloane,' I hear my name as Elodie repeats it time and again, 'Sloane, Sloane, *ouvre-moi la porte*, Sloane, *je t'en prie*. Open the door. Please, Sloane, open. You were right. I was wrong. *C'est elle, c'est toujours elle*. It is the wife, *ma* Sloane; it is she who wins. It is always the wife who wins.'

I want to go to her, to let her in and to comfort her but I cannot. There is nothing I can do. I do not have the power.

Epilogue

People Talk!
Issue 34; September 2011

Bidding Wars for Posthumous Publication as Heiress Comes Back from the Dead!

A fierce bidding war has broken out in New York following the mysterious death of two celebrated authors, and the equally mysterious reappearance of what looks set to be one of the wealthiest women in America.

Police were called to a building in central Paris last week in response to an anonymous call. Uniformed officers entered the apartment in the desirable Left Bank of the capital by force to find Nicholas Bride, author, art critic and CEO of Harper Enterprises in a critical condition. The distinguished writer, a Harvard graduate, was rushed to hospital, but was pronounced dead on arrival.

Sloane Granger, novelist and author of best-selling self-help manual, *All you ever wanted to know about loss and hoped you would never need to ask* was found dead at the scene.

The apartment is registered to an eminent former member of the French government, who is being questioned in connection with the deaths. The police have, however, released a statement to say they have ruled out Olivier Martragnol as a suspect.

Sources reveal that up until last week, it was 60-year-old Martragnol's long-term PA and alleged girlfriend, Elodie Delavigne, who occupied the exclusive and elegant two-storey penthouse. It has been reported that the couple have recently split. The married former senator, who has three teenage children with wife, Danielle, has also been linked with actress, Emmina Mannering, 26 years his junior, since the two were seen together last year at the film festival in Cannes.

It is understood that Bride, 57, whose first novel, *In the Hands of The Mistress,* enjoyed several weeks at the top of the *New York Times* Bestseller List, started dating Granger, 46, after his wife, Marcia Harper, was missing and later presumed dead in the World Trade Centre disaster on September 11 2001. Granger's daughter, Libby, died suddenly on that very same date and shortly after her death, Granger split from her husband, Stuart Bone.

On hearing the news of his ex-wife's death at his home in Surrey, England, 45-year old teacher, Bone, who remarried in 2004, declined to offer comment.

According to reports, Bride and Granger first met in 2005 at the prestigious London Book Fair. The pair has since been spotted together at literary events around the globe.

Cause of death has not yet been released but police are seeking no further parties in their investigations.

In a bizarre twist of fate, Marcia Harper, 56, appeared later on in the week at the Harper Foundation on the Avenue of the Americas, having apparently risen from the dead. Sue-Anne Lerma, her former PA, said, 'I was just so shocked at seeing her. I thought I'd seen a ghost. It surely is terrific to see her come back to us like that.'

Eye witness, Kirk Appleby, long-term Head of Acquisitions for Harper said, 'When I saw her get out of the car, I couldn't believe my eyes. I guessed it must be for real given that it was Caesar, the family chauffeur driving her, but you just don't expect things like that to happen. I'm just so sad that Ms Marcia's mom and her dad are no longer with us to see their daughter alive again. It's a real tragedy, that's what it is.'

So far, no explanation for her absence has been offered.

Her lawyers are in talks with the authorities, but it is understood that Marcia Harper, whose name has been romantically linked with that of musician, Jake Jacobson, is the sole heir to Harper.

In an even more bizarre twist of fate, Harper looks set also to inherit Granger's estate.

According to sources, having no natural heir, Granger's entire estate, which comprises the recent sale of a house in London plus the considerable royalties from the sale of her books, was left in her will to Bride. His estate in turn goes to his wife, now very much alive.

As if that's not enough, Marcia Harper looks set to cash in on Bride and Granger's final work.

A manuscript, rumoured to be a collaborative novel, was recovered from the scene of their death. Already there is a fierce bidding war amongst publishers for the writers' one and only joint oeuvre.

Whilst speculation remains about Harper's legal situation, the heiress' lawyers are confident that Ms Harper's claim will stand up in court; 'Ms Harper is understandably distraught at the death of her husband. She is determined to ensure that Harper Enterprises goes from strength to strength in honour not only of Mr Bride but also of her late father, Abe Harper. We have no reason to believe that the final wishes of Ms Granger and Mr Bride will not be upheld in court and are confident that Ms Harper will receive everything that is rightfully hers at this tragic time.'

Marcia Harper declined to comment.

Sleeping People Lie

About the Author

Half Dutch and born in London, Jae De Wylde is the best selling author of *The Thinking Tank*. She graduated with BA Joint Hons in Modern Languages from the University of Bristol and went on to teach in independent schools in the UK before taking up a career in writing and journalism, including several years as Editor of Travelsphere Holidays. Jae has travelled widely and has lived in France, Germany, Spain and the Middle East. She now lives in Lincolnshire with her husband and three Chihuahuas.

www.jaedewylde.com

Acknowledgements

Thank you to everyone who has helped me along the way with this, my second novel.

Janna Gray, an enormous thank you for your amazing PR skills and for your fantastic support. Antonia Hoyle (www.antoniahoyle.com) — thank you for your superb journalistic skills. Martin, you are a saint for putting up with my obsession. I am truly sorry for the burnt fish curry. Rebecca, I love your encouragement — it makes my heart sing!

Jo Parfitt, your fine example always keeps me on track. Thank you to Leslie Ann Bosher. You always get there first and keep me chasing after!

My wonderful readers – Lynda Renham, Samantha Buckley, Sue Webb, Sue Mannering, Kala and Gordon Chappel, Gilly Bleakley, Helen Steele, Yvonne Muntaner, Peter and Mary Moore and Loraine Slessor — such helpful feedback. I am grateful to you all.

The lovely Sonja Crossan – thank you for the help with up-to-date French. Thanks also to the charming and perfectly bilingual jazz drummer, Louis Hansen, whom I met in *Les Bien Assises* campsite in Guînes – one of the fabulous Castels Camping group – where, in the friendly, lively bar, the dénouement of this novel took shape.

Walkers Bookshops, Bookmark and Waterstones – thank you for your incredible support, which spurred me on and gave me confidence that my readers wanted number two!

Thanks also to Leyla Ahu Urfali and Cello Dubai as well as Stamford Arts Centre, Claire at Renu in Bourne and the Guildhall Arts Centre in Grantham; you gave me a platform to dance and with it the sanity to sit back down and write.

Finally, a huge thank you to the many reading groups who so kindly invited me along to chat about my first novel *The Thinking Tank*. Your feedback and enthusiasm has been inspiring. A special mention must go to the Stamford Arts Centre Cellar Bar group and the Haconby team who meet at Derek and Mary's brilliant Hare and Hounds pub for providing my baptism of fire.

Author's notes

The school in *Sleeping People Lie* is fictitious as are the events that take place within it. The system used to deposit, collect and care for students doing exchange visits in Paris, is, however, a genuine model, as is the system for birthday buns!

The story of Camille Claudel and Rodin is factual and there is more information on www.camille–claudel.fr courtesy of relatives of the extraordinarily talented sculptress. The film by Bruno Nuytten, mentioned in *Sleeping People Lie*, is readily available as a DVD (Camille Claudel: Studio Canal 1988).

The Château de l'Islette (www.chateaudelislette.fr) exists and is not far from Azay-le-Rideau in the Loire Valley in France. Claudel and Rodin did indeed spend time there as described. Please go and visit this beautiful place, which, as in my novel, has been open to the public since 2011.

Tragedy comes in many forms. When my daughter died in 1999, it was at the time of the war in Kosovo. I remember telling myself that there were mothers out there who not only had lost their children and other family members but also their homes; a far worse situation than my own, being amongst friends and family in a safe environment. This inspired me to examine the situation presented to a mother whose child died in other circumstances on September 11 2001, where the world is mourning a global tragedy. Honour and respect to those who have lived through this tragedy and to those who have lost loved ones.

I am sorry for any mistakes – they are all my own.

Extra Material for Reading Groups

1. The reader does not know who *Em* is until very near the end. In the course of your reading, what possibilities crossed your mind as to who *Em* might be?

2. What, in your opinion, are the main themes of the novel?

3. Sloane seeks redemption in *Sleeping People Lie*. Who do you think bears the most blame for what happened?

4. Cathy insists she is Sloane's friend. Do you think this is true? Comment on your answer.

5. Elliott and Patricia-May, Nicholas' parents are particularly keen on their son marrying the girl next door. What is their role in the tale?

6. Comment on the story of Camille Claudel and Rodin and the part it plays in the novel.

7. What influence did Elodie have on Sloane's actions?

8. What did Sloane mean by her final words, do you think? Was she right, bearing in mind the fact that Marcia plays the role of both mistress and wife?

9. Did the ending alter in any way what you felt about the following characters; Sloane, Nicholas and Marcia?

10. The report in the Epilogue suggests that Nicholas and Sloane met in 2005, once Marcia and Stuart had left their lives. In your opinion, was it a memoir or the manuscript of a collaborative novel that was found? What makes you think this – and what have you decided happened in the end?

11. '*Sleeping People Lie is all about perception.*' Comment on this statement, giving reasons for your point of view.

The Thinking Tank
by Jae De Wylde

1969, London, England and Sally, a little girl dressed in brown, visits Father Christmas at a church fair. He rescues her as she trips and stumbles into his arms. As he hoists her onto his lap she thinks she feels the breath of a kiss on her cheek.

It is 2003 and in Rutland, England, Sarah's relationship with her daughter Rebekah is going from bad to worse. Torn apart by family secrets yet locked together by a solemn promise, the future for both seems bleak. But the mysterious and haunting circumstances of a hospital visit set Sarah on a path of discovery from which there is no turning back.

Sarah travels to Spain in search of answers – but even before she arrives, it becomes clear that offers of help rarely come without strings...

Only by confronting the truth can Sarah move forward, but that means revealing the one secret she herself cannot face.

Jae De Wylde steers us masterfully through the twists and turns of this splendidly paced, poignant and compelling story of love, identity and belonging.

designed by

Lightning Source UK Ltd.
Milton Keynes UK
UKOW04f1942130315

247870UK00004B/226/P